Matt wasn't going to let some woman—some lady cop—best him.

Grinning crookedly in the night, he drew her to him again. "You're not so tough, are you, Detective?" he asked, knowing he was stepping into dangerous territory. He should just leave well enough alone, but the challenge in her eyes, the defiant lift of her chin, the passionate woman hidden beneath the cop's uniform zeroed in on his male pride. "Don't lecture me about caveman tactics," he warned, "or I just might accuse you of being a tease."

"That wouldn't destroy me."

"No?" His fingers tightened over her arms. "And I'll bet it's not true."

"Wait a minute. I was just—"

"You were just curious and it backfired. You're not as immune as you thought you were. You're not an ice woman after all."

"And you're not a gentleman."

"Never said I was."

Dear Reader,

It's the little things that mean so much. In fact, more than once, "little things" have fueled Myrna Temte's Special Edition novels. One of her miniseries evolved from a newspaper article her mother sent her. The idea for her first novel was inspired by something she'd heard a DJ say on her favorite country-western radio station. And Myrna Temte's nineteenth book, *Handprints,* also evolved in an interesting way. A friend received a special Mother's Day present—a picture of her little girl with finger-painted handprints and a sweet poem entitled "Handprints." Once the story was relayed to Myrna, the seed for another romance novel was planted. And the rest, as they say, is history....

There are plenty of special somethings this month. Bestselling author Joan Elliott Pickart delivers *Single with Twins,* the story of a photojournalist who travels the world in search of adventure, only to discover that *family* makes his life complete. In Lisa Jackson's *The McCaffertys: Matt,* the rugged rancher hero feels that law enforcement is no place for a lady—but soon finds himself making a plea for passion....

Don't miss Laurie Paige's *When I See Your Face,* in which a fiercely independent officer is forced to rely on others when she's temporarily blinded in the line of duty. Find out if there will be a *Match Made in Wyoming* in Patricia McLinn's novel, when the hero and heroine find themselves snowbound on a Wyoming ranch! And *The Child She Always Wanted* by Jennifer Mikels tells the touching tale of a baby on the doorstep bringing two people together for a love too great for either to deny.

Asking authors where they get their ideas often proves an impossible question. However, many ideas come from little things that surround us. See what's around you. And if you have an idea for a Special Edition novel, I'd love to hear from you. Enjoy!

Best,
Karen Taylor Richman, Senior Editor

Please address questions and book requests to:
Silhouette Reader Service
U.S.: 3010 Walden Ave., P.O. Box 1325, Buffalo, NY 14269
Canadian: P.O. Box 609, Fort Erie, Ont. L2A 5X3

The McCaffertys: Matt

LISA JACKSON

Silhouette

SPECIAL EDITION™

Published by Silhouette Books

America's Publisher of Contemporary Romance

SILHOUETTE BOOKS

ISBN 0-373-24406-1

THE McCAFFERTYS: MATT

Copyright © 2001 by Susan Crose

Visit Silhouette at www.eHarlequin.com

Printed in U.S.A.

Books by Lisa Jackson

Silhouette Special Edition

A Twist of Fate #118
The Shadow of Time #180
Tears of Pride #194
Pirate's Gold #215
A Dangerous Precedent #233
Innocent by Association #244
Midnight Sun #264
Devil's Gambit #282
Zachary's Law #296
Yesterday's Lies #315
One Man's Love #358
Renegade Son #376
Snowbound #394
Summer Rain #419
Hurricane Force #467
In Honor's Shadow #495
Aftermath #525
Tender Trap #569
With No Regrets #611
Double Exposure #636
Mystery Man #653
Obsession #691
Sail Away #720
Million Dollar Baby #743
He's a Bad Boy #787
He's Just a Cowboy #799
He's the Rich Boy #811
A Husband To Remember #835
He's My Soldier Boy #866
†*A Is for Always* #914
†*B Is for Baby* #920
†*C Is for Cowboy* #926
†*D Is for Dani's Baby* #985
New Year's Daddy #1004
‡*A Family Kind of Guy* #1191
‡*A Family Kind of Gal* #1207
‡*A Family Kind of Wedding* #1219
§*The McCaffertys: Thorne* #1364
§*The McCaffertys: Matt* #1406

Silhouette Intimate Moments

Dark Side of the Moon #39
Gypsy Wind #79
Mystic #158

Silhouette Romance

His Bride To Be #717

Silhouette Books

Silhouette Christmas Stories 1993
"The Man from Pine Mountain"

Fortune's Children
The Millionaire and the Cowgirl

Montana Mavericks: Wed in Whitehorn
Lone Stallion's Lady

*Mavericks
†Love Letters
‡Forever Family
§The McCaffertys

LISA JACKSON

has been writing romances for over ten years. With over forty-five Silhouette novels to her credit, she divides her time between writing on the computer, researching her next novel, keeping in touch with her college-age sons and playing tennis. Many of the fictitious small towns in her books resemble Molalla, Oregon, a small logging community where she and her sister, Silhouette author Natalie Bishop, grew up.

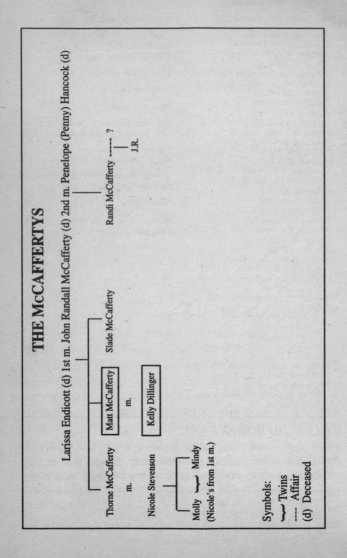

THE McCAFFERTYS

Larissa Endicott (d) 1st m. John Randall McCafferty (d) 2nd m. Penelope (Penny) Hancock (d)

Thorne McCafferty
m.
Nicole Stevenson

Matt McCafferty
m.
Kelly Dillinger

Slade McCafferty

Randi McCafferty ----- ?
J.R.

Molly ⌣ Mindy
(Nicole's from 1st m.)

Symbols:
⌣ Twins
----- Affair
(d) Deceased

Prologue

Early May

"**Y**ou miserable piece of horseflesh," Matt McCafferty growled as he climbed to his feet, dusted the back of his jeans and glowered at the wild-eyed Appaloosa colt. There was a reason the damned beast was named Diablo Rojo, the orneriest two-year-old on the Flying M Ranch. A challenge. In all his thirty-seven years, Matt had never met a horse he couldn't tame. But he was having second thoughts about Red Devil Major ones. The horse had spirit. Fire. Not easily tamed. Like a lot of women Matt had run across. "Okay, you bastard, let's start over."

He reached down and picked up his hat. Slapping it hard against his thigh, he squinted into the lowering Montana sun as it started its slow descent behind the western hills. "You and I, Devil, we're gonna come to a reckoning and we're gonna do it this afternoon."

The colt tossed his fiery head and snorted noisily, then lifted his damned tail like a banner and trotted along the far fence line, the empty saddle on his back creaking mockingly. *Damned fool horse.* Matt squared his hat on his head. "It isn't over," he assured the snorting animal.

"It may as well be."

Matt froze at the sound of his father's voice. Turning on the worn heel of his boot, he watched as Juanita pushed John Randall's wheelchair across the parking lot separating the rambling, two-storied ranch house from the series of connecting paddocks that surrounded the stables. Matt didn't harbor much love for his bastard of a father, but he couldn't help feel an ounce of pity for the once-robust man now confined to "the damned contraption," as he referred to the chair.

John Randall's sparse white hair caught in the wind and his skin was pale and thin, but there was still a spark in his blue eyes. And he loved this spread. More than he loved anything, including his children.

"I tried to talk him out of this," Juanita reprimanded as she parked the wheelchair near the fence where Harold, John Randall's partially crippled old springer spaniel, had settled into a patch of shade thrown by a lone pine tree. "But you know how it is. He is too *terco*...stubborn, for his own good."

"And it's served me well," the old man said as he used the sun-bleached rails of the fence to pull himself to his full height. Lord, he was thin—too thin. His jeans and plaid shirt hung loosely from his once-robust frame. But he managed a tough-as-old-leather smile as he leaned over the top bar and watched his middle son.

"Maybe you can talk some sense into him," Juanita said, sending Matt a worried glance and muttering something about *loco,* prideful men.

"I doubt it. I never could before."

The older McCafferty waved Juanita off. "I'm fine. Needed some fresh air. Now I want to talk to Matt. He'll bring me inside when we're through."

Juanita didn't seem convinced, but Matt nodded. "I think I can handle him," he said to the woman who had helped raise him. Clucking her tongue at the absurdity of the situation, Juanita bustled off to the house, the only home Matt had known growing up.

"That one," John Randall said, hitching his chin back to the wayward colt. "He'll give ya a run for your money." He slid a knowing glance at his second-born. "Like a lot of women."

Matt was irritated. He wiped the sweat from his forehead and swatted at a horsefly that got a little too close for comfort. "Is that what you came all the way out here to say to me, the reason you had Juanita push you outside?"

"Nope." With an effort the older man dug into the pocket of his jeans. "I got somethin' here for ya."

"What?" Matt was instantly suspicious. His father's gifts never came without a price.

"Somethin' I want ya to have—oh, here we go." John Randall withdrew a big silver buckle that winked in the bright Montana sun. Inlaid upon the flat surface was a gold bucking bronco, still as shiny as the day John Randall had won it at a rodeo in Canada more than fifty years earlier. He dropped it into his son's calloused hand.

"You used to wear this all the time," Matt observed, his jaw growing tight.

"Yep. Reminded me of my piss-and-vinegar years." John Randall settled back in his wheelchair, and his eyes clouded a bit. "Good years," he added thoughtfully, then squinted upward to stare at his son. "I don't have much longer on this earth, boy,'' he said, and before Matt could protest, his father raised a big-knuckled hand to silence him. ''We both know it so there's no sense in arguin' the facts. The man upstairs, he's about to call me home…that is, if the devil don't take me first.''

Matt clenched his jaw. Didn't say a word. Waited.

''I already spoke to Thorne about the fact that I'm dyin', and seein' as you're the next in line, I thought I'd talk to you next. Slade…well, I'll catch up to him soon. Now, I know I've made mistakes in my life, the good Lord knows I failed your mother….''

Matt didn't comment, didn't want to even think about the bleak time when John Randall took up with a much younger woman, divorced his wife and introduced his three sons to Penelope, ''Penny'' Henley, who would become their stepmother and give them all a half sister whom none of them wanted to begin with.

''I have a lot of regrets about all that,'' John Randall said over the sigh of the wind, ''but it's all water under the bridge now since both Larissa and Penny are dead.'' He rubbed his jaw and cleared his throat. ''Never thought I'd bury two wives.''

''A wife and an ex-wife,'' Matt clarified.

The old man's thin lips pursed, but he didn't argue. ''What I want from you—from all my children—is grandchildren. You know that. It's an old man's dream, I know, but it's only natural. I'd like to go to my grave in peace with the knowledge that you'll find yourself a good woman and settle down, have a family, and that the McCafferty name will go on for a few more generations.''

''There's lots of time—''

''Not for me, there ain't!'' John Randall snapped.

Feeling as if he was being manipulated for the umpteenth time by his father, Matt tried to hand the buckle back. "If this is some kind of bribe or deal or—"

"No bribe." The old man spit in disgust. "I want you to have that buckle because it means something to me, and since you rode rodeo a few years back, I thought you might appreciate it." He wagged a finger at the buckle. "Turn it over."

Matt flipped the smooth piece of metal and read the engraving on the backside. "To my cowboy. Love forever, Larissa." His throat closed for a minute when he thought of his mother with her shiny black hair and laughing brown eyes, which had saddened over the years of her marriage. From a free spirit, she'd become imprisoned on this ranch and had sought her own kind of solace and peace that she'd never found in the bottles she'd hidden in the old house she'd grown to despise.

Matt's gut twisted. He missed her. Bad. And the old man had wronged her. There were just no two ways about it.

"Larissa had it engraved after I won it. Hell, she was a fool for me back then." The wrinkles around John Randall's mouth and eyes deepened with sadness, and there was a tiny shadow of guilt that chased across his eyes. "So, now I want you to have it, Matthew."

Matt's fingers tightened over the sharp edges of the buckle, but he didn't say a word. Couldn't.

"And I want me some grandbabies. That's not too much for an old man to ask."

"I'm not married."

"Then get yourself hitched." His father gave him a head-to-toe once-over. "Fine, strappin' man like you shouldn't have too much trouble."

"Maybe I don't believe in marriage."

"Then maybe you're a fool."

Matt traced the silhouette of the bucking bronco with one finger. "It could be I learned from the best."

"So unlearn it," John Randall ordered, just as he always did. His way or the highway. Matt had chosen the latter.

"I've got me a horse to break," he said. "And my own place to run."

"I was hopin' you'd be stayin' on." There was a hint of desperation in his father's voice, but Matt stood firm. There was just too much water under the damned bridge—muddy, treacherous water fed by a swift current of lies and deceit, the kind of water a man could slowly drown in. Matt had come to the ranch to mend some emotional fences with the old man and to help the foreman, Larry Todd, for a week or so, but his own spread, a few hundred acres close to the Idaho border, needed his attention.

"I can't, Dad," he said finally as he followed the path of a wasp as it flew toward the back porch. "Maybe it's time to get you inside."

"For God's sake, don't try to mollycoddle me, son. It's not like I'm gonna catch my death out here today." John Randall folded his hands in his lap and looked between the old slats of the fence to the hard pan of the paddock where the Appaloosa, still wearing an empty saddle, pawed the ground, kicking up dust. "I'll watch while you try to break him. It'll be interesting to see who'll win. You or Diablo."

Matt lifted a disbelieving eyebrow. "You sure?"

"Ye-up."

"Fine." Matt squared his hat on his head and climbed over the fence. "But it's not gonna be much of a contest," he said, more to the horse than the man who had sired him. He strode forward with renewed determination, his eyes fixed on the Appaloosa's sleek muscles that quivered as he approached. Few things in life beat Matt McCafferty.

A high-strung colt wasn't one of them.

Nor was his father.

Nope. His weakness, if he had one, was women. Fiery-tempered, bullheaded women in particular.

The kind he avoided like the plague.

And now his father wanted him to find a woman, tie the knot and start raising a passel of babies.

He nearly laughed as he reached for the reins, and Diablo had the nerve to snort defiantly.

No way in hell was Matt McCafferty getting married. Not today, not tomorrow, not ever. That's just the way it was.

Chapter One

The following November

She'd met him before.

Too many times to count.

That didn't mean she had to like him.

No, sir.

As far as Detective Kelly Dillinger was concerned, Matt McCafferty was just plain bad news. Pure and simple, cut from the same biased, sanctimonious, self-serving cloth as his brothers and his bastard of a father before him.

But that didn't mean he didn't look good. If you liked the rough-and-tumble, tough-as-rawhide cowboy type, Matt McCafferty was the man for you. His rugged appeal was legendary in Grand Hope. He and his older and younger brothers had been considered the best catches in the entire county for years. But Kelly prided herself on being different from most of the women who wanted to swoon whenever they heard the McCafferty name.

So they were handsome.

So they were sexy.

So they had money.

So what?

These days their reputations had tarnished a bit, notoriety had taken its toll, and the oldest of the lot, Thorne, was rumored to be losing his status as an eligible bachelor and marrying a local woman doctor.

Not so the second brother, Matt. The one, it seemed, she was going to have to deal with right now.

He was muscling open the door to the Grand Hope office of the sheriff's department with one broad shoulder and bringing with him a rush of frigid winter air and snowflakes that melted instantly the minute they encountered the sixty-eight degrees maintained by a wheezing furnace hidden somewhere in the basement of this ancient brick building.

Matt McCafferty. Great. Just…damned great. She already had a headache and was up to her eyeballs in paperwork, a ream of which could be applied to the McCafferty case—no, make that cases, plural—alone. But she couldn't ignore him, either. She stared through the glass of her enclosed office and saw him stride across the yellowing linoleum floor, barely stopping at the gate that separated the reception area from the office, then sweep past the receptionist on a cloud of self-righteous fury. Kelly disliked the man on sight, but then she had her own personal ax to grind when it came to the McCaffertys.

There was fire in McCafferty's brown eyes and anger in his tight, blade-thin lips and the stubborn set of his damnably square jaw. Yep, cut from the same cloth as the others, she thought as she climbed to her feet and opened the door to the office at the same time as he was about to pound on the scarred oak panels.

"Mr. McCafferty." She feigned a smile. "A pleasure to see you again."

"Cut the bull," he said without preamble.

"Okay." He was blunt if nothing else. "Why don't you come in…" But he'd already crossed the threshold and was inside the small glassed-in room, pacing the short distance from one wall to the other.

Stella Gamble, the plump, nervous receptionist, had abandoned her post and was fidgeting at the door, her bright red fingernails catching light from the humming fluorescent tubing overhead. "I tried to stop him, really I did," she said, shaking her head as her tight blond curls bounced around her flushed cheeks. "He wouldn't listen."

"A family trait."

"I'm sorry—"

"It's all right, Stella. Relax. I needed to talk to one of the McCafferty brothers, anyway," Kelly assured her, though that was stretching the truth quite a bit. A conversation with Thorne, Slade or especially Matt wasn't on her agenda right this minute, not when Nathaniel Biggs was calling every two hours, certain that someone had stolen his prize bull last night, Perry Carmichael had reported an odd aura suspended over the copse of oak trees behind his machine shed out on Old Dupont Road and Dora Haines was missing again, probably wandering around the foothills in nineteen-degree weather with a storm threatening to blast in from the Bitterroots by nightfall. Not that the McCafferty case wasn't important—it just wasn't the only one she was working on. "Don't worry about it," she said to Stella. "I'll talk to Mr. McCafferty."

"No one should get by me," the receptionist said, blinking rapidly.

"You're right, they shouldn't," Kelly agreed, and glared at the uninvited guest. "But, as I said, I need to talk to him, anyway, and I don't think he's dangerous."

"Don't count on it," McCafferty countered. Standing near the file cabinet, he looked as if he could spit nails.

The phone rang loudly at Stella's desk.

"I'll deal with this," Kelly said as the receptionist hurried back to her desk and immediately donned her headset.

Kelly closed the door behind her and snapped the blinds shut for privacy, as she didn't want any of the deputies witnessing the dressing-down that was simmering in the air of her postage-stamp-size office.

"Have a seat," she offered, sweeping off the files that were stacked in the single chair on the visitor's side of her metal desk.

He didn't move, but those eyes followed her as she plopped into her ancient desk chair. "I'm tired of getting the runaround," he announced through lips that barely moved.

"The runaround?"

"Yep." He planted his hands between her in-basket and the computer monitor glowing from one corner of the desk and leaned across the reports that were strewn in front of her. "I want answers, dammit. My sister's been in a coma for over a month because of an accident that I believe is the result of someone running her Jeep off the road, and you people, *you people,* are doing nothing to find out what happened to her. For all we know someone tried to kill her that day and they won't stop until they finish the job!"

"That's just speculation," Kelly reminded him, the short fuse on her temper igniting. There was a chance that

Randi McCafferty's rig had been forced off the road up in Glacier Park. With no witnesses it was hard to say. But the sheriff's department was checking into every possibility. "We're trying to locate another vehicle if one is involved. So far, we haven't found one."

"It's been over a month, for crying out loud," he said as she sat on the corner of her desk, watching a battery of emotions cross his face. Anger. Determination. Frustration. And more—a fleck of fear darkened his brown eyes. Fear wasn't an emotion she considered when thinking of any of the roguish, tough-as-rawhide McCafferty men. The three brothers, like their father, had always appeared an intrepid, fearless lot. "And over two weeks have passed since Thorne's plane went down. You think that was an accident, too?"

"It's possible. We're looking into it."

"Well, you'd better look harder," he suggested, his nostrils flaring.

The guy was getting to her. Again. He had a way of nettling her—getting under her skin and irritating her. Kind of like a burr caught beneath a horse's saddle. McCafferty straightened, swept his hat from his head and raked stiff fingers through his near-black, wavy hair. "Before someone actually dies."

"The feds are involved in the plane crash."

"That doesn't seem to be helping a whole helluva lot."

"We're doing everything in our power to—"

"It's not enough," he cut in. Again fire flared in his eyes. "Are you in charge of this investigation, Detective?" he asked, casting a glance at the badge she wore so proudly. He was crushing the brim of his Stetson in fingers that blanched white at the knuckles.

She held on to her patience, but just barely. "I think we've been over this before. Detective Espinoza has been assigned the case. I'm assisting him, as I was the first on the scene of your sister's wreck.''

"Then I'm wasting my time with you.''

That stung. Kelly gritted her teeth and stood.

"Tell Espinoza I want to talk to him.''

"He's not in right now.''

"I'll wait.''

"It might be a while.''

Matt McCafferty looked as if he might explode. He dropped his hat on a nearby folding chair and leaned over her desk again, shoving some file folders out of the way as he pushed his face closer, so that the tip of his nose nearly touched hers. The air seemed to crackle. The smell of wet suede, horses and a faint hint of pine reached her nostrils. Snow had melted on the shoulders of his sheepskin jacket, and there were a few damp spots on his face. His fists opened and closed in frustration on the desktop. "You have to understand, Detective, this is my family we're talking about,'' he said in a low whisper that had more impact than if he'd raged. "*My* family. Now, the way I see it, my sister was nearly killed, and not only that but she was nine months pregnant at the time.''

"I know—''

"Do you? Can you imagine what she went through? She went into labor when her Jeep careered over that embankment and crashed. She was just lucky someone came along and called 911. Between the paramedics and the doctors over at St. James Hospital and a lot of help from the man upstairs, she pulled through.''

"And the baby survived,'' she pointed out, remembering all too clearly the condition of mother and son.

Matt wasn't about to be deterred. Like a runaway freight train gathering steam, he kept right on. "*After* a bout of meningitis.''

Her fingers coiled over a pen on the desk. "I understand all this—"

"Fortunately little J.R. is a McCafferty. He's tough. He pulled through."

"So he's fine," she reminded him, trying to keep emotions out of the conversation, which, of course, was impossible.

"Fine?" He snorted. "I guess you might say so, except that he needs his mom, who is still comatose and lying in a hospital room." For a brief second Matt McCafferty actually seemed as if he cared about his nephew, and his brown eyes darkened in concern. That got to Kelly, though she refused to show it. Of course he was worried about the kid—McCaffertys always looked after their own. To the exclusion of all others. "And that's not all, Detective," he added.

"I'm sure not," she drawled, and he scowled at her patronizing tone.

"It's a miracle that Thorne survived the plane crash and ended up with only a few cuts and bruises and a broken leg."

Amen to that. Thorne was the eldest McCafferty brother, a millionaire oilman who hailed from Denver. He'd been flying the company jet back to Grand Hope, hit bad weather and gone down.

"The way I see it, either the McCaffertys are having one helluva string of bad luck, or someone's out to get us."

"Randi was driving and hit an icy patch. Your brother was flying alone in the middle of a snowstorm. Bad luck? Or bad judgment?"

"Or, as I said, a potential murderer on the loose."

"Who?" she asked, meeting his glare, not backing down an inch though she was beginning to sweat, and the office, filled by his presence, seemed even smaller than usual.

"That's what I was hopin' you'd tell me."

God, he was close to her. Too close. The desk between them seemed a small barrier.

"Believe me, Mr. McCafferty—"

"Matt. Call me Matt. There're too damned many McCaffertys to call us by our last name."

She wouldn't argue that point.

"And somehow I have the feelin' that you and I, we'll be workin' real close together on this one. I intend to stick to you like glue until you find out who the hell is behind this, so we may as well cut the formalities."

The thought of working closely with anyone named McCafferty stuck in Kelly's craw, and this one, this damnably sexy, cocksure cowboy, was the most irritating of the lot, but she didn't have much choice in the matter. "All right, *Matt*. As I was saying, we're trying our best here to find out the truth behind both accidents. Everyone in the department is busting their hump to figure this mess out."

"Not fast enough," he growled.

"And none of us, me especially—" she hooked a thumb at her chest "—needs anyone looking over her shoulder." She stuffed the pen in the mug on her desk. "Didn't you hire your own private detective?"

His thin lips tightened a fraction.

"A man by the name of Kurt Striker?" She folded her arms across her chest.

He nodded. "We thought we needed more help."

"So what has he got to say?"

"That he thinks there's foul play," McCafferty said, his eyes narrowing on Kelly as if he couldn't quite figure her out. Tough. She was used to men distrusting her as a detective because she was a woman, and that's what Matt McCafferty was saying; she could read it in his eyes. Well, that was just too damned bad. She wasn't about to be bullied or intimidated. Not by anyone. Not even one of the high-and-mighty McCaffertys. Matt's father, John Randall, had once been a rich, powerful and influential man in the county, and his descendants thought they could still throw their collective weights around. Well, not here.

"Has Striker got any proof that someone's behind the accidents?" she asked.

Hesitation.

"I didn't think so." She slipped from the desk. "That's it. Now, listen, I have work to do, and I don't need you barging in here and making demands and—"

"Striker says there's some paint on Randi's rig. Maroon. Maybe from the other car when she was forced off the road."

"*If* she was forced off," Kelly reminded him. "She could have scraped another vehicle in a parking lot at home in Seattle for all we know. And we already know about the paint, so don't come in here and insinuate that the department is inefficient or incompetent or any of the above, because we're just being thorough. Got it?"

"Listen—"

"No, you listen to me, okay?" Her temper was stretched to the breaking point as she stepped around the desk and went toe-to-toe with him. "This force is doing everything in its power to try and find out what happened to your sister and your brother. Everything! We don't take either accident lightly, believe you me. But we're not jumping off the deep end here, either. Your sister's Jeep could have hit ice. It's just possible she lost control of the vehicle, it slid off the road up in Glacier and she ended up in the hospital in a damned coma. As for your brother, he was taking a big chance with his life flying a small craft in one helluva snowstorm. The engines failed. We'll determine why. We haven't yet ruled out foul play. We're just being careful. The department can't afford to go off half-cocked and making blind assumptions or accusations.''

''Meanwhile someone might be trying to kill off my family.''

''Who?'' she demanded as she rounded the desk again, plopped down in her worn chair and took up her pen. Yanking a yellow legal pad from the credenza behind her, she dropped it on the desk and sat ready, ballpoint pressed against the clean sheet of paper. ''Give me a list of suspects, anyone you know who might hold a grudge against the McCafferty clan.''

Matt's eyes narrowed. ''There are dozens.''

''Names, McCafferty, I want names.'' She hoped she sounded professional, because he was cutting a little too close to the bone with his damned insinuations.

''You should know a few,'' he said, and though she wanted to, she didn't allow herself to rise to the bait.

''Don't beat around the bush.''

''Okay, let's start with your family,'' he shot out.

Kelly's back went up. ''No one in my family has any ax to grind with your brother or half sister.'' She raised her eyes and met the simmering anger in his.

''Just my dad.''

''Lots of people had problems with him. But he's gone. And my family aren't potential murderers, okay? So let's not even go there.'' She bit out the words but wouldn't give in to the white-hot anger that threatened to take hold of her tongue. The nerve of the man. ''Now...'' She clicked the pen again. ''Who would want to harm your sister, Randi, and your brother Thorne?''

Some of the anger seemed to drain from him. "I don't know," he admitted. "I'm sure Thorne's made his share of enemies. You don't get to be a millionaire without someone being envious."

"Envious enough to try and kill him?" Kelly said.

"Damn, I'd hope not, but..." He closed his eyes for a second. "I don't know."

That, at least, sounded honest. "He's based out of Denver, isn't he?"

"He was. The corporate headquarters are there."

"But he's moving back here and getting married." It wasn't a question, but Matt nodded and Kelly noticed the way his dark hair shone under the humming fluorescent lamps. He unbuttoned his jacket, revealing a flannel shirt stretched over a broad chest. Black hairs sprang from the opening at the neck. She tore her eyes away, gave herself a swift mental kick for noticing any part of his male anatomy and scribbled down some notes about Thorne, the oldest of the brothers.

"Yeah, he's marrying Nicole Stevenson." Matt managed a half smile that was incredibly and irritatingly sexy. "Lots of people are losing that particular bet."

Kelly understood. Thorne, like his brothers, had been a confirmed bachelor. He, along with Matt and the youngest brother, Slade, had raised holy hell in high school and cut a wide swath through the local girls. Rich, handsome and smart to the point of arrogance, they'd soon been regarded as the most eligible bachelors in the county and thereby broken more than their share of hearts. Matt, in particular, had earned the reputation of being a ladies' man. *Love'Em and Leave'Em McCafferty*.

But now it seemed that the first of the invincible and never-to-be-wed brothers was about to fall victim to matrimony. The bride was an emergency room doctor at the local hospital, a single mother with twin girls.

"Okay, so what about your sister?" she asked, trying to keep her mind on business. "Any known enemies?"

Annoyance pulled the smile off of Matt's cocky jaw. This wasn't new territory. Ever since the accident, the sheriff's department had been looking into Randi's life. "I don't know," Matt admitted. "I'm sure she had her share. Hell, she wrote a column for the *Seattle Clarion*."

"Advice to the lovelorn?" Kelly filled in.

"More than that. It's more like general, no-nonsense advice to single people. It's called—"

"'Solo.' I know. I've got copies on file," she said, not admitting that she'd found his sister's wry outlook on single life interesting and amusing. "But most of the advice she gave was about a single person's love life."

"Ironic, wouldn't you say?" Matt said, walking to the far side of the room and shaking his head. Turning, he leaned his shoulders against a bookcase. "She gave out all this advice—the column was syndicated, picked up by other papers as well—and yet she winds up pregnant and nearly dies behind the wheel and no one even knows who the father of her kid is."

"I'd call that more than ironic, I'd call it downright odd." She clicked her pen several times, then motioned to the one empty chair on the far side of her desk. "You could have a seat."

He eyed the chair just as the phone in her office rang.

"Excuse me." Lifting the receiver, she said, "Dillinger."

"Sorry to bother you, but Bob is on the line," Stella said, still sounding nervous from her failed attempt to keep Matt McCafferty in line.

"I'll talk with him." She held up a hand toward Matt

as Roberto Espinoza's voice boomed over the wires. He was out at the Haines farm and was reporting that they'd found Dora, carrying her cat as she trudged through the snow in her housecoat and slippers, following a trail that cut through the woods to a steep slope where, she had explained to Detective Espinoza, her father had taken her sledding as a girl.

"A sad case," Bob said on a sigh, then added that Dora was now on her way to St. James Hospital by ambulance. The paramedics who had examined her were concerned about exposure, frostbite and senility, which could translate into something deeper. Her husband, Albert, was beside himself. "I'm heading over to St. James myself and I'll see you when I'm finished there," Bob added.

"I'll meet you," Kelly said, and glanced at the McCafferty brother filling up a good portion of her office. "When you've got a minute you might want to speak to Matt McCafferty. He's here now." While Matt listened, his expression intense, Kelly explained the concerns of the McCafferty family to her boss.

"Arrogant son of a bitch." Espinoza let out a whistling breath. "As if we're not doing everything humanly possible." She heard the click of a lighter and then a deep sigh. "Tell him to cool his jets. I'll see him as soon as I'm finished dictating a report on Dora."

"Will do." Kelly hung up and relayed the message. "He'll see you soon. In the meantime you're supposed to stay cool."

"Like hell. I've been cool way too long and nothing's being done."

She let that one slide. As far as Kelly was concerned the meeting was over. She stood and reached for her hat and coat, then flipped open the blinds. "I've got work to do, McCafferty. Detective Espinoza said he'd call you and he will.'' She opened the door and stood, silently inviting him to leave. ''Got it?''

''If that's the best you can do—''

''It is.''

He crammed his Stetson onto his head and threw her a look that told her she wasn't about to see the last of him, then she watched as he swung out of her office, past Stella's desk and through the creaking gate. His jeans had seen better days and they'd faded over his buttocks, it seemed, from the glimpse she caught at the hemline of his jacket. He didn't bother with the buttons or gloves; he was probably overheated from the anger she and Bob Espinoza had fired in him. Well, that was just too damned bad.

He shouldered open the door and again a blast of air as cold as the North Pole rushed into the room. Then he was gone, the glass door swinging shut behind him. ''And good riddance,'' Kelly muttered under her breath, irritated that she found him the least little bit attractive and noticing that Stella had forgone answering the telephones or typing at her computer keyboard to watch Matt's stormy exit.

Yep, Kelly thought, squaring her hat on her head and sliding her arms through the sleeves of her insulated jacket. The man was bad news.

Chapter Two

Matt drummed his fingers on the steering wheel of his truck. Snow was blowing across the highway, drifting against the fence line and melting on his windshield. He flipped on the wipers and switched the radio to a local country station, searching for a weather report and settling for a Willie Nelson classic.

Squinting against the ever-increasing flakes, he scowled as he headed out of town toward the Flying M Ranch. Maybe he'd made a mistake, driving like the devil was on his back into town and barreling into the sheriff's department demanding answers.

He hadn't gotten squat.

In fact that red-haired detective had put him in his place. Time and time again. It was unsettling. Infuriating. Downright insulting. Kelly Dillinger had a way of bothering him more than she had the right to. And he couldn't get her out of his mind. Her skin was pale, her eyes a deep chocolate brown, her hair a bright, vibrant red which, in his estimation, accounted for her temperament. Redheads were always a fiery, hot-tempered lot. Then there was her no-nonsense, I-won't-deal-with-any-bull attitude. Like she was a man, for God's sake. That would be the day. Her build was basically athletic, but definitely female. He'd noticed, and kicked himself for it. Her uniform had stretched tight over her breasts and hugged her waist and hips. The woman had curves, damned nice curves, even if she tried her best to conceal them.

He'd always heard that women were attracted to men in uniforms, but he damned well didn't expect it to work in reverse. Especially not with him. Nope. He liked soft, well-rounded women who reveled in and showed off their feminine attributes. He was partial to tight T-shirts, miniskirts or long dresses with split skirts, open enough to show a good long length of calf and thigh. He'd seen slacks and silk blouses that were sexy, but never a uniform, for crying out loud, and especially not one of those from the local sheriff's department, but he'd noticed Kelly Dillinger. Angry as he'd been when he'd stormed into the sheriff's department, he'd found it damned hard to keep his mind on business.

But then he'd always had trouble with his libido; around attractive women it had always been in overdrive. Tonight was worse than it had been in a long, long while.

So there it was. He was attracted to her.

But he couldn't be. No way. Not to a woman cop—especially not this one who was working on his sister's case and who, he knew, held a personal grudge against the McCafferty family. But the bare facts of the matter were that he was lying to himself. Even now, just thinking about her, he felt his crotch tighten. He glanced at his reflection in the rearview mirror. ''Idiot,'' he chastised, then shifted down as he approached the Flying M, the ranch that had been his father's pride and joy.

"Great," he grumbled as he cranked the steering wheel and his tires spun a little as they hit a patch of packed snow. The woman was off limits. Period. If for no other reason than she lived here in Grand Hope, far from his own ranch. If he was going to be looking for a woman, which he wasn't, he reminded himself, he'd be looking for one a lot closer to home. God, where did those thoughts come from? He didn't want or need a woman. They were too much trouble. Kelly Dillinger included.

His headlights caught the snowflakes dancing in front of the truck and a few dry weeds poked through the mantle of white, scraping against the undercarriage as he navigated along the twin ruts leading to the heart of the spread. A few shaggy-coated cattle, dark, shifting shapes against the white background of the snow, were visible, but most of the herd had sought shelter or was out of his line of vision as he plowed down a long lane and rounded a final bend to a broad, flat parking area located between the main house and the outbuildings.

The truck slid to a stop beneath a leafless apple tree near a fence that was beginning to sag in a spot or two.

Matt yanked his keys from the ignition, threw open the door and was across the lot and up the three steps of the front porch in seconds. He only stopped to kick some of the snow off his boots, then pushed open the front door.

A wave of warm heat and the sound of piano keys tinkling out a quick, melodic tune greeted him. He sloughed off his jacket and felt his stomach rumble as he smelled roasting chicken and something else—cinnamon and baked apples. Hanging his jacket and hat on a peg near the front door, he heard the quick, light-footed steps of tiny feet scurrying across the hardwood floor overhead. Within seconds the twins were scuttling down the stairs.

"Unca Matt!" one little dark-haired cherub sang out as she rounded the corner of the landing and flew down the rest of the worn steps.

"How're ya, Molly girl?" Crouching, opening his arms wide, he swept the impish four-year-old off her feet.

"Fine," she said, her brown eyes twinkling at a sudden and uncharacteristic hint of shyness. She sucked on a finger as her sister, blanket in tow, scampered down the steps.

"And how about you, Mindy?" he asked, bending down and hauling the second scamp into his arms. The music was still playing and so he dipped and swooped, dancing with a niece in each arm. He'd only known the little girls over a month, but they, along with Randi's baby, were a part of his family, now and forever. He couldn't imagine a life without Molly, Mindy or the baby.

The girls giggled and laughed, Mindy's tattered blanket twirling as Matt sashayed them into the living room where their mother, Nicole, was seated on the piano stool, her fingers flying over the keys as she played some ragtime piece for all it was worth.

"Is Liberace playing?" Matt asked.

"No!" the girls chimed, throwing back their heads and giggling loudly.

"Oh, you're right. It must be Elton John?"

"No, no!" They screamed in unison, their little noses wrinkling. "It's Mommy."

"And she's a hack," their mother said, twirling around as the final notes faded and the sound of the fire crackling in the grate caught Matt's attention. Nicole's daughters wiggled out of his arms and scrambled to their mother.

"But then, you're not exactly Fred Astaire or Gene Kelly."

"Oh, damn, and I thought I was." Matt walked to the fireplace and warmed the back of his legs against the flames. "I'm crushed."

"That'll be the day." Nicole shook her head, her amber eyes bright with mischief.

Harold was lying in his favorite spot on the rug near the fire. He lifted up his head and yawned, stretching his legs before he perked up one ear and snorted, looked as if he might climb to his feet, but didn't bother and let his snout rest upon his paws again.

"Well? What did you find out?" Thorne, on crutches, hitched his way into the room and plopped into the worn leather recliner where he propped up his injured leg. He was wearing baggy khaki pants that covered up the cast running from foot to thigh, and his expression said more clearly than words, "I'm tired of being laid up."

"Nothing. The damned sheriff's department doesn't know diddly-squat."

"You talked to Espinoza?" Thorne asked.

Boots pounded from the back of the house, heralding the arrival of their youngest brother.

"Wait a minute!" Juanita's voice echoed through the hallways. "You take off those boots! I just mopped the floor. *Dios!* Does anyone ever listen to me? No!"

"Hey!" Slade appeared in the archway separating the living room from the foyer and staircase. He didn't bother to answer Juanita, nor did he shed his coat. "Where the hell have you been?" Black eyebrows were slammed together over intense, laser-blue eyes as he stared at Matt. "We've got stock to feed, and Thorne's not a helluva lot of help these days."

"Cool it." Thorne's gaze moved from his youngest

brother to Nicole's daughters who, if they'd heard the swearing, were too busy banging on the piano keys to notice. "Matt was down at the sheriff's office."

"They found anything?" Slade asked, his belligerence fading as he walked to the liquor cabinet set into the bookcase and unearthed an old bottle of Scotch. "How 'bout a drink?"

"No, they don't know anything else and yeah, I could use a shot." Matt couldn't hide his irritation that he hadn't gotten more definitive answers.

"None for me." Thorne shook his head. "What did Espinoza have to say?"

"He wasn't around. I talked with the woman."

"Kelly Dillinger," Nicole said as the twins, bored with making their own kind of music, climbed down from her lap and hurried out of the room. A tall woman with brown hair, a sharp wit and a medical degree, Nicole Stevenson was more than a match for his brother. She was smart, savvy, and as an emergency room physician, wasn't used to taking orders from anyone—just the kind of woman to tame Thorne and settle him down.

"She's the one." Matt accepted a short glass from Slade, took a swallow and felt the warm fire of liquor burn a welcome path down his throat. And he shoved any wayward thoughts of Detective Dillinger from his mind. It wasn't easy. In fact it was damned near impossible. That fiery redhead had a way of catching a man's attention. Big time.

"A drink?" Slade asked Nicole as he poured another glass.

"I'd better take a rain check. I'm scheduled at the hospital later," she said, and as her words faded she froze and cocked her head. "Uh-oh, it sounds like someone's waking up."

Matt heard the first cough of a baby's cry, and he was amazed at how women seemed to have a sixth sense about that sort of thing.

"I'll get him," Nicole said, then turned her head and looked over her shoulder at Thorne. One sleek eyebrow rose as she added, "but you uncles are going to be pulling duty later this evening."

"We can handle it," Thorne said, as if a baby were no problem at all. But then Thorne thought he could handle the world. And he wasn't too far off.

"Yeah. Right." Nicole wasn't buying her fiancé's confident routine. She climbed the stairs to the nursery, and her laughter drowned out the baby's fussy noises.

"So what did the detective say?" Thorne asked Matt as he pushed the recliner into a more upright position.

"Same old runaround. They're looking into all possibilities. They have no evidence of foul play. There are no suspects. When Randi wakes up, then maybe they'll be able to piece more of it together. All a load of bull if you ask me." He downed his drink, irritated all over again. The heat from the fire felt good against the back of his legs, the liquor warmed him on the inside, but he was restless, anxious, needed to take action. He'd been staying at the Flying M for nearly a month, ever since he'd been called and told about his half sister's accident. He'd driven like a madman, camped out and done what he could, but he was frustrated as hell because he felt like he was spinning his wheels. He had his own place to run, his ranch near the Idaho border. His neighbor, Mike Kavanaugh, was looking after the place while he was gone and had hired a couple of high school boys to help out, but Matt was beginning to feel the need to go back and check on the ranch himself.

"Detective Dillinger is a looker, if ya ask me," Slade offered up as he took a swallow from his drink.

"No one did," Matt grumbled.

Slade's chuckle was deep and wicked, and Matt caught the teasing glint in his brother's blue eyes. "Don't tell me you haven't noticed."

Matt snorted. Lifted a shoulder.

"Come on, admit it." Slade wasn't about to give up. "You've always had an eye for the ladies."

"It takes one to know one."

"Enough," Thorne said just as Nicole returned toting the baby. Matt's heart melted at the sight of little J.R., the name the brothers had come up with since Randi was still in a coma, didn't even know she had a son. They figured they could call him Junior or John Randall, like the kid's grandfather. As he had dozens of times, Matt wondered about the baby's father. Who was the guy? Where the hell was he? Why hadn't Randi ever mentioned him?

Matt felt a slash of guilt. The truth of the matter was that he, and the rest of his brothers, had been so caught up in their own lives, they'd lost touch with their half sister, a firebrand of a girl who, for years, had been the bane of her older siblings' existence, the daughter of the woman whom they blamed for wrecking their parents' marriage.

Now, looking down at the baby, his downy reddish-gold hair sticking up at odd angles, Matt felt a bit of pride and something more—something deeper, something that scared him, as it spoke to the need for roots, and settling down and marriage and children of his own.

Nicole handed the bundle to the man she intended to marry. "Here, Uncle Thorne, you deal with J.R. while I see if Juanita needs some help with dinner."

"Me, too. I help," Molly offered, dashing into the

room only to take a spin around her mother and race off toward the kitchen.

"How about you?" Nicole asked Mindy, who was tailing after her more exuberant sister.

"Yeth. Me, too."

"Come on, then," she said, casting one final glance at her soon-to-be husband and shepherding the girls down the hallway. Harold gave up a disgruntled "woof" and slapped his tail onto the braided rug. Matt swallowed a smile at the sight of his eldest brother—millionaire, CEO of McCafferty International, heretofore international jet-setter and playboy—reduced to juggling a one-month-old infant in his awkward hands while propping up his broken leg.

"Hey, I could use some help here," Thorne grumbled, though he grinned down at the baby.

"Didn't you say something about feeding the stock?" Matt asked Slade.

"That I did." The two younger McCaffertys left Thorne in charge of the infant. Matt thought it was only fitting as he snagged his jacket from the peg near the front door and stepped outside into the frigid air. Seeing as Thorne couldn't help out much with the heavy work around the ranch, he could damned well baby-sit.

The woman in the hospital bed looked horrible, though by all accounts she was healing. Nevertheless, in Kelly's estimation Randi McCafferty had a long way to go. There were tubes and monitors running into and out of her body and she lay on the bed unmoving, thin and pale, her skin still showing some signs of discoloration, though some of the bruises and cuts had healed.

"If only you could talk," Kelly said, biting her lower lip. For all the pain the McCaffertys had put on her family,

Kelly still didn't like seeing anyone like this. A nurse walked to Randi's bedside and began taking her vital signs. "Has she shown any sign of waking?" Kelly asked.

"I can't really say," sighed the petite woman with shiny black hair, olive skin, eyes rimmed with excessive mascara and a name tag that read Kathy Desmond. "With this one, we might need a crystal ball," she joked as she picked up Randi's wrist and took her pulse, then slipped a blood pressure cuff over her arm. "It seems to me that she should wake up soon. Certainly she's had plenty of eye movement beneath her lids, she's yawned, and one of the night nurses thinks she moved her arm. Whether this means she'll be waking up today, tomorrow or next week, I don't know."

"But soon."

"I would think." The nurse's highly arched brows pulled together. "But I'm not sure."

"I understand," Kelly said, wishing Matt McCafferty's half sister would rouse and open her eyes, be cognizant and clearheaded enough to answer questions about the day her car slid off the road. Had someone intentionally forced her over the embankment? Had she gone into labor and lost control? Had she just hit a patch of black ice that sent her vehicle into a skid? The McCafferty brothers seemed to think there was some person or persons behind the accident. Kelly wasn't convinced. Right now only Randi McCafferty had the answers to what had happened up at Glacier Park and only she knew who was the father of her child.

The nurse left the room and Kelly stepped closer to the unmoving form on the bed. She wrapped her fingers around the cool metal rails, then touched the back of Randi's hand, willing some life into Randi's battered body. "Wake up," she urged. "You've got so much to live for…a new baby, for starters.'' *And three stubborn, intense half brothers.*

''Besides that you've got a lot of explaining to do when you wake up.'' She squeezed Randi's hand, but there was no response. ''Come on, Randi. Help me out here.''

''She can't hear you.''

Kelly released the comatose woman's hand quickly and flushed. She recognized Matt McCafferty's voice instantly. Her heart jumped.

''I realize that.'' Turning, she found him in the doorway, still dressed in the jeans and shirt he'd had on a few hours earlier. His jacket was unbuttoned, his hat in his hands, his face not as hostile as it had been earlier, but there were still silent accusations in his dark eyes. Roguishly handsome and mad as a wet hornet.

''What're you doing here?'' he demanded.

''I met Detective Espinoza in the ER, then decided to check on your sister.''

''You should be checking out leads, trying to find the bastard who did this to her.'' Matt stepped into the room, closer. Kelly's nerves tightened and she silently chided herself for her reaction.

He stared down at his sister, and the play of emotions across his bladed features showed signs of a deeper emotion than she would have expected from the rogue cowboy, who had become, according to town gossip, a solitary man. Yes, there was anger in the set of his jaw, quiet determination in his stance, but something else was evident—the flicker of guilt deep in his near-black eyes. At some level Matt McCafferty felt responsible for his sister's condition. He reached over the rails just as Kelly had minutes before and took Randi's small, pale hand in his big, tanned fingers. ''You hang in there,'' he said huskily, his thumb rubbing the back of his sister's hand, only to stop less than an inch from the spot where the IV needle was buried in her skin.

Kelly's throat tightened as she recognized his pain.

"Your little man, J.R., he's needin' ya." Matt cleared his throat, slid an embarrassed glance at Kelly, then turned his attention back to his sister. Obviously he felt more comfortable shoeing horses, mending fence or roping calves than he did trying to come up with words of encouragement to a comatose sibling. And yet he tried. Kelly's heart twisted. Maybe there was more to Matt McCafferty than first met the eye, than rumor allowed. "And the rest of us, we need ya, too," he added gruffly. With a final pat to his kid sister's shoulder, he turned on his heel.

Kelly let her breath out slowly. *Who* was this man and why did she react to him—dear Lord, her hands were sweating, and if she didn't know better, she'd swear her heartbeat accelerated whenever she saw him. But that was crazy. Just plain nuts.

Giving herself a quick mental shake, Kelly followed him through the door into the central hallway to the hub that housed the nurses' station.

"Where's Espinoza?" he asked, sliding a glance her way.

"Probably back at the office. He finished up here on another case, but he's aware that you're concerned. He'll call you tonight, but I don't think he can give you any more information than I have."

"Damn." They walked to the elevator and stepped into a waiting car. She ignored the fact that her pulse had accelerated, and she noticed that he smelled faintly of leather and soap. As the doors to the elevator shut and they were alone, his dark eyes focused on her. Hard. She wanted to squirm away from his intense, silently accusing eyes. Instead she stood her ground as he asked, "So why were you in Randi's room?"

"Just to keep my focus. I hadn't seen her for a while and after your visit this afternoon, I thought I'd see how she was getting along. I've kept in contact with the hospital, of course, gotten updates, but I thought seeing her might make me clearer on some points."

"Such as?"

"Such as why was she up in Glacier Park? Where was she going? Who were her enemies? Who were her friends? Why did she fire the foreman of the ranch a week or so before she left Seattle? What happened at her job? Who's the father of her child? Those kind of questions."

"Get any answers?" he asked sarcastically.

"I was hoping someone in the family might know."

"I wish. No one does." He leaned against the rail surrounding the interior as the elevator car landed and the doors opened to the lobby. He straightened, his jacketed arm brushing hers. She stepped out of the car, ignored the faint physical contact. "What do you know about a book your sister was writing?"

"I'm not sure there is one," he said as they crossed a carpeted reception area where wood-framed chairs were scattered around tables strewn with magazines and a few potted trees had been added to give some illusion that St. James Hospital was more than a medical facility, warmer than an institution.

"Your housekeeper, Juanita Ramirez, said she was in contact with your sister before the accident and that Randi had been working on a book of some kind, but no one seems to know anything more about it."

"Juanita didn't even know that Randi was pregnant. I doubt if she was privy to my sister's secrets," Matt muttered as he made his way to the wide glass doors of the main entrance.

"Why would she make it up?"

"I'm not saying Juanita's lying." The first set of doors opened automatically, and as Kelly stepped into the vestibule, she felt the temperature lower ten or fifteen degrees. Thank God. For some reason she was sweating.

"But maybe Randi fibbed. She'd talked about writing a book since she was a kid in high school, but did she ever? No. Not that my brothers or I ever heard of."

The second set of doors opened and a middle-aged man pushed a wheelchair, where a tiny elderly woman was huddled in a wool coat, stocking cap and lap blankets. Outside the snow was falling, flakes dancing and swirling in the pale blue illumination from the security lamps.

Matt squared his hat on his head, the brim shadowing his face even further. "Talk to anyone and sooner or later they tell you about the book they're gonna write someday. Trouble is that 'someday' never comes."

"Spoken like a true cynic," Kelly observed as she buttoned her coat and felt the chill of Montana winter slap her face and cool her blood, which seemed a few degrees higher than normal.

"Just a reality check. If Randi was writing a book, don't you think one of us, either Thorne, Slade or I, would know about it?"

"Just like you knew all about her job and her pregnancy," Kelly threw back at him, using the same argument he'd given her earlier about the housekeeper's belief that Randi had penned some literary tome.

Matt was about to step off the curb, but stopped and turned to face Kelly. "Okay, okay, but even so. Big deal. So what if she was writing her goddamned version of *War And Peace?* What's that got to do with the price of tea in

China, or more specifically what happened to her up in Glacier Park?''

"You tell me."

"*You're* the cop," he pointed out, his eyes flaring angrily. "A detective, no less. This is your job, lady."

"And I'm just trying to do it."

"Then try a little harder, okay? My sister's life is on the line." With that he stepped off the curb, hunched his shoulders against the wind and strode through the blowing snow to his truck. Kelly was left with her cheeks burning hot, her temper in the stratosphere, her pride taking a serious blow.

"Bastard," she growled under her breath, and headed to her own car, an unmarked four-wheel drive. She didn't know who she was more angry with, the hard-edged cowboy, or herself for her reaction to him. What was wrong with her? She was nervous around him, nearly tongue-tied, so…*unprofessional!* Well, that was going to change, and now!

Once behind the wheel, she twisted on the ignition, flipped on the wipers and drove to her town house on the west end of town. With a western facade, the two-storied row house had been her home for three years, ever since she'd scraped up enough of a down payment to buy her own place.

She parked in the single garage and climbed up a flight to the main floor, where she kicked off her boots in the tiny laundry room, then padded inside. Tossing her keys onto the glass-topped table that served as her eating area and desk, she walked into the kitchen and hit the play button on her answering machine while shedding her coat.

"Kelly?" her sister's voice called frantically, bringing a smile to Kelly's lips as her sibling was nothing if not overly dramatic. "It's Karla and I was hoping to catch you. Look, it's about six and I'm still at the shop, but I'm gonna close up soon and pick up the kids at the sitter's then run out to Mom and Dad's. I thought maybe you could meet me there…call me at the shop or try and reach me out at their place."

Kelly checked the wall clock and saw that it was nearly seven-thirty. There were no other messages so she placed a call to her folks' house and Karla picked up on the second ring.

"Got your message," Kelly said.

"Kelly, great! Mom just pulled this fantastic pork roast from the oven, and from the smell of it, it's to die for."

Kelly's stomach rumbled and she realized she hadn't eaten anything since the carton of yogurt and muffin that had sufficed as lunch.

"We were hoping you could join us."

With a glance at the paperwork on the table, Kelly weighed the options. She wanted to go over every ounce of information she could on Randi McCafferty, but she figured she could wedge in some time for her family first. "Just give me a few minutes to change. I'll be there in half an hour."

"Make it twenty minutes, will ya? My kids are starved and when they get hungry, they get cranky."

"Do not," one of the boys countered, his high voice audible.

"Just hurry," Karla pleaded. "The natives are restless."

"I'll be there in a flash."

"Good idea. Put on the lights and siren, clear out traffic and roar on over."

"I'll see ya." Kelly whipped off her uniform and changed into soft, well-worn jeans and her favorite cowl-necked sweater. She took half a minute to run a brush through her hair, then threw on a long coat and boots and dived into her old Nissan, a relic that she loved. Fifteen years old, a hundred and eighty thousand miles on the odometer and never once had the compact left her stranded. At a stoplight, she applied a fresh sheen of lipstick but still made it to her parents' house, the bungalow where she'd grown up, in fifteen minutes flat.

"Kelly girl!" her father called as he pushed his wheelchair into the dining room where the table was already set. Once tall and strapping, Ron Dillinger had been reduced to using the chair for twenty-five years, the result of a bullet that had lodged in his back and damaged his spinal cord. He'd been a deputy at the time, and had been on disability ever since. "Glad you could join us."

"Me, too, Dad," she said, and bent down to kiss his forehead where thin strands of white hair couldn't quite cover his speckled pate.

"You've been busy, I see," he said, holding up a folded newspaper. "Lots going on."

"Always."

"That's the way I remember it. Even in my day, there weren't enough men on the force."

"Or women."

Ronald snorted. "Weren't any women at all."

"Maybe that's why you weren't so efficient," she teased, and he swatted at her with his newspaper. She ducked into the kitchen and was greeted with squeals of delight from her nephews, Aaron and Spencer, two dynamos who rarely seemed to wind down.

The boys charged her, nearly toppling their mother in the process. "Aunt Kelly!" Aaron cried. "Up, up." He held up chubby three-year-old arms and Kelly obligingly lifted him from the floor. He had a mashed sandwich in one hand and a tiny toy truck in the other. Peanut butter was smeared across the lower half of his face. "You comed."

"That I did."

"Came, she came," Karla corrected him.

"You're such a baby," Spencer needled.

"Am not!" Aaron rose to the bait as quickly as a hungry trout to a salmon fly.

"Of course you're not," Kelly said, swinging him to the ground and wondering just how much peanut butter was transferred to her sweater. "And neither are you," she said to her older nephew, who grinned, showing off the gap where once had been two front teeth. Freckled, blue-eyed and smart as a whip, Spencer enjoyed besting his younger sibling, a half brother. Karla, two years younger than Kelly, had been married twice, divorced as many times, and had sworn off men and marriage for good.

"Here, you can mash the potatoes," Karla said as she snatched a wet dishrag from the sink and started after a squealing Aaron, who took off into the dining room.

"Papa!" Aaron cried, hoping his grandfather would protect him from his mother's obsession with cleanliness.

"He won't save you," Karla said, chasing after her youngest.

Kelly's mother, Eva, was adding a dab of butter and a sprinkle of brown sugar to already-baked acorn squash. The scents of roast pork, herbs and her mother's favorite perfume mingled and rose in the warmth of the kitchen as she shook her head at the melee. "Never a dull minute when the boys are around."

"I see that." Kelly rumpled Spencer's hair fondly, cringed at the wail coming from the dining room, then rinsed her hands and found the electric beaters so that she could whip the potatoes. Over the whir of the hand mixer,

Aaron's screams, the microwave timer and comments from Charlie, her parents' pet budgie, who was perched in his cage near the front door, Kelly could barely hear herself think.

"I'll make the gravy," Karla said as she tossed the dirty rag into the sink.

"Mission accomplished?" Kelly glanced down at a more subdued Aaron. His face was clean again, red from being rubbed by the washcloth.

"Yeah, and it'll last all of five minutes. *If* we're lucky."

Kelly's mother chuckled. A petite woman with fluffy apricot curls and a porcelain complexion, she doted on her two grandsons as if they were truly God's gifts, which, Kelly imagined, they were. It was just too bad they had such louses for fathers. Seth Kramer and Franklin Anderson were as different as night and day—their only common trait being that they couldn't handle the responsibilities of fatherhood.

"Are we about ready?" Eva asked, and Kelly clicked off the beaters.

"I think so."

It took another five minutes to carry everything into the dining room, find a booster chair for Aaron, get both boys settled and served up, but soon Kelly was cutting into a succulent slab of herb-seasoned pork. She finally relaxed a little, the tension in her shoulders easing as they ate and talked, just as they had growing up. Except there were two more chairs crowded around the Formica-topped table now, for two boys who were as dear to her as if they'd been Kelly's own.

"So what gives with all that business with the Mc-Caffertys?" her father asked around a mouthful of pork. "I read in the paper there's speculation about foul play."

"Isn't there always?" Kelly asked.

"With that group there is." Eva's eyebrows pulled together, causing little lines to deepen between them. "Yeah, they're an untrustworthy lot, there's no doubt of that."

"Amen," Karla said as she cut tiny pieces of meat for her youngest son.

Kelly didn't comment. For years the name McCafferty had been tantamount to Beelzebub or Lucifer in the Dillinger home. She saw her mother give off a soft little sigh as Eva poured gravy onto her potatoes. "I suppose it's all water under the bridge," she said softly, but the pain of the old betrayal was still evident in the lines of her face.

Ron scowled into his plate. "Maybe so, but it doesn't mean I have to like 'em."

"John Randall is dead."

"And I hope he rots in his grave."

"Dad!" Karla said sharply, then glanced pointedly at her sons.

"Well, I do. No reason to sugarcoat it. That son of a bitch didn't care a whit about anyone but his own kin. It didn't matter how many years your mother put in working for him, passing up other good jobs, he still cut her loose when times got a little rocky. And what happened to her pension, huh? There wasn't any, that's what happened. Bad investments, or some such crock of—"

"Dad!" Karla said again.

"Karla's right. There's no use discussing it in front of the boys," Eva agreed, but the sparkle in her eyes had faded. "Now, if you'll pass me the pepper..."

And so the subject was gratefully closed for the duration of the meal. Their father even found his smile again over a piece of his wife's lemon meringue pie.

After the plates had been cleared and the dishwasher

was humming with a full load, Ron challenged the boys to a game of checkers on a small table near the fire. Aaron climbed onto his grandfather's lap and they played as a team against Spencer, who thought he could beat them both as he'd practiced how to outmaneuver an opponent on a computer.

"The boys could really use a father figure," Karla observed, watching her sons relate to their grandfather as she fished in the closet for her sons' coats and hats. Sadly, she ran a hand through her spiky strawberry-blond hair. "All they've got is Dad."

"They do have fathers," Kelly reminded her.

Karla rolled her expressive green eyes. "Oh, give me a break. They have sperm donors, nothing else. Boy, can I pick 'em. Some people are athletically challenged, I'm love challenged."

"You and the rest of the women on the planet."

"I'm not kidding. I can see when anyone else is making a mistake, but I seem to have blinders on when it comes to my choice in men."

"Or rose-colored glasses."

"Yeah, those, too." She was pensive, running long fingers along the stitching in Aaron's stocking cap. "But then you never take a chance, Kelly. I mean, not on love. You take lots of chances in your career."

"Maybe I've been too busy."

"Or maybe you're just smarter than I am," Karla said with a sigh. "I don't see you making the same mistakes I did."

"You forget I'm a career woman," Kelly said, reaching for her coat. "A cop."

"So am I—a career woman, that is—and don't tell me that being a beautician and owning your own shop doesn't count."

"I wouldn't dream of it," Kelly said, laughing.

"So…when are you going to tuck your badge away long enough to fall in love?"

"As soon as you put down the perm rollers, shampoo and clippers."

"Very funny."

"I thought so." She slipped her arms through the sleeves of her coat, hiked it up over her shoulders and began working on the buttons.

"I think we both could take some advice from Randi McCafferty. You know she wrote a column for single people?" Karla asked, then added, "Of course you do—what was I thinking? You've been working on the case for weeks." She held up Spencer's coat, then called toward the living room. "Come on, boys. Time to go." Both kids protested and Karla said to Kelly, "I was only kidding about Randi McCafferty's column. The last person I would take any advice from is a McCafferty."

"Maybe they're not all as bad as we think," Kelly said as she reached into her pocket for her keys.

"Oh, yeah? So now they're sprouting wings and halos?" Karla shook her head. "I don't think so."

There was a whoop from the living room as Spencer actually beat Aaron and his grandfather. Aaron burst into tears, and from the twinkle in Ron Dillinger's eyes, Kelly was certain he'd let his eldest grandson win.

"Come on, boys, time to go," Karla called again. In an aside to Kelly, she added, "Getting them out of here is like pulling teeth."

"No!" Aaron cried, refusing to budge from his grandfather's lap while Spencer just ignored his mother, no matter what tack she took. Eventually she wrestled her youngest into his ski coat, hat and mittens while Spencer, lower lip protruding in an exaggerated pout, shrugged into a quilted pullover with a hood.

"You boys be good, now," Eva said as she emerged from the kitchen without her apron. She planted a kiss on each boy's cheek and slipped them each a tiny candy bar left over from Halloween into their hands.

"I be good!" Aaron said, trying to tear off his mittens to get at the bit of chocolate.

"Mom!" Karla admonished.

"I just can't help myself."

"Here, let me get it." Kelly unwrapped the chocolate morsel, then plopped it into Aaron's open mouth.

"He's like one of those nestlings you see on the nature shows," Karla grumbled good-naturedly. "Aren't ya, little eaglet?"

Aaron grinned and chocolate drooled down his chin.

"I've got to get out of here. Come on, Spence." With that she bustled out the door, leaving Kelly to say goodbye to her parents.

"Everything good with you?" her father asked, worry in his dark eyes as he rolled his wheelchair into the foyer.

"Couldn't be better."

"But the boys on the force, they're not giving you any trouble?"

"None that I don't deserve, Dad. This isn't the 1940s, you know. There are thousands of female cops these days."

"I know, I know, but it just doesn't seem like a job for a woman." He held up his hands as if warding off the verbal blow he was certain was heading his way. "No offense."

"Oh, none taken, Dad, none at all. You've just denigrated every woman police officer I know, but am I offended? Oh, no-o-o. Not me."

"Fine, fine, you've made your point," he said with a chuckle. "Just don't let anyone give you a bad time. None of the boys you work with and especially none of the McCaffertys."

"Can't we just forget about them?" Eva asked.

"Impossible." He cranked the wheelchair into the living room and returned with a copy of the *Grand Hope Gazette,* folded to display an article on the third page of the main section, an article about Thorne McCafferty's small plane crash. "And this is after a couple of weeks have passed." He skimmed the article. "Seems as if there's some question as to whether or not there was foul play involved, and this here reporter thinks maybe the plane crash and the sister's wreck might be related. Bah. Sounds like coincidence to me." He glanced up at Kelly, his bristly white eyebrows elevated, inviting her opinion.

"I'm not at liberty to discuss the case."

"Oh, cut the crap, Kelly. We're family."

"And I'll confide in you when I need to, okay? Now... I've got to run. Duty calls."

She bussed each of her parents on the cheeks, then hurried outside to her car. The snow had stopped falling, but because of the dark clouds, she couldn't see a solitary star in the dark heavens. Her breath fogged in the air, her windshield was frozen, and she shivered as she cranked on the ignition.

Like clockwork, the engine fired and she drove away from the warm little bungalow with its patches of golden light and wide front porch. Her parents were aging, more rapidly as the days went by. Her father had never been his robust self after the gunshot blast that had ruined his career and crippled him for life, and her mother, strong woman that she was, had never complained, had taken care of a convalescing, depressed husband and two young

daughters. She'd landed a job with John Randall Mc-
Cafferty as his personal secretary to help make ends meet.
John Randall had promised her raises, promotions, bo-
nuses and a retirement plan, but his fortunes had changed,
and after his second divorce and a downturn in the econ-
omy, he'd been left with nothing but the ranch. Eva had
lost her job and all the promises of a substantial nest egg
had proved to be empty, the money that was supposed to
have been set aside dwindled away by bad investments—
oil wells that had run dry, silver mines that had never
produced, stock in start-up companies that had shut down
within months of opening their doors.

There had been talk of a lawsuit, but Eva hadn't been
able to find a local attorney ready to take on a man who
had once been a political contender in the area, a man
who had been influential and still had connections to
judges, the mayor and even a senator or two.

"Don't dwell on it," Kelly told herself. She drove
across the town where she'd grown up, wheeled into the
parking lot of her row house and used the remote to open
her garage door.

Though there hadn't been a lot of money in her family,
she'd grown up with security and love from both her parents. That was probably more than any of the McCafferty
children could say. She climbed up the stairs to her bedroom on the upper floor, changed into her flannel pajamas
and a robe, then made herself a cup of decaf coffee and
sat at the kitchen table, scouring the notes she'd taken on
Randi McCafferty's accident and Thorne McCafferty's
plane crash.

So many questions swirled around John Randall's only
daughter and no one, it seemed, could come up with the
answers. Kelly had interviewed all the brothers, everyone
who worked on the Flying M Ranch, all of Randi Mc-

Cafferty's friends in the area. All the while she'd kept in contact with the Seattle police, who had handled interviewing Randi's friends and associates there, in the city where Randi had lived and worked. It wasn't usual procedure, but this case was different with Randi being pregnant, giving birth, then lying comatose in the hospital, her half brothers crying foul play.

But until Randi McCafferty came out of the coma, the mystery shrouding the youngest of John Randall's children would most likely remain unsolved.

Kelly glanced down at the notes she'd taken and two questions loomed larger than the others. First and foremost, who was the father of Randi's son, and second, was she writing a book and what was it about?

Doodling as she sipped her coffee, she thought about the case, then, as a headache began to cloud her mind, she finished her coffee and leaned back in her chair. In her mind's eye she saw Matt McCafferty as he had been at the office and later in the hospital. Chiseled features, dark eyes, square jaw and hard, ranch-tough body. He came on like gang busters, looking as if he was ready to spit nails, but there was more to him, deeper emotions she'd witnessed herself as he'd stood over his sister's bedside. Feelings he'd tried to hide had crossed his features. Guilt. Worry. Fear.

Yes, she decided, there was more to Cowboy Matt than met the eye.

She stretched and yawned, scraped her chair back and started for the bedroom when the phone jangled loudly. She picked it up on the extension near the bed and glanced at the clock. Eleven forty-seven. "Hello?" she said into the receiver, knowing it was bound to be an emergency.

Espinoza's voice boomed over the line. "Kelly? We've

got a situation. Meet me down at St. James Hospital ASAP.''

''What happened?'' she asked, already stripping off her robe.

''It's Randi McCafferty. Someone just tried to pull the plug on her.''

Chapter Three

Somewhere a phone was ringing, jangling, intrusive, but the woman, naked to the waist, her uniform tossed over the back of a chair in the unfamiliar room, didn't seem to notice.

Brring!

She walked forward, tossed her long red hair over her shoulder and flashed him a naughty smile. With a wink, she said, "So come on, cowboy, show me what you're made of." Her dark eyes sparked with a wicked, teasing fire and her lips were full, wet and oh so kissable.

Aching, he reached forward to pull her close and lose himself in her.

Brring!

Matt's eyes flew open. He'd been dreaming. About Kelly Dillinger, and he was sporting one helluva proof of arousal. He blinked, the image disappearing into the shadows of the night. Down the hallways of the old ranch house, the phone blasted again. Groggily, he glanced at the digital display of his clock. Nearly twelve. Meaning whoever was calling wasn't waking up the McCaffertys with good news.

Randi. His heart nearly stopped. Slapping on the light, he didn't wait for his eyes to adjust but yanked on the pair of jeans he'd tossed over the foot of the bed and threw a sweatshirt over his head. He was striding barefoot down the hall when the door to the master suite was flung open, and Thorne, wearing boxer shorts, his cast and a robe he hadn't bothered to cinch, was hobbling toward the stairs.

"That was Nicole from the hospital. Someone tried to kill Randi," he said tersely.

"*What?*"

"Someone put something into her damned IV."

"Hell!" Matt broke out in a cold sweat. His mind began running in circles. "Is she okay?"

"Far as anyone can tell," Thorne said, frowning darkly. By this time they were both working their way toward the center staircase.

"How could that happen?"

"No one's sure yet. It's pandemonium down there. Her heart stopped beating. They had to use paddles."

"Son of a bitch!"

"My thoughts exactly." Thorne stopped at the door to Slade's room and pounded hard, then shoved it open to find their youngest brother half dressed, his hair sticking up at odd angles, his fingers fumbling with the buttons of a flannel shirt.

"I heard the phone ring. Figured it was bad news," Slade muttered.

"You figured right." Thorne filled him in quickly and the youngest McCafferty's expression clouded over.

"For the love of Mike, we told them this would happen! The police are out to lunch, for God's sake!" He swung a fist in the air. "Who's doing this?"

"And why?" Thorne's gray eyes narrowed with cold fury.

"Let's go." Slade stuffed his shirttails into his jeans.

"We all can't go to the hospital," Thorne pointed out as Slade swore a blue streak and reached for a pair of hiking boots. "Someone's got to stay with J.R. and the girls."

"That's your job," Matt decided. "You're gonna be stepfather to the twins and you're not a helluva lot of use, anyway, what with the bad leg."

"But I can't just stay here and—"

"Don't argue. We've heard it all before," Matt said. "You think you're in charge of 'the Randi situation,' the one calling the shots. But you're laid up, whether you like it or not. So you have two choices. Wake up the baby and Nicole's daughters and drag them out in the freezing cold to a hospital that's sure to be chaos, or stay here and wait for one of us to call or relieve you."

Thorne's gray eyes darkened. Thick black eyebrows slammed together in frustration. "But I think—"

"For once just trust us, okay? We can handle things." Matt was already halfway to his room, where he found his socks, boots and a pair of gloves. He yanked them on as Thorne filled the doorway, his shoulders nearly touching each side of the frame.

"I don't like this."

"Of course you don't. You can't stand not being in charge." Matt tugged on his socks and started with his cowboy boots.

"I'd feel better if—"

"For God's sake, just give it up, okay? I'll feel better

if you'd just shut the hell up and stay here with the kids. Coordinate. Take calls. Be Communications Central. Someone will relieve you soon and you can drive yourself to the hospital and take charge of things there again, okay? Until then, you're on, 'Uncle Thorne.' Now, get out of my way.'' Matt shouldered past his older brother, collected Slade and hurried down the stairs. He didn't have time for any of Thorne's bogus authority trips. Not now. He grabbed his jacket and hat.

His jaw tightened when he thought of Randi lying vulnerable in the hospital. God, you'd think she'd be safe there!

Outside, the snow had started again and it was cold as hell. Not bothering to button his jacket, he slid behind the wheel of his pickup and, with the flick of a wrist, twisted on the ignition. Slade climbed into the passenger side. ''Let's go.''

Matt threw his truck into gear before Slade had a chance to shut the door.

Who tried to kill his sister?

Why would someone go to such lengths to see that she was dead?

Did someone want to shut her up?

Was it revenge?

Did it have anything to do with her baby and J.R.'s mystery father?

''What the devil's going on?'' he growled, his breath fogging in the frigid air. Worry and fear took turns clawing at his gut, and his fingers clamped around the steering wheel until his knuckles showed white. He squinted through the foggy windshield as the wipers slapped haphazardly over the glass.

What if Randi didn't make it? What if whoever was trying to kill her was successful?

"I don't know," Slade admitted, reaching into the inside pocket of his jacket for a crumpled pack of cigarettes as Matt cranked the wheel at the highway, then gunned the engine. "But I'm sure as hell gonna find out."

Amen. If nothing else, Matt intended to find out who'd done this to his sister and then he'd beat the living hell out of the bastard.

St. James Hospital was a madhouse. Word had leaked out to the press that someone had tried to murder a patient, and a television van, camera crew and reporters from two stations were already staked out in front of the front doors. Kelly managed to dodge a microphone thrust toward her by muttering a quick "No comment" as she walked outside. Another reporter was camped out in the lobby, and Kelly shoved her way through doors marked Staff Only to avoid him. She flew up the staircase to the third floor, her boots ringing on the steps, her heart pounding as if it were a drum. Outside the doors of the ICU unit, she nearly ran into Detective Espinoza, two deputies from the sheriff's department and a policewoman with the Grand Hope force.

"Okay, so what happened?" she demanded.

"Randi McCafferty went into cardiac arrest, and it looks like someone might have helped her along by slipping something into her IV."

"What?"

"That's what we're trying to determine."

"But Randi's okay?"

"Out of the woods for now," Espinoza said, running a hand around his neck. His uniform, always neatly pressed, was rumpled, his usually spit-polished boots dull under the harsh hospital lights.

"Fill me in."

"One of the doctors here, Nicole Stevenson, stopped by on her break to look in at her soon-to-be sister-in-law. She's engaged to Thorne McCafferty."

"The oldest brother, I know."

"Anyway, Randi was in a private room up on the fourth floor. As Dr. Stevenson stepped off the elevator, she spotted a person in a lab coat emerging from Randi's room. The guy—or it could have been a woman, Dr. Stevenson didn't get that much of a look—anyway, the suspect turned and hurried down the hallway, then cut back into the employee stairwell. Dr. Stevenson didn't think much of it, thought the person was another doctor, until she checked on Thorne's sister. Randi wasn't breathing. Nicole started CPR and yelled for the nurses."

"She didn't recognize the person running away?"

"Can't even say if it was a man or woman." Espinoza snorted. "All she remembers is that the suspect was about five nine and had brown hair—long for a man, short for a woman. Medium build. She didn't get much of a glimpse of the person's face, but thinks he or she might have been wearing glasses." Espinoza's dark eyes seemed weary. "Not much to go on."

"But better than nothing."

"Unless it's not our guy."

"Or gal," Kelly said.

"Right. Or woman." Espinoza told Kelly that he'd already secured Randi's private room and a crime team was going over it, though the chances of lifting the perpetrator's fingerprints or finding other incriminating evidence were small. Espinoza had also sent the two deputies to check St. James's staff roster and were instructed to interview anyone on duty. The policewoman was posted here, near the ICU, and for the moment, Espinoza thought, Randi was safe.

Rubbing a day's growth of stubble along his jaw, he added, "Whoever struck earlier won't take another chance tonight. He'll lay low for a while. Let things cool off."

"Unless he can't afford to. Obviously he's worried that when Randi wakes up, she'll finger him."

"We'll keep a guard posted," Espinoza said. "If the guy's stupid enough to try again, we'll be ready."

"So what about the patient? Is she still in a coma?" Kelly asked.

Espinoza nodded and glanced at the closed double doors of the ICU unit. "So far. Before the attack a couple of the nurses thought she might be coming around."

"Maybe that's why the perp struck when he did."

"Looks like."

"Then he'll be back." Kelly was certain of it.

The doors to the elevator opened and two of the McCafferty brothers strode through. Kelly's insides tightened and her stupid pulse jumped at the sight of Matt, his jaw thrust forward, his eyes burning bright in their sockets. "What the hell happened?" he demanded as if she were somehow to blame. "Where's Randi?" His head swiveled toward the closed doorway and he took two steps toward the ICU ward.

"You can't go barging in there," Kelly warned, and stuck out her hand as if to physically restrain him.

"Like hell." Matt's gaze sliced clear to her soul. He had one hand on the door and his brother Slade was only a step behind.

"She's right." Espinoza flashed his badge.

"Randi's my sister," Matt said flatly. "And it's gonna take a helluva lot more than a badge to stop me from seeing for myself that she's okay. You people," he snorted, and brushed past Espinoza. Bob stepped forward, but Kelly, recognizing Matt's need to see for himself that his sister was alive, put a hand on Espinoza's arm as the two McCafferty brothers entered the ICU ward.

"The nurses will shoo them out," she said under her breath, and within seconds, Matt and Slade were back in the hallway. They were more subdued, but the anger in the set of Matt's mouth hadn't disappeared. "This might not have happened," he stated, his brown eyes drilling into hers before centering on Espinoza, "if the police hadn't been sitting on their backsides while a killer was on the loose."

Espinoza's dark gaze flashed fire. "We don't know that."

"Like hell." Matt went nose-to-nose with the detective. Broad shoulders were tense, the cords in the back of his neck stretched taut, his muscles flexed, as if ready for a fight. "Maybe you didn't before, but I'd say that all doubt is gone."

"Things have changed."

"Damned straight. My sister nearly died." His furious gaze burned a path from Roberto Espinoza to Kelly. His lips were blade-thin, bracketed by thin white lines of rage. "Now, let's get on with the investigation."

"Maybe you should let us do our jobs," Kelly snapped, more at her own reaction to the man than at Matt. Just being around him made her tense, edgy, and that silly feminine part that she so long had penned screamed to be set free whenever he was near. Her emotions were a mess. While maintaining her professionalism, she was trying to cut the guy some slack, but he was coming on pretty strong out here in the hushed corridors of St. James Hospital.

"Do your jobs? Let me know when you've started," Matt growled.

"Wait a minute—"

"No." He pushed his nose to within inches of hers and jabbed a finger in the air. His dark skin was red, his nostrils flared, his eyebrows rammed into a single line. "*You* wait a minute. My sister nearly died, got it? *Died.* Twice. I don't think we can give you permission to take your own sweet time."

"We're doing everything possible to find out what happened," she said, squaring her shoulders, not giving in an inch when she wanted nothing more than to put some distance between her body and his, to give herself more room to think.

"Then what about the maroon Ford? Kurt Striker found where Randi's rig was scraped by another vehicle. The paint samples he took from the fender matched any number of Ford products."

"We know that and we're checking into it," Espinoza said firmly as the elevator doors opened and a petite, smartly dressed woman emerged. Kelly recognized the local news reporter in her three-inch heels and tailored suit.

"How'd she get past security and get up here?" Kelly asked, stepping forward, blocking the woman's path. "You'll have to go downstairs," she ordered.

"I'm with the news."

"Jana Madrid. KABO. We've met before." Kelly didn't budge.

"I just want to talk to someone to get the facts." She managed a camera-perfect smile. "You're a police officer. Is it true that there was an attempt on Randi McCafferty's life tonight, here, in the hospital?"

"No comment."

"But—" The reporter was craning her neck, trying to see past the nurses' station to the small crowd clustered around the ICU. "Matt McCafferty's here."

"You know him?" Kelly asked.

"We've met. Yes." Jana's large eyes narrowed and Kelly could almost see the gears turning in the woman's mind. "So someone did make an attempt on his sister's life. If you'll excuse me, I'd like to get a statement from him."

"Later."

"What, exactly, happened here?"

"Leave, Ms. Madrid. Now." Kelly was firm, sensing one of the deputies approaching her to help.

"I just need a few facts for a story," Jana persisted, throwing a friendlier smile in Kelly's direction. "Come on. If a killer's on the loose, the public needs to be aware of it."

"The department will issue a statement at the appropriate time, as will the hospital. Until then I'm not at liberty to answer any questions." Kelly slapped the elevator call button.

"But the people have the right to know."

"The people need to know facts. When we have some. Now, please, either leave the hospital alone, or I'll have someone escort you."

"I'll handle it," the deputy who'd come to assist her offered. Six three or four, with his blond hair shaved to barely a quarter of an inch, he stepped forward. About twenty-six and beefy, Mike Benedict was a force to be reckoned with. The reporter hesitated, started to say something, then with a quick appraisal of the no-win situation, frowned.

"Television could help with the investigation, you know. If we got a sketch of a suspect, we could air it to the community, be involved in a community watch. It's the public's right."

"We'll let you know. Now, please," Kelly said firmly, and the woman reluctantly stepped into the elevator. The doors closed and Kelly returned to find Matt McCafferty ready to jump down Espinoza's throat.

"So check the hell faster, would ya? Find out what's going on and arrest the bastard who did this to Randi before she winds up dead!"

From the corner of her eye Kelly caught sight of a slim woman in a white coat striding purposefully along the hallway. Her hair was tossed off her face, and her worried gold eyes, sculpted cheekbones and full lips were set into a regal countenance. Her name tag read Nicole Stevenson, M.D.

"Where's Thorne?" she asked without preamble. She seemed cool and sophisticated, but just beneath the surface of her eyes there was a deeper emotion. Worry. Maybe even fear. Obviously a strong woman, one who was in charge of her life professionally and personally, she was nonetheless frightened. Kelly had seen enough trauma to recognize when someone's calm life had been breached. The killer had broken into Nicole Stevenson's workplace, a spot she considered a haven, and attacked someone the doctor was close to. Beneath her veneer of cool professionalism, Dr. Nicole Stevenson was anxious.

"We left Thorne home with the kids," Slade said.

"But I thought he was going to get Juanita or Jenny to stay...oh, it doesn't matter. I thought I'd check on Randi again," Nicole said before her gaze landed on Kelly. "Detective Dillinger." She didn't bother forcing a smile she didn't feel. Obviously she, too, thought the police weren't doing everything possible to track down Randi's enemies or protect her from attack.

"Do that—check on Randi," Slade said, shoving a hand nervously through his rumpled black hair.

"I'll be back in a minute." Nicole swept through the

doors to Intensive Care with the quiet authority of a medical professional on her own turf.

"You questioned her?" Kelly asked Espinoza.

He nodded.

"I think I'll have a few words with her."

"Have at. But she didn't see much. I'll be up on the fourth floor in the private room where she was attacked," he said, with one last glance at the McCafferty brothers as he headed toward the elevators.

"How's your sister doing?" Kelly asked, hitching her chin at the closed doors to ICU.

White lines of irritation were visible at the corners of Matt's mouth, but he'd calmed a bit and the self-righteous fury she'd seen burning in his eyes had faded to some extent. "I guess we should be thankful she's alive."

Slade nodded. "Now, if only she'd wake up."

"That would help," Matt agreed, and slid his jaw to the side. "Why don't you tell me any theories you have?" he said. "Surely you must have some idea who's behind this."

"Ideas, no suspects, no hard evidence." Kelly shook her head thoughtfully. "Not much to go on. How about you? Or you?" She cut a glance toward Slade. "I'll buy you a cup of coffee in the cafeteria."

Matt looked at the closed door to the ICU. "Just as soon as we talk to Nicole."

"You go along," Slade said to Matt, and braced himself against the wall with his shoulders. "I think I'll hang out here and I'll let Nicole know where you are so she can fill you in."

"Fair enough." Matt nodded sharply and fell into step with Kelly as they took the back stairs.

On the first floor, Matt walked directly toward the cafeteria, a path he'd obviously traveled often while his half sister, nephew and brother were patients at St. James. The coffee was complimentary, and they found a quiet table near the windows and a shedding ficus tree.

"I want to know what you guys have," Matt said, sipping from a paper cup, his dark eyes blazing above the rim. "And don't keep anything back. I'm not buying into anything being top secret or any other mumbo-jumbo. I want the facts about my sister."

Kelly had nothing to hide. She took a sip of her coffee and leaned her elbows on the table, so that she was closer to this middle McCafferty brother and could keep her voice at a lower level. "I'll tell you what I can, but I'm not going to compromise the investigation."

"I'm *family,* for Pete's sake."

"But they're not." Lifting an eyebrow, she scanned the tables, noting that a few nurses sat at one, at another, doctors in scrubs, and at a third, a few people were drinking from cups while others milled nearby. Jana Madrid, the pushy reporter who had pushed her way onto the floor housing the ICU, was among them.

"The press." Matt scowled darkly.

"Some of them. Who else would be up at this hour?"

"Hell."

"So let's just talk in general terms."

"Shoot."

"As I said, we're investigating the possibility that your sister might have been run off the road, and we're checking any vehicles that might have needed body work after the time of the accident, specifically maroon Fords. We've narrowed that down to probably an Explorer. Also, we're checking on the people she worked with and the men she dated...." Kelly let her voice drift off as one of the men near the table of reporters, a thin man with sandy hair, a clipped mustache and an affable smile wended his way through the empty tables in their direction. Not far behind was the petite newswoman.

"Excuse me," the man said, flashing a brilliant smile. "I'm Troy White with KAB—"

"I've seen you on television," Kelly said, cutting the reporter off. "I've already said 'No comment' to one of your associates." She pointed toward Jana Madrid, and the woman took it as a cue to step forward. Inwardly groaning, Kelly leveled her censorious gaze at Troy.

"I'd just like a few words with Mr. McCafferty. You're Matt, right?"

Matt glared at him as if he could see right through the man. "Yep."

"If you don't mind."

"I do." Matt's expression was hard as granite.

"But it'll only take a few seconds." This from Jana, who despite her brashness stood a step behind Troy as if the small man were some kind of shield. Doctors, nurses and the woman behind the cafeteria counter all stopped to watch.

"Another time," Matt said, standing and towering over the shorter man by three or four inches. He was spoiling for a fight, if ever anyone was. His shoulders were bunched, his right hand clenched into a fist, his nostrils flared.

The reporter either didn't pick up on Matt's mood, or didn't give a damn. "Just tell me about Randi. Do you have any idea who would attack your sister?"

"That's it!" Kelly shot to her feet. "Maybe you weren't listening, but Mr. McCafferty here said he didn't want to be bothered, so maybe you'd better wait for your interview until it's more convenient for him." Kelly wedged her angry body between the reporter and Matt and glowered at both reporters, then allowed her gaze to skate across the room to include the cameraman hanging out near the coffeemaker. "Now, if you people aren't careful, I'll personally escort you out of here."

Troy White took offense. His mustache shivered. "Listen, lady, the American people have the right to know—"

"Stuff it, Troy," Kelly said, cutting him off. "I already heard the spiel from Jana here." She glanced at the woman next to him. "Both of you will have to wait for a statement."

Jana's lips pinched. "Let it go," she said, touching Troy's sleeve, though her eyes were fastened to Matt. Despite her professionalism, Kelly felt an unlikely spurt of jealousy squirt through her veins. The woman was pretty, proud and predatory. "We've got enough tape for the morning news," Jana said, and managed a smile that seemed to be trained only on Matt. "Thank you for your trouble."

Troy White somehow managed to grit his teeth and give Kelly and Matt a quick cursory nod. "Another time."

"Call first," Matt warned. He strode out the doors and Kelly caught up with him near the reception area. He slid her a glance as he kept walking. "Look, Detective, I don't need anyone to fight my battles." He glanced down at her small frame. "Especially not a woman."

"I'm a cop," she reminded him as they reached the elevators.

"A female cop."

Stung, she slapped the call button. "But a cop just the same. I can handle myself," she asserted, angry with herself for letting his remarks get under her skin. He was so damned unsettling and his opinion mattered way more than it should.

"I don't remember asking for your help."

The nerve of the man. Of all the pompous, self-serving…simmering, she turned on him, ready for a fight. "I was just doing my job, okay? I didn't mean to step on your fragile male ego if that's what you're insinuating."

He grabbed her arm. "Nothing about me is fragile." Her heart leaped and blood pounded in her ears as she stared into a face raw with emotion.

The doors to the elevator slid open. Nicole Stevenson nearly collided with them. "Oh! Matt?" She stopped on the tracking and the doors started to close only to open again. The bell chimed. Her surprised gaze moved from the middle McCafferty brother's eyes to Kelly's before she glanced down at Matt's fingers, wrapped so tightly over Kelly's arm.

"Vulture alert," Matt said, dropping Kelly's elbow as if it were hot. "The press."

"They just don't let up," Nicole muttered. She frowned at Kelly. "Maybe that's something you should handle."

"I have."

"Just like you and your department handled Randi's safety?" she asked, then, as if hearing herself, sighed and stepped back into the elevator car. "Sorry," she said, leaning her shoulders against the back wall of the elevator. She shoved stiff fingers through her hair, pushing the locks off her forehead. "That was uncalled for." Matt pushed the button to the third floor. "I'm just worried sick," Nicole admitted. "Not only for Randi, but for Thorne as well."

"He'll be fine. Tough as nails," Matt said, and offered her an encouraging smile, hinting at a softer, kinder man beneath his cowboy-thick skin. There was definitely more to the man than met the eye, more than he wanted most people to see. More than Kelly wanted to glimpse. The last thing she needed was to start softening to any member of the McCafferty family. Especially this man who sent her pulse skyrocketing for no tangible reason.

"I hope he'll be okay," Nicole whispered.

The rest of the ride was tense silence. On the third floor Slade was still standing, one shoulder propped against the wall near the doors to the ICU. A self-imposed security guard. "Your boss is looking for you," he said to Kelly. There wasn't a bit of warmth in his laser-blue eyes; he was as cold to her as the McCaffertys had always been.

"Espinoza?"

"Yeah. He's up on the fourth floor."

"Thanks." Kelly noted that the policewoman was still hanging around. Espinoza was leaving nothing to chance. "I'll need to talk to all of you again."

"You know where to find us," Matt said, and she felt his gaze drilling into her back as she hurried to the stairwell. Inhaling deeply, she forced him from her mind. She couldn't, wouldn't think of him as anything more than the brother of a victim…nothing more.

Jaw set, she took the stairs two at a time. Whether anyone in the McCafferty household believed it or not, she was determined to unearth the slime who had run Randi McCafferty off the road and, when that hadn't killed her, had found the guts to walk into a hospital and try to finish the job. Not that murdering a comatose victim took much bravery.

Kelly couldn't wait to nail the bastard.

Because she wanted to solve the crime, because she wanted to insure Randi's safety and because, damn it, she wanted to prove herself to Matt McCafferty.

Chapter Four

"So the police have nothing," Thorne said the next morning while huddled over a cup of coffee, his broken leg propped on another chair at the scarred kitchen table, the same table where they'd prayed, eaten and fought as kids. The maple surface was nicked and half the original chairs had been replaced, but the biggest change was that John Randall no longer took his seat at the head of the table near the window, where he could rest his elbow on the ledge, sip coffee and stare out at the vast acres of the ranch he loved.

Not that Matt cared. But, in a way, it seemed odd that the old man was missing. "I think the police don't have a clue as to who's behind the attacks."

"Hell." Storm clouds gathered in Thorne's gray eyes and Matt knew that his older brother was silently cussing his broken leg for keeping him housebound. Thorne couldn't stand being cooped up. A control freak from the get-go, he needed to be in charge, to make decisions, to be able to be on the front lines. "Has anyone heard from Striker?" he grumbled.

"Not for a couple of days." Matt stretched one arm over his head and yawned. He'd spent a restless night, tossed and turned, his mind spinning in endless circles of concern for his sister, her baby, and with disturbing thoughts about a certain red-haired cop, the one who seemed determined to infiltrate his dreams and keep him awake at night. He'd woken up this morning and beelined for the shower, turning on the cold stinging spray to chase any remaining thoughts of her from his mind…and body. Why he was attracted to Kelly Dillinger, he couldn't imagine. She was a policewoman, for crying out loud. Not exactly his type.

As Matt drained his cup, Juanita bustled through the back door. A blast of cold air swept through the room and Harold found his way to his favorite spot on the braided rug under the table. Absently Matt leaned over to scratch the old dog behind his ears.

"*Dios,* it's cold out there. *Frío.*"

"That it is, Juanita," Matt agreed, as he'd already trudged to the barn and stables to feed the stock, then checked the troughs, making certain they hadn't iced over. He'd called Mike Kavanaugh, his neighbor, this morning and learned that his own place on the Idaho border was still standing. Mike was making noise about buying it again, but Matt resisted. He'd fought too hard and long to own a ranch of his own and his stay here at the Flying M was temporary. Just until things calmed down, Thorne was back on his feet again and Randi was out of the woods. Then he'd leave Grand Hope and any lingering fascination he had with Kelly Dillinger behind him.

"You mentioned that Randi was writing a book,"

Thorne said as Juanita unwrapped herself from several layers of coats and sweaters.

"*Sí.*" She hung her wraps on hooks near the back door and fussed with her hair, tucking a few wayward strands from the braid she pinned to the base of her neck.

"You saw it?"

"No."

"But you think it existed?" Another dead end in Matt's estimation. He stood and refilled his coffee cup from the glass pot warming on the coffeemaker.

"She said it did. The last time she was here." Juanita poured herself a cup of coffee, took one long gulp, placed her mug on the counter and started searching through the pantry. Her voice was muted as she said, "Señorita Randi, she worked on it for hours, sitting on the couch in the living room."

Thorne's eyes met Matt's as he lounged against the counter by the coffeepot. "So where is it? Her laptop computer?"

From the depths of the pantry, Juanita snorted. "How would I know?"

"Maybe Kurt'll find it," Matt said to his brother.

"If he's as good as Slade says he is," Thorne scoffed as Juanita reappeared, paused to take another swallow of coffee, then slid into an apron and tied it around her waist.

"He figured out another vehicle was involved in Randi's accident before the police did," Matt pointed out. "My money's on him."

Juanita was starting to bang some pans on the stove and the sounds of tiny scurrying feet approached. Thorne's harsh expression melted as the twins raced into the room, their footed pajamas sliding on the worn floor.

"I wondered when you two would wake up," he said with a chuckle.

"The baby was crying!" Molly wrinkled her nose and put her hands over her ears.

Mindy, who had crawled onto Thorne's lap, copied her sister, placing her chubby palms to the sides of her head and making a face as if she'd tasted something disgusting. "He cried and cried."

At that moment Nicole walked into the kitchen carrying little J.R. Her eyelids were still heavy, her normally crisp steps dragging. "We're up," she said around a yawn. "Whether we want to be or not." She was dressed in a fluffy white robe and pink scuffs, her hair mussed, her face devoid of makeup, but she radiated a quiet beauty that came from deep inside. And Thorne was captivated. Never in a million years would Matt have thought his older brother—a harsh, determined businessman hell-bent to make his next million—ever capable of falling in love and settling down, but this lady doc with her twin scamps had captured his heart.

"I'll take the baby," Thorne offered, and she shook her head and smiled.

"You've got your hands full already." She motioned toward the twins, both of whom decided they wanted to climb onto Thorne's lap.

"Here, sit down. Have a cup of coffee. I'll take over," Matt said, standing and reaching for the tiny bundle that was his nephew. Bright eyes stared up at him. "Don't panic," he ordered the little one. "No matter how clumsy I appear, it's just an act. I'm really a complete and utter idiot when it comes to taking care of a baby."

"You certainly instill confidence," Nicole observed as she poured herself a cup of coffee from the glass carafe. "Hey, girls, what do you say to pancakes?"

"With blueberries and syrup?" Molly asked.

"Well...syrup for sure. I don't know if we have any berries."

"In the freezer. I'll get some," Juanita said as she wiped her hands and walked into a small alcove by the pantry.

"You want the same?" Nicole asked her other daughter.

Mindy nodded vigorously. "Yeth."

"Easy deal," Thorne said, and Matt wondered about Thorne and his built-in family. It appeared to work. He was nuts for those kids and crazy about Nicole, acting as if she was the only woman on this entire planet for him.

Matt had trouble swallowing it. For years Thorne had dodged marriage, though many a beautiful and smart woman had set her matrimonial sights on him. But he'd never been interested and certainly hadn't committed. Until Nicole. And then all bets had been off.

Matt settled into a chair. He couldn't blame Thorne. Nicole was beautiful, smart, ambitious and a helluva mother. A catch.

Without preamble Kelly Dillinger's image sparked unexpectedly through Matt's mind. She, too, was beautiful...well, he supposed she would be if she ever shed her uniform and cop attitude, and she was smart as a whip, could handle herself in most situations, suffered no fools and, even in uniform, was sexy as hell. Too bad she lived here, so far from his ranch on the western Montana border, he thought, then caught himself up short. What the hell was he thinking? He wasn't even close to settling down, and certainly not with a woman—a cop—who lived hundreds of miles away from his home.

"So is that the consensus?" Nicole asked, searching the faces around the table. "Pancakes?"

Thorne nodded. "And bacon, eggs—"

"Cholesterol, fat..."

"Exactly." Thorne winked and Nicole laughed, a deep husky laugh.

"Well, okay. I know a great heart surgeon just in case we have a problem."

"Load me up!" Thorne said as the twins scrambled out of his lap. For the first time in his life Matt felt a touch of envy. What Thorne shared with Nicole was deep. True. With the kind of bond Matt hadn't believe existed. His father and mother, Larissa, had split up when Penelope had come into the picture. John Randall had married the younger woman, becoming a father again within six months of the wedding date, and that union, too, had crumbled, unable to stand the test of time.

Restless, Matt watched as his brother hobbled into the kitchen, gave Nicole a playful swat on her rump, then actually helped make breakfast around Juanita's sharp protests.

The self-made millionaire and CEO, playboy in his own right, was flipping flapjacks as if he'd done it all his life. Matt's gaze caught Juanita's and he saw that she was just as surprised as he. She didn't say it, but the words *will wonders never cease* came to mind as surely as if the housekeeper had sent them via mental telepathy.

Holding the baby and letting his cup of coffee grow cold, Matt stared through the window where ice had collected and snow gathered in the corners of the panes. What about his own life? He'd never considered marriage, had thought it all a waste of time, and children, well, there was plenty of time before he needed to become a father. And when he did, he'd find a homebody, not a career woman, someone who would want to live on his ranch, someone who cared as much for the land as he did, a woman who would want to share his life the way he wanted to live it. But that was someday. Not today. He just wasn't ready for a family.

He glanced down at the baby snuggled in his arms and for the first time second-guessed himself.

Maybe he'd been wrong.

"I think it was one of the brothers," Karla asserted as she worked on her last client of the day. Standing in the first station of her small salon, she swiped the strands of Nancy Pederson's hair with a small brush dipped into a red color, then wrapped the lock in foil until Nancy's head looked like it could pick up radio signals from Pluto.

Nancy, while twisting her head this way and that to accommodate Karla's ministrations, was doing a cross-word puzzle. The pounding beat of a Shania Twain song underscored the sound of Karla's popping gum and conversation. Plants grew in profusion near the windows at the front of the shop, and on an antique armoire painted salmon-pink, bottles of shampoo and conditioner were displayed. The faint odors of a recently developed perm mixed with traces of perfume. The counters were a deep purple, the walls brown, and head shots of celebrities adorned the area around each individual station. Karla had been a beautician for ten years. She'd owned this shop for two.

"You think one of the McCafferty brothers tried to kill his sister?" Kelly said as she leaned against the manicurist's table and stared at the bottles of polish.

"One of them, two of them, maybe all three." Karla glanced into the mirror and met Kelly's dubious gaze.

"A conspiracy, I see." Kelly couldn't keep the sarcasm from her voice.

"Don't mock me." Karla waved a rattail comb at her sister. "Those brothers never liked Randi, and don't let them tell you any different. She was the reason their father divorced their mom and married Penelope. And then he left each of his sons one sixth of his ranch, a measly *sixth,* while she got half. Is that fair?'' Karla rolled her expressive eyes and sectioned off another lock of Nancy's wet mane.

''Then why are they so adamant that I locate the killer?'' Kelly asked as the song faded and a country deejay gave a weather report.

''To throw you off track, of course. Jeez, Kelly, don't be so dense. You're a detective, for crying out loud. The McCaffertys need to *pretend* that they're concerned for Randi or how would it look?''

''I'm not buying it.'' Kelly fingered a bottle of Pink Seduction nail polish and shook her head.

''Hey, I'm just telling you what I think, and I'm not the only one. I've had three clients sitting in this very chair and Donna's had four.'' Karla pointed toward the second station where Donna Mills, pregnant with twins, was sweeping up snippets of blond curls from the floor around her chair.

''That's right,'' Donna said with a smile.

''Everyone's talking about the attempt on Randi's life. I mean, the attempts. *Plural,*'' Karla continued, managing to hold up two condemning fingers before she picked up another tiny piece of aluminum foil. ''I even overheard a couple arguing about it at Montana Joe's when I was picking up a pizza for lunch. They were standing in line and started to argue over which one of the brothers actually did the deed.''

''That's ridiculous.''

''Maybe. Maybe not. Alexis Bonnifant, she grew up with Slade. I gave her a perm not two hours ago. The way she tells it, he hated Randi. They're in it together, I tell you, just so they can provide one another with alibis!''

"I doubt if they'd want to kill their sister."

"Murder's been committed for a lot less than half a Montana spread."

"Amen," Nancy added, looking up from her puzzle for just a second. "Who else would want Randi dead?"

Who else indeed, Kelly thought as she left a few minutes later. She'd just dropped by the Bob and Weave to offer to watch her sister's kids if Karla needed a night out, but she figured it didn't hurt to listen to gossip and see what the townspeople thought of the case. So far the odds were stacked against the McCafferty brothers.

She walked three blocks to the Pub'n'Grub and ordered a sandwich and bag of chips to go from a kid she'd sent to juvenile court on more than one occasion. He gave her correct change, but avoided eye contact as he placed the order in a computer. As she waited she stood on one side of a brick planter and couldn't help overhearing conversation from a booth on the other side of the silk philodendrons and ferns.

Over Reuben sandwiches and clam chowder two women were deep in conversation about the biggest news to hit Grand Hope since the mayor's wife had run off with one of the city councilmen.

"Always out for themselves, those McCafferty boys. Chips off the old block, if you ask me," Roberta Fletcher said, nodding her head emphatically, her earrings catching in the shivering fluorescent lighting overhead.

"Never got along with their stepmother or little sister. Never tried. Blamed them for their parents' divorce and well…you know, their mother had her share of problems. The drinking, you know. Probably all started when she was married to John Randall. I would've drunk, too, if that son of a gun was my husband." Kelly didn't know the other woman by name, but thought she was married to one of the insurance men in town…she also helped out with the local rodeo association.

"And what if he was your father?" Roberta clucked her tongue as she reached for her cola. "Poor girl—grew up with all those hellions, and now look. It's a shame, I tell you. When I think about that baby, with no father, at least none that we know of, his mother in a coma, three bachelors trying to raise him… Someone should call Child Services."

"If one of the brothers is a killer."

"Hard to believe, but stranger things have happened. The poor baby. He's the cutest little guy you've ever seen, I've heard," Roberta added. "My daughter's a friend of Jenny Riley's. Jenny, she looks after the baby and the Stevenson twins when Nicole's working, you know. Jenny says little J.R. is the most adorable baby in the world."

"Well the McCaffertys always were a good-looking lot. Every last one of 'em."

"Too handsome for their own good." Roberta swirled her straw in her cola. "It's always been a problem."

"But you'd think that baby's father would step forward," Roberta's friend rolled expressive eyes as she bit into her sandwich.

"Maybe the father doesn't know about the little tyke."

"Why wouldn't she tell him?" Roberta asked.

"Maybe they weren't together."

"Or maybe she doesn't know who the father is." Roberta cackled nastily, and the other woman hadn't commented on the gossip. Kelly had tried to turn a deaf ear as she waited for her order.

Later, back at the office, Kelly picked at her sandwich while she cruised through the notes she'd entered into her computer files. Dozens of questions burned through her brain. Who wanted to kill Randi? Why? Because of the baby? Because of her work? A love affair gone wrong? Did she owe someone money? Did someone take offense to her column? Who were her enemies? Her friends?

She studied the list of people who knew Randi—co-workers in Seattle, people she'd grown up with and gone to school with around Grand Hope, people she'd dated or befriended throughout her life. Nothing made any sense. Randi McCafferty had been a tomboy, probably because of her older half brothers. She'd been adored by her father and mother, a "princess" who had managed not to become too spoiled. She'd graduated from high school here in Grand Hope, gone to college at Montana State and eventually become a journalist. She'd worked on her father's ranch as well as having a part-time job at the *Grand Hope Gazette* while in high school, and eventually, after a series of jobs, she ended up in Seattle, where she'd landed the job with the *Clarion*. Her column had become syndicated, picked up by a few other papers, and she'd done some freelance work.

Then she'd had the accident.

Kelly bit into the pickle that came with her ham and cheese and scanned her notes again. Juanita Ramirez, the housekeeper and the one person who seemed to have kept in contact with Randi in the past few months, claimed Randi was writing a book, that the reason that she was returning to the ranch was to finish the book—wherever the blazes it was. If it existed. Juanita, for all her communication with Randi, hadn't known she was pregnant. So maybe she'd gotten the book thing wrong as well.

If only Randi McCafferty would wake up.

Before the killer tried to strike again.

Kelly tossed her hair over her shoulder and scowled at her computer screen. There wasn't anything new. Even the recent lab reports hadn't helped much. The hospital room where Randi was attacked had heretofore given up no clues as to the identity of the person who had sneaked into her room and slipped a deadly dose of insulin into her IV. Interviews with everyone on duty had provided no new information and no one had witnessed anything suspicious aside from Nicole Stevenson's claim that she'd seen someone—man or woman—she didn't recognize near Randi's private room. According to hospital records and the pharmacy on the first floor, no insulin was missing from the locked cabinets, but records could be falsified and someone could have had enough in a vial hidden deep in a pocket.

Not much to go on. Not much at all. Kelly wadded up the uneaten portion of her sandwich in the sack from the Pub'n'Grub and tossed it into the wastebasket in frustration. "We'll get you," she promised, as if the perpetrator was in her office and could hear her. "And it's gonna be soon. Real soon."

She spent a few hours in the office returning phone calls and catching up on paperwork, then decided to finish the interview she'd tried to start with Matt McCafferty in the cafeteria the night before.

He wouldn't be happy to see her, as she didn't have any more information on the case, but that was just too bad.

She threw on her jacket and grabbed her gloves. What was it about that guy that got to her? Sure he was handsome in that cowboy, rough-and-tumble way that so many women found irresistible, and yes, he had a certain charm, but she'd met tons of charming cowboys over the course of her life and she'd never felt this attraction—and that's what it was—before.

Maybe she was just another silly woman who couldn't resist one of the McCafferty brothers, still the most eligible bachelors in the county. "Oh, give me a break," she mumbled to herself as she buttoned her jacket, yanked on her gloves and walked outside to the parking lot where her car was parked.

Don't do it, Kelly. Don't fall for him. He's the worst possible choice. She pulled out of the lot and eased into the sluggish traffic. What was she even thinking? She wouldn't fall for a McCafferty; she wouldn't fall for anyone.

Cautious by nature, she'd always protected her heart. She didn't trust easily and she had only to look at Karla's failed marriages and twice-broken heart to keep a rein on her emotions. No man, especially a McCafferty, was worth the heartache. But the image of Matt, tall, broad-shouldered, chiseled features, beard-darkened jaw, came to mind. She envisioned him in the saddle upon a racing horse, moving easily with the animal, looking for all the world as if he belonged astride a stallion galloping hell-bent-for-leather. Her mouth went dry at the image and she glanced in the rearview mirror. "You're a fool, Dillinger," she growled, disturbed, as she trained her attention to the road again.

She drove north, through the outskirts of town where pumpkins and cornstalks, leftovers from Halloween or precursors of Thanksgiving, adorned some of the porches. Eventually the houses gave way to wide, snow-covered fields.

The McCafferty ranch was located twenty miles out of town, and Kelly fought the weather all of the way. Snow swirled from the heavens, blowing across the highway and melting on her windshield as she squinted against the few oncoming headlights heading toward town. The sky was dark, the hills invisible, the wintry night cold enough to chill the bones.

She listened to the police radio, though she was officially off duty, and reminded herself that Matt McCafferty was only the brother of a crime victim. Nothing more. Her fingers shouldn't be sweating at the thought of him, her pulse should return to its normal, steady rate. She shouldn't be feeling one drip of anticipation.

And yet she did. Oh, Lord, she did. Even her stupid stomach knotted, and she imagined what it would be like to feel his arms around her, his anxious lips on hers...and...she shifted down before her wayward thoughts could take her into forbidden territory.

Eventually, thank God, she reached the turnoff.

So this is the Flying M, she thought as she wheeled into the snow-covered lane. She'd driven past it a million times, of course, but had never once turned down the twin ruts leading to the heart of the ranch. Until now. A few hardy dry weeds poked through the snow to scrape the undercarriage of her car, and she passed fields where cattle huddled against the wind and snow.

The lane widened to a large lot and a series of paddocks around a barn, stables and several other sheds. On a rise, the ranch house overlooked it all. Tall and rambling with weathered siding and windows glowing bright against the wintry night.

Kelly parked near a few other vehicles, flipped up the hood of her jacket and braved the elements, hunching her shoulders against the wind as she dashed to the front porch and climbed the steps. Stomping the snow from her boots, she rang the bell and the door swung open immediately.

"Detective Dillinger," Matt McCafferty drawled, his dark eyes silently appraising. Dressed in faded jeans and a denim work shirt tossed over a navy T-shirt, he stood in stocking feet. Some of the animosity had disappeared from his expression and a dark stubble covered his jaw. He was, without a doubt, sexy as hell.

And she was far from immune. Her heart was racing, her knees unsteady.

He swung the door open and stepped to one side. "Come in."

Suddenly she felt as if she'd just been invited into a viper's lair.

She cleared her throat. "I wanted to talk to you, ask a few more questions."

"Well, isn't that a coincidence?" His brown eyes held hers. "As it just so happens, I've got some for you."

Chapter Five

"You have questions?" Standing toe-to-toe with him on the porch, she lifted an eyebrow, encouraging him while trying to ignore his innate sexuality. "Shoot."

"Obviously you haven't found the person who tried to kill Randi."

"We're still working on it."

"Put more men and women on the job." His gaze intensified, left Kelly a little breathless.

She forged on. "It's not the only case we have, you know."

"Yeah, but someone bull-bustin' through a neighbor's fence, or...kids using mailboxes as target practice aren't quite in the same league, now, are they?"

"Trust me," she assured him, though she sounded more forceful than she felt beneath his assessing glare, "the attempt on your sister's life is top priority."

He stepped out of the way and threw the door to the ranch house open a little wider. "It had better be."

Kelly didn't respond, just scraped her boots on the porch mat, then walked inside. She turned her attention away from the cowboy and inspected the place where he'd grown up, the house Randi McCafferty had called home.

Inside, the old ranch house was warm, and despite its size, had a cozy feel. Soft golden light splashed upon pine-paneled walls and plank floors that had withstood three generations of McCaffertys. A faded runner covered stairs that wound upward from the entryway, and the aromas of burning wood, roasting pork and ginger tinged the air. From the floor above high-pitched giggles erupted. Young voices. Girls. Nicole's twins, Kelly deduced.

"Is there somewhere we could talk?" she asked as she unbuttoned her coat. He helped her remove it, the tips of his fingers brushing the back of her neck. She tried not to notice, it wasn't much contact, but still she felt an unwanted tingle as he hung her jacket on the hook near the door.

"This way." He led her around a corner to a living room where Thorne McCafferty, one leg bound in a cast and elevated on the extension of his recliner, was talking with a tall, blond man who hadn't bothered to take off his jacket and was holding his hat in one hand. "Larry Todd, Detective Dillinger," Matt introduced. "Larry's the foreman here and Detective Dillinger is with the sheriff's department, trying to find out who attempted to kill Randi."

"Any luck?" Larry asked.

"Not enough," she admitted, noticing a cheery fire burning in the grate of a river-rock fireplace. Mounted above a mantel strewn with framed photos was an expansive set of antlers holding an antique rifle. An upright piano filled one wall while worn chairs, tables and the leather couch surrounded a braided rug.

"Get the son of a bitch." Thorne was struggling to get to his feet.

Kelly held up a hand, indicating that he shouldn't bother standing. "We will."

"Make it soon," Matt persisted, and her back went up a bit.

"That's why I'm here. As I said, I'd like to ask you a few more questions. You, too," she added, motioning to Thorne.

"Well, it looks like you've got some business to take care of, so I'd better shove off." Larry hitched his pants up. "Think about trading some of the yearlings for Lyle Anderson's broodmares. I think it would really improve the herd."

Thorne glanced at Matt.

Matt nodded. "I'm in favor of introducing new blood-lines in the stock."

"Then do it," Thorne said to the foreman. "I'll go along with whatever you and Matt decide."

"Done." Larry started for the door.

"Wait a minute, Mr. Todd," Kelly interjected. "Since you're here maybe you could give me some insight." She reached into her pocket and found a small notepad. While Thorne pushed himself out of the chair and braced himself with a crutch and Matt folded his arms over his chest, she said, "A couple of weeks before her accident, Randi McCafferty let you go, isn't that right?"

The big man flushed. His lips flattened over his teeth. He rubbed the back of his neck nervously. "Yep. That's just about how it happened," Larry admitted, not bothering to hide his irritation. "And it pissed me off royally. I'd been running this place ever since her father died and all of a sudden, out of the damned blue, she calls me and says she doesn't need me anymore.''

"Did she give a reason?''

He shook his head. "Nope. I'd always gotten along with her and the last I'd heard she was satisfied with my job—liked having me look over things. I guess she changed her mind," he added, frowning slightly. "She didn't bother to explain, but I had the feeling that she was moving back here and that she had someone else in mind to run the spread. She didn't say so, but it was just the way she handled the conversation. She was nice enough, I suppose," he added, glancing at the brothers. "Even paid me for an extra three months, which was supposed to be my severance package, then she thanked me and basically showed me the door. And that was that. Years of work, down the drain. I was pretty mad about the whole thing, but figured there wasn't much I could do about it. She was the boss as she owned half this ranch.''

"But she didn't ask any of her partners before letting you go," Kelly clarified.

"Not that I know of.''

"None of us heard a word," Matt said. He grabbed a poker from the blackened tool set on the hearth and jabbed at the logs in the fire. Flames crackled and embers spit sparks. "Since Dad died, Randi was in charge. She's always been pretty independent.''

"To a fault," Thorne grumbled.

"And since each of us—Slade, Thorne and I—only owned a sixth of the spread apiece, we let her do her thing. We—well, at least I figured if she needed my help, she'd ask for it." Matt's mouth tightened and he seemed a bit ashamed as he tossed a chunk of mossy oak onto the old andirons. "To tell you the truth, I thought she'd give it all up after one winter of ranching. Even though she was in Seattle, working at the newspaper, she was responsible for what went on here. I figured she'd want to sell out.''

"To you?" Kelly asked.

"To whoever would buy, but yeah, I thought she'd come to either me or one of my brothers." He let out a disgusted breath. "Guess I was wrong."

Larry's anger had dissipated. "It's a helluva thing," he said, his lips folding in on themselves. "She fires me, then within two weeks ends up having a baby and fighting for her life."

"And you took your old job back."

"The brothers asked me." His green eyes narrowed a bit. "It took a little persuadin', let me tell you. I don't like bein' let go."

"I understand. Did you ask her who would be handling the place after you left?" Kelly asked. "This is a pretty big ranch, and since she didn't live here, how did she expect to keep things running smoothly?"

"Good question. One I didn't ask. Guess I was too hot under the collar." He took a step closer to Kelly and a shadow of concern darkened his gaze. "You know, I have this feeling...and it's nothing she said, mind you...but just a sense that she wanted to just hole up and be alone. She didn't fire the hands, just me, so maybe she thought she could run the place herself, but " he hesitated as he squared his hat upon his head "—I guess we won't know until she wakes up."

"Hell's bells," Thorne grumbled as he reached for a single crutch tucked to the side of his recliner.

Larry checked his watch. "I'd better get home."

"If you think of anything else she may have said, call me." Kelly slipped her wallet from her jacket pocket and handed him a card.

"Will do." Larry nodded curtly, then swept his gaze to Thorne and Matt. "I'll see you in the morning." Within seconds the door was slamming shut behind him.

"I don't suppose either of you can shed any further light on why your sister fired him?" Kelly asked, hitching her chin toward the window. Through the icy glass she watched Larry climb into a king-cab pickup. The sound of an engine rumbling to life reached her ears just as the truck's headlamps blazed through the swirling snow.

"Neither of us had talked to Randi in a while," Matt admitted, and Thorne scowled darkly. Larry Todd's truck tore off, plowing through the drifts.

"What about the father of her baby?"

"We're still trying to locate him—whoever he is. Kurt Striker is looking into it." Thorne hobbled to the fireplace and, bracing his shoulders on the mantel, picked up a photograph of his sister that had been propped against the old bricks. Sighing, Thorne shook his head. "Striker's supposed to be back here tomorrow."

"I'd like to talk to him."

Matt hesitated. "Is that standard procedure?"

Kelly's temper snapped. "Listen, Mr. McCafferty, nothing about this case is standard."

"I thought we established that you could call me Matt."

"Whatever," she said, bristling. "Now, what about her boyfriends?"

"I never met any of the guys she was dating, even if she was...well, obviously there was someone in her life." The lines bracketing his mouth became more pronounced. "But I don't have a clue as to which one of the men she'd been seeing is little J.R.'s father." Matt raked his fingers through his near-black hair and frustration was evident in the tension of his muscles and set of his jaw.

"J.R.'s father might be someone that no one knew about, a man she was seeing on the sly," Thorne said as the fire popped and bright sparks and smoke floated up the chimney.

Matt swore under his breath. "The truth of the matter is we all feel foolish, not knowing this basic stuff about our sister."

"I have several names of people she dated." Kelly flipped through her notes. "Joe Paterno, who worked freelance for the Seattle *Clarion,* Brodie Clanton, a lawyer whose father is a judge, and Sam Donahue, an ex-rodeo rider who ranches outside of Spokane, Washington." She glanced up and noticed the thunder in Matt's stare.

"I don't know the other two guys, but Donahue's a miserable piece of work," he growled, dusting his hands then shoving them into the front pockets of his jeans. "But I still can't believe that Randi was ever involved with him."

"You don't know that she was," Thorne rebutted. From his expression, Kelly guessed he didn't like the idea of Randi and Donahue any better than Matt did. Using the crutch, he hitched his way across the braided carpet to the bookcase. "Kurt Striker is checking blood types, which should help. Even if we can't determine who is the father of Randi's kid, we can rule out those who aren't."

"Exactly. We're working on the same premise," she said as a clatter of footsteps on the stairs caught her attention.

Nicole Stevenson, twin girls tagging behind her, and baby—presumably Randi McCafferty's infant—in her arms, made her way down the stairs.

Gone was the all-business, tough doctor whom Kelly had run up against. In her stead was a smiling mother listening to the little girls babble and giggle as she tended to the baby.

Kelly's heartstrings pulled a bit just as Nicole, who had reached the bottom of the stairs, looked up and caught sight of a policewoman in her home. Her jaw hardened just a fraction before a smile tugged the corners of her mouth upward. "I think I owe you an apology," she admitted, striding into the room. "Last night I was very upset when hospital security had been breached and Randi was attacked. I shouldn't have taken it out on you."

"It was tense for everyone."

"I know, but it wasn't very professional on my part." She was sincere. Kelly decided her apology was heartfelt.

"It's fine. Really." Even though she reminded herself not to be suckered in by anyone in the McCafferty family, Kelly couldn't help but warm to the slim woman with her forthright gold eyes and proud lift of her chin. In other circumstances, Kelly thought, she and Nicole might be friends.

"Thank you."

"This is Randi's baby?"

Matt crossed the room to peek at his nephew. "Yep. He's what all the fuss is about." To Kelly's surprise, Matt plucked the baby out of Nicole's arms. Big, calloused hands drew the infant to his chest, and though he seemed a tad awkward with J.R., Matt smiled down at the boy. "If only he could talk."

Or his mother could, Kelly thought, amazed at the transformation in both McCafferty brothers. Matt was ranch-tough and no-nonsense, but his leathery touch-me-not exterior softened as he gazed down at his nephew. Thorne, with the use of a crutch, had crossed the room and stood by Nicole, his free arm slung over her shoulder, the edgy, hard-as-nails corporate executive evaporating into a proud, caring husband-to-be. He ruffled one twin's crown with his free hand while the other twin, a shier girl, hid behind his cast. For the briefest of seconds, Kelly felt an emotion akin to envy for this tightly knit family.

Nicole's gaze moved from Thorne to Matt. "Hasn't either of these gentlemen, and boy, do I use the term loosely, offered you anything? Coffee…tea…a glass of wine?"

"I'm fine, really."

"I wants a drink," one of the girls said, tugging on her mother's blouse. "I wants a drink."

"In a minute, Molly. Now—" she eyed the men speculatively "—which uncle is on J.R. duty?" Nicole asked. "The baby could use a bottle, and then, no doubt, he'll need to be changed. Uncle Thorne? Uncle Matt?" From Matt's arms the baby let out a soft little coo that had the amazing effect of pulling on Kelly's heartstrings.

"I think it's my turn," Thorne grumbled good-naturedly, reaching for the child as Matt handed the baby to him. "But you'd better carry him into the kitchen and get me settled in with a bottle."

"I do it!" One of the curly-haired girls, Molly, Kelly guessed, volunteered, then she dashed down the hall.

"Me, too." Her sister raced after her, tiny feet pounding on the hardwood floor. Two bright-eyed dynamos.

"I think I'd better supervise. I'll meet you in the kitchen," Nicole said to Thorne as she took the baby from his arms and started out of the living room, only to pause midstep. "Oh, but one last thing." She was looking at Kelly. "Has it been proved that something was slipped into Randi's IV? I haven't been back at the hospital since last night."

"Insulin," Kelly supplied. "It can kill if the victim overdoses. Remember the Sunny von Bulow case? Where her husband was accused of trying to kill her by injecting her with insulin?''

"He got off, right?" Matt asked.

Kelly nodded. "But his wife remained in a coma. Alive, but hospitalized. Nearly dead. For years."

"Damn."

Nicole frowned and sighed. "I suspected as much. From the symptoms. Any ideas who could have done it?''

"Not yet," Kelly admitted.

"Well, do me a favor, will you?" she asked. "Nail the bastard who did this."

"We will," Kelly said fervently.

There was a crash and a wail at the far end of the hall and Nicole, still carrying the baby, took off toward the sound. Thorne was on her heels, hurrying after her on one crutch.

"*Dios, niña!* Look what you've done," a husky woman's voice cajoled, then muttered a Spanish phrase Kelly didn't understand.

Within seconds there was the sound of sobbing from one small girl and a series of denials from the other. "I didn't do it!" one of the twins cried.

"Did, too," the other responded.

One side of Matt's mouth lifted as he listened to the exchange from the living room. "Never a dull minute around here, I'm afraid."

"It seems that way."

Nicole, now carrying one of the twins, winked at Kelly and Matt as she reached the bottom of the stairs. The little girl had her head burrowed in her mother's shoulder and wouldn't look up, just sobbed as if her heart was breaking. "Good thing I'm an emergency room doc," Nicole confided, swallowing a smile as she toted her daughter upstairs. "Mindy might need major surgery."

The girl, aware that her mother was teasing, buried her tear-streaked face in Nicole's neck even further and muttered, "No."

"Is she okay?"

Nicole nodded. "Fingers got smashed when the sugar jar broke. I'm not sure how it happened—"

"Molly did it!" the girl insisted, finally lifting her head in self-righteous indignation. She sniffed loudly and her lower lip quivered. "She pushed my chair."

"Did not," the other twin denied as she streaked from the kitchen to proclaim her innocence. "You falled."

"I think Mindy will live," Nicole said as she turned at the landing and disappeared up the remaining stairs.

"You falled, you falled, you falled," Molly chimed, clambering up the remaining stairs.

"Damned three-ring circus," Matt grumbled as he checked his watch. "Look, I've got to check the broodmares." He slid her a glance that was unreadable. "You have any more questions?"

"A few."

"Then come along." He walked through the foyer, snagged a jacket and hat from a tarnished brass coatrack, then continued toward the back of the house through a hallway adorned with pictures of the McCafferty family at different stages in their lives—Thorne in a football uniform, Slade tearing down a mountain on skis, Randi in a long dress with her arm linked through that of a tuxedoed beau, and Matt astride a rodeo bronc. The buckskin horse, front feet planted firmly in the sod of an arena, head ducked, back legs shooting skyward, had been frozen in time trying to throw his rider—a lean, hard-muscled cowboy who seemed as determined to stay on as the stallion was to send him skyrocketing. Matt's right hand was lifted to the sky, his other buried in the strap surrounding the buckskin's chest.

"Who won?" she asked, motioning toward the glossy eight-by-ten.

"I did."

"Of course."

"Not always, especially when I drew Zanzibar." He motioned toward the picture. "He was a tough one." A nostalgic gleam sparked in his eye and Kelly suspected that he missed the excitement and thrill of the rodeo. From all accounts, though he often wore a wide belt buckle depicting a bucking bronco, Matt had given up the rodeo circuit years ago and contented himself ranching on a spread he owned in the western hills of Montana.

Through an archway, they stepped into a large kitchen where the fragrance of roasting pork and cooling pies tickled her nostrils. A battered butcher-block counter surrounded a stainless steel sink and electric range where pots were simmering, steam rising to the copper bonnet. In a corner, shards of delft-blue pottery and white crystals were gathered together in a dustpan, testament to the accident with the twins. Thorne was seated at the table, the heel of his cast on a nearby chair, the baby in his arms suckling at a bottle and staring up at him.

Matt clucked his tongue as he shrugged into his jacket. "I never thought I'd see the day—"

"Don't say another word," Thorne warned Matt, but there was a twinkle in his gray eyes, as if the millionaire CEO enjoyed his newfound role of temporary father.

"Who's gonna stop me? A man with a broken leg holding a baby?"

"Try me."

"Anytime, man. Anytime."

"Enough!" A hefty, dark-skinned woman with flashing

black eyes and a strong chin emerged from the pantry. She placed bags of onions and potatoes on the counter. "You two are like two old...*toros*. Always pawing at the dirt and snorting... *Dios!*" She threw up a hand. Her gaze fastened on Kelly. *"Policia?"*

"Detective Kelly Dillinger, with the sheriff's office," Matt explained. "Our cook, housekeeper and angel of mercy, Juanita Ramirez."

"Angel?" Juanita snorted her disdain, but smothered a smile as she rounded the counter and picked up the dustpan, then shook it into the trash. "You two, you could have taken care of this..." she admonished as she dusted her hands. "So you," she said to Kelly, "you are searching for the person who is behind Randi's trouble?"

"Yes."

"But you have not found him?"

"Not yet."

Juanita sighed heavily, her ponderous breasts heaving at the injustice of the world. "So much trouble for that one. The baby. Her job...and the book." She reached for a knife and began skimming the skins off onions with expert dexterity. "If you ask me, this is about her *libro.*"

"You've read it?" Kelly asked.

"Me?" Juanita glanced up, the knife poised over the onion that oozed juice. "No." Shaking her head, she tossed a pile of thin, paperlike skins into a trash basket.

"But you saw it, know that it existed."

"She talked about it. She was here for a few days and she was on the phone all the time."

"Because of the book?" Kelly asked, trying to follow the older woman's line of reasoning.

"Sí. With her..." She snapped her fingers, as her forehead wrinkled in thought. *"Dios,* her...her...*agente.*"

Thorne's head snapped around. "Her agent?" he repeated, his eyes narrowing thoughtfully. "Randi had an agent?"

"Sí."

"Who?" Matt demanded, and Kelly's heartbeat accelerated. Here was a fresh clue, one no one had picked up on before.

"I don't know." Juanita shrugged. "You will have to ask her when she wakes up."

"When was this?" Kelly asked. "How long before the accident?"

"Oh…let me see…the middle of summer, I think," Juanita said, and Kelly scribbled frantically in her notebook. "Yes, not long after Señor John passed on." Deftly, not bothering to drop the knife, she made the sign of the cross over her chest. "She came for a visit."

"And you didn't see that she was pregnant?" Matt asked, unable to hide his incredulity. "She would have been five or six months pregnant."

"No. *Sí,* she was…rounder…heavier…but I thought she had just gained weight."

"Did you see her working on the book?" Kelly asked. Juanita cut thick slabs of the onion, frowned and blinked against tears that were probably brought on by her task rather than her ragged emotions. "I saw her working on something on her computer. She said it was a book. But no, I did not read any of the pages."

"So we're back to square one," Matt said, sliding his arms through the sleeves of his rawhide jacket in disgust.

Kelly disagreed. Now they had more information to work with. It could very well turn out to be another blind alley, but it was something. She stuffed her notebook into her jacket pocket and followed Matt through the back door and across the porch.

Outside the air was sharp. The wind slapped her face

and snow swirled in the dark night. She trudged through the path Matt broke to the stables. He threw open the door and snapped on the lights.

One horse nickered nervously. Another snorted at the intrusion, poking a large head over the top rail of the stall. "How're ya, girl?" Matt asked, and scratched the blaze that ran crookedly up the mare's broad nose. Outside the raw winter wind raged and howled, but in this old building with its ancient siding, hayloft overhead, tack room visible through an open door, the stables felt warm and safe, filled with the scents of horses, oiled leather, dust and straw. Cobwebs hung from the support posts, surrounded the windows and feathered in the corners. Barrels of oats and mash were stacked in an old bin, and pitchforks, shovels and buckets were held by nails pounded into the siding years ago.

"These are the ladies of the Flying M," Matt explained to Kelly as other mares stretched their necks over the gates. "Expectant mothers."

Curious eyes blinked from the heads thrust over the railings. One mare seemed skittish, another jerked away as Kelly approached, but others allowed her to pet their muzzles.

Matt checked feed and water, patted each velvet-soft nose and spoke in low, soft tones as he scratched an ear or patted a sleek shoulder. All the while his eyes moved from one mare to the next.

It was hard to imagine him or any of his brothers as a murderer intent on killing their half sister for her share of the Flying M. No, that was just gossip whispered around the coffee shops and taverns of Grand Hope, nothing more. In Kelly's estimation the harsh talk was far-fetched and probably fueled by jealousy. Despite her own family's run-ins with the McCafferty family, she found it difficult to believe that Thorne, Matt or Slade was a potential murderer.

All of the brothers seemed more than concerned for their sister's well-being. They were clamoring for the police to find Randi's assailant.

And they all doted on the baby.

Now, as she watched Matt's ease with the mares, his strong hands gentle as he patted a shiny neck or scratched beneath a strong equine jaw, she was more certain than ever that someone outside the McCafferty family was behind the attacks on Randi and possibly Thorne.

"So what is it you wanted to ask me?" Matt glanced over one shoulder as he poured oats from a coffee can into the empty mangers.

She climbed onto the top rail of a stall and hooked the heels of her boots on a lower slat while bracing herself with her hands, the way she used to do years ago at her grandmother's farm. "I hoped you could tell me about why your father left half the ranch to your sister."

He slid her a troubled glance she didn't understand.

"Each of his sons got a sixth, but Randi inherited half of it, the half with the house and outbuildings, right? While you boys each got a sixth."

"That's about the size of it. I guess Dad felt he had to take care of Randi, more than he did with the rest of us."

"Because she was a woman?"

"Bingo." His lips thinned.

"Did she know anything about ranching?"

"Not enough."

"So how do you feel about that? I mean, don't you and your brothers resent the fact that she inherited the lion's share?"

He lifted a shoulder and something stirred in his gaze. "She was always Dad's favorite."

"Why?"

"Because she was Penelope's daughter," he said coldly. "He would have gone through hell for that woman, and in the end, she tossed him over. Kinda tit for tat, if ya think about what he did to Mom." His jaw tightened. "But it's all water under the bridge now. Doesn't matter a whole helluva lot."

"So you think John Randall didn't split things equally because of favoritism?"

"Probably, but I can't second-guess my old man. At the time the old man realized he was facing the grim reaper, Thorne was already a millionaire, I had my own place, Slade...well, Slade plays by his own rules, never gave Dad the time of day, and Randi, she had a job in Seattle, yeah, but Dad never approved. Not that it mattered. She did pretty much as she damned well pleased."

"A family trait."

"You noticed." He walked to a ladder built into the side wall and climbed up to the hayloft. Kelly dragged her gaze away from the faded buttocks of his worn jeans as he disappeared through an opening overhead.

Thud!

One bale of hay landed on the floor.

Thud! Thud!

More bales rained from above. Within seconds Matt had swung down to the main floor again and cut the bailing twine with his jackknife. As he leaned over, her eyes were drawn again to his hips and strong legs. Her blood heated and she turned her attention to the mare in the stall behind her. Lord, what was wrong with her? Why did she wonder what he wore, if anything, beneath those disreputable Levi's? Why did she envision hard, muscular thighs and strong calves? She'd never in her lifetime ever so much as contemplated what a man would look like naked. Until now. And now she wondered what his body would feel like stretched out over hers, touching, sweating, tasting...

He clicked his knife shut and she started, brought back to the here and now. Matt snagged a pitchfork from its hook on the wall and began shaking huge forkfuls of hay into the mangers.

"You know," he said, his shoulders moving fluidly beneath his shirt as he worked, "I hadn't seen Randi in a while. Neither had Slade nor Thorne and we all feel bad about it. We should have kept up with her."

"So, as you said, you didn't know about the men in her life, right?"

"Well, of course I knew Randi had boyfriends, not only here when she was growing up but also when she was away at college. But I never heard that she was ever serious about any one guy, not even lately." He jabbed the pitchfork into a fresh bale and looked over his shoulder, his gaze meeting Kelly's in the light from the few iridescent bulbs suspended from the ceiling. Her throat went dry, but she managed to concentrate on the conversation. "For someone who tosses out advice, she's pretty private," Matt added. "The independent kind. Well, you know about that."

"We're not talking about me," she retorted, stung a bit.

"No, but I thought you could relate." He leaned on the pitchfork and sighed. "It really doesn't surprise me that she was involved with a man who I didn't know about, but it's strange that she didn't tell any one of us, not me, or Thorne, or Slade that she was pregnant."

"Maybe she planned to give the baby up for adoption," Kelly suggested.

He shook his head. "I doubt it. It's not like she's a

teenager who hasn't finished school and doesn't know what she wants in life, or that she couldn't afford a baby. No, I'm sure she intended to have the baby and keep him, but there was something she had to do before she told us about him.''

"Write a book?" Kelly suggested.

"More likely deal with the father." He turned and faced her, and she noticed the lines of irritation pinching the corners of his eyes. "What's the deal with that guy? Where is he? If he cared a lick about my sister he would've shown up by now."

"If he knows about her accident."

"He should, dammit. If he cared enough...enough to get her pregnant, then he damned sure should be hanging around.''

"Maybe they broke up before he found out she was pregnant. Maybe she didn't tell him just like she didn't tell you. Maybe she doesn't want him to know." She thought long and hard, avoiding staring into Matt's angry eyes. "Or maybe you're right, he just doesn't care."

"Damn it all." Matt kicked at a bale of hay as he walked up to her, and as she balanced on the top rail, he pressed his nose close to hers. "Let me tell you, if my woman was in the hospital and that kid was mine—" he jerked his thumb in the general direction of the ranch house where, presumably, little J.R. was sleeping "—things would be a lot different. A whole lot different.'' Matt's lips had thinned, his nostrils flared and one fist was clenched in impotent rage. He smelled of horses and hard work. A vein near his temple became more pronounced. Tiny crow's feet fanned from eyes set deep behind a ledge of thick black eyebrows.

Kelly's heart took off. She licked suddenly dry lips.

Matt McCafferty was just too damned sexy for his own good.

Her stupid, feminine heartbeat accelerated to the rate of hummingbird's wings and she noticed the corners of his mouth, where anger pulled the skin tight. In another surreal moment, she wondered what it would feel like to kiss those blade-thin, furious lips and have his big, work-roughened hands rub against her skin. Just what kind of a lover would he be?

The best.

She caught herself up short.

This was silly.

Ridiculous.

Damned unprofessional.

His gaze caught hers for a second and held. Something dark and dangerous sizzled in those scorching brown depths, connected with a part of her she didn't want to examine any too closely. He was dangerous. Emotionally. But not a killer. Not a man who would plot to murder his half sister, no matter what the stakes.

The moment stretched long. Horses shifted and snorted in their stalls. Kelly heard her heartbeats count off the seconds.

Her throat was arid as a windswept Montana prairie.

His gaze flicked to her mouth, as if he, too, felt the sudden intimacy, sensed the unseen charge in the air.

This couldn't be happening. She...couldn't want him to gather her into his strong arms, pull her off the top of the stall, drag her close and kiss her until...oh, dear...

As if he, too, felt the atmosphere in the musty building thicken, he took a step back and cleared his throat. But his dark gaze still held hers and she saw sex and promise in his eyes.

Oh, God, no.

With more agility than she thought possible at the moment, she dropped to the cement floor. "If...if..." She licked her lips, felt a wash of heat stain her cheeks, realized with disgust that her legs had gone weak. What in the name of God was she thinking? "If you think of anything else, call me," she added, her voice louder than she'd intended.

He hesitated.

"I'm talking about the case."

"I know."

Her heart galumphed. Somewhere nearby a horse whinnied softly. Kelly tore her gaze from his. Dear Lord, what was wrong with her? This never happened to her. *Never.* She worked with dozens of men, interviewed witnesses, suspects and victims on a regular basis, and she'd never even brushed the emotions that were battling within her now.

"And you keep me posted on the investigation," he said.

In your dreams, she thought as she reached for the door. Yes, the family would be informed, but some of the evidence the department collected would be kept under wraps, privy only to law enforcement until the investigation was closed, used for the purpose of trapping the assailant.

As if he read her mind, Matt grabbed the crook of her elbow and spun her around.

"I mean it," he said with a quiet, deadly determination. "I want to know what's going on every step of the way in this investigation. And if there's anything I can do to nail the son of a bitch who did this to Randi, I will." His jaw was set, his eyes on fire, his skin tight over his cheekbones. "This guy can't get away."

"I know."

"Otherwise I might be forced to take the law into my own hands."

"That would be a mistake."

"Just be sure it doesn't have to happen. Get the creep."

"We will," she promised.

The fingers around her arm tightened. "I'm not kidding, *Detective,* I want this murdering bastard caught and punished. Big time. And I'm tired of waiting around while my sister's life is in danger. Either you arrest the son of a bitch, or I'll find him, and when I do, I won't wait around for the courts to decide what to do with him. I'll handle it myself."

Chapter Six

"I just don't know why they don't have a man in charge of the investigation," Matt grumbled as he sat at the table cradling a cup of coffee two days later. It was only a few days until Thanksgiving. Juanita, Nicole and Jenny, the babysitter, had been bustling around, planning a big spread, inviting friends and relatives and decorating the house with those stupid accordion-pleated turkeys and pumpkins, gourds and squash. Randi's condition had stabilized but not improved much, little J.R. was getting cuter by the minute, and Mike Kavanaugh had called again, trying to press Matt into selling the place he'd thrown himself into the last six years.

On top of all that, he was losing sleep. Ever since Kelly Dillinger had been at the house the other night he'd been bothered with thoughts of her. Big time. While working with the stock, his wayward mind would bring up the image of her face. At night he'd tossed and turned, dreamed of kissing her, woken up with an ache in his groin just as hard as it had been in high school. During the days, whenever he was at the hospital, he'd looked for her, hoped to run into her, found himself concocting excuses to call her.

So far he hadn't.

It was stupid. She wasn't even his type. He liked softer, quiet women with round curves, long blond hair and dulcet-toned voices. Whenever he'd considered settling down, which hadn't been all that often until Thorne had decided to marry, Matt had thought he'd like a nice, home-grown woman who wanted nothing more than to be a rancher's wife and a mother to his children. Never once had he considered that he might fall for a career woman, a gun-toting, no-nonsense, sharp-tongued cop, for crying out loud, one who lived too far from the ranch he'd bought with hard work, sweat and determination. He'd paid a hefty price for that scrap of land that signified his independence and he wasn't going to give it up for any woman, especially a detective.

Not that he was falling for anyone, he reminded himself, and took a gulp of coffee that burned the back of his mouth. He sputtered and coughed. Where the hell had that wayward thought sprung from?

"A man is in charge of the investigation," Thorne said. "Last I heard, Roberto Espinoza was leading the team."

Slade leaned low on his back and observed his brothers over the rim of his mug. "That's not what this is all about. Unless I miss my guess, I'd say the lady detective bothers you for the same reasons Nicole being Randi's doctor got under Thorne's skin."

"What's that supposed to mean?" Matt growled, not liking the turn of the conversation.

"Face it, brother, you're attracted to her."

His gaze bore straight into his younger brother's eyes. "No way. She's a cop. I'm *not* interested in a woman detective. It's just that she's working on the investigation."

Slade slid a wide grin toward Thorne, silently inviting him in on the razzing. Ignoring Matt's protests, he feigned deep thought and said solemnly, "I think I know what it is. You've got yourself a reverse authority-figure fascination going on here."

"What?" Matt had to keep himself from shooting to his feet. His hands clenched his cup tightly.

"Oh, you know how they always say that women get off on men in uniforms…maybe that's what's going on with you—you like the idea of having some woman boss you around."

Matt snorted in disdain. "Don't you have something constructive to do?" Matt asked, draining his cup and not wanting to examine Slade's theory too closely.

"Yeah." The youngest McCafferty brother scraped his chair back. "I suppose I'd better put in another call to Kurt Striker. He said he'd be back in Grand Hope this afternoon. Maybe he learned something while he was in Seattle." He carried his cup to the sink and tossed the dregs down the drain. "I'll ask him to stop by this evening."

"Good." Thorne pushed out his chair. "The sooner we get to the bottom of this, the better."

Amen, Matt thought.

"No medications were missing from the cart, cabinets or pharmacy," Kelly said, tossing a file onto the corner of Roberto Espinoza's desk. It landed next to a picture of Espinoza's son's baseball team from last spring.

"I'd guess that someone brought the insulin in." Espinoza was leaning back in his chair, staring through windows reinforced with wire and glazed with ice.

"So the hospital staff is clean?"

"Or smart."

"Or both," she said, resting one hip on the corner of the desk and pointing to the file folder. "We'll check anyone connected with the McCaffertys. See if there's a diabetic in the crowd, and then find out if he's missing any medication."

Kelly made a mental note to herself, then asked, "What about fingerprints?"

"None that can't be accounted for, but given the amount of latex gloves floating around St. James that's not a big surprise." His eyebrows drew into a heavy single line. "But the good news is that Randi McCafferty is out of immediate danger and has been moved from ICU to a private room."

"With a guard?"

"You bet. I don't want to risk another attack or the McCafferty boys slapping a lawsuit our way." His eyes met Kelly's. "They're a passel of hotheads, y'know. All three of them were on their way to juvenile detention when they were in school. Their old man bailed 'em out, time and time again, and in my opinion it didn't do any of 'em any good."

"That was a long time ago."

"Yeah, I suppose." He cocked his head to one side and regarded her as if he had the right to. "They've got reputations. Broke more than their share of hearts around this town in their younger days."

"That's not relevant to the case."

"No?"

"Don't tell me, you think I need some advice, right?" she asked, deciding to take the bull by the horns. Espinoza was leading up to it. "S̶̶ ̶ ̶ ̶

me? About what?" Kelly bra̶

she saw brewing in his eyes. Ever̶

pinoza took on the role of older brother ̶ ̶

because he'd worked with her father years ̶ ̶

joined the force.

He tented his hands under his chin and his eyes narrowed a fraction as if he wasn't sure he should share his
thoughts.

"You started this," she said. "You may as well finish
it. If you've got something to say to me, just spit it out."

"Okay." He leaned back in his chair until it creaked,
but he never took his eyes off Kelly. "My sister, Anita,
had a thing for the middle McCafferty boy. It was a long
time ago, probably fifteen years ago. She was in her senior
year of high school when she hooked up with Matt."

Matt, Kelly thought wryly. Of course it had to be the
middle son of John Randall. She fought a prick of disappointment, but managed to hide it as she stood.

"McCafferty took her out a few times and it got pretty
hot and heavy, at least from Anita's point of view. He
acted interested in her, and then, out of the blue, took up
with the rodeo circuit again and within a month had
moved on. It was kind of a whirlwind thing, but my sister
was crushed." Espinoza's jaw tightened.

"Let me guess. You've held a grudge ever since."

He clicked his pen. "Let's just say I wouldn't want it
to happen again to anyone I know."

"Wait a minute. Are you talking about me? Are you
warning me off Matt McCafferty?" Kelly demanded, her
spine stiffening.

"Just making an observation."

"Well, observe something else, okay? It's none of your
business who I see."

seeing him?''

No! I mean, only professionally—not that it's any of your damned business.'' She was overreacting and knew it, but couldn't stop the sharp edge of her voice or the color she felt climbing up the back of her neck. ''Let's get back to the case, okay? What about the men Randi McCafferty was interested in?''

He nodded. Apparently the older-brother-type lecture was over, at least for a while. ''The three men we've linked to her—Paterno, Donahue and Clanton—have alibis, if that's what you mean. All of 'em were miles away from Grand Hope at the time she was forced off the road. They were also elsewhere when the attack at St. James occurred. Now, I'm not saying they have watertight alibis, but there are people who say they saw them during the dates of the attacks. Seattle PD's double-checking, though, to make sure.''

''What about paternity?''

''Still checking.'' Espinoza's scowl deepened and he dropped his feet to the floor. ''As far as blood types go, all three men—Joe Paterno, Brodie Clanton and Sam Donahue—could be the kid's father. It'll take paternity tests to narrow the field down and then maybe none of these guys would end up being the father.''

''What have they got to say for themselves?''

''They're not a very talkative group, but a detective in Seattle is interviewing them. We really don't have a helluva lot to go on.'' He leaned forward and reached for the file she'd brought in. ''I'm thinking about sending someone to Seattle to interview the men, just so we have a better handle on it.''

And because the McCaffertys are breathing down our necks, demanding answers. He didn't have to say it.

''Are you interested?''

"Sure," she said quickly, eager to do anything to keep the investigation moving forward. She plopped down in the one chair on the opposite side of his desk. "When?"

"This week. Before Thanksgiving." He picked up the file folder and tapped it on the desk as if he'd just made the decision final in his mind.

"Count me in."

"Good. Now, we've still got a guard posted at the hospital. So far, there's been nothing suspicious happening, thank God, so if Randi McCafferty would just cooperate and wake up, maybe we'd get some answers."

He opened the file folder. Leafing through the pages, he scanned the lab reports on the crime scene about the latest attack on Randi McCafferty, though Kelly suspected he knew the contents by heart.

"What about Thorne McCafferty's plane?" she asked as he flipped to the final typewritten page. "The McCafferty brothers seem convinced that foul play was involved."

"Again, the jury's still out." He slapped the manila folder onto his desk. "There was one helluva storm that day. The crash could have been the result of pilot error or equipment malfunction. Or maybe it was just coincidence that his plane went down. It doesn't make a lot of sense to me that someone is trying to bump off the entire McCafferty family one at a time, and there hasn't been another attempt on his life." He clicked his pen again and shook his head, gray hairs catching in the fluorescent bulbs that hummed overhead. "Nope. I'll bet my badge that McCafferty just had a run of bad luck on that one."

"But Randi's another matter."

"Yep." Espinoza stuffed his pen into a mug labeled Coach Espinoza. "Someone's definitely trying to make sure that she doesn't wake up. We just have to figure out who.''

"And why."

"Yeah." His thick eyebrows elevated a fraction. "A motive would be nice. Some people around town think the brothers are involved, that Thorne staged the plane crash just to throw us off guard and that Randi and her son are the primary targets."

"No way. They could have come up with better ways to kill her off if they really wanted to." The thought soured her stomach and fired her blood. "They're three big, strapping men whom she trusted, they could have been one another's alibis, and as for the baby... I've seen the uncles with little J.R. They'd defend him with their lives."

Espinoza nodded. "Agreed. So who does that leave?"

Who indeed, Kelly wondered off and on for the rest of the day. She helped investigate an accident scene, interviewed witnesses in a hit-and-run, and took statements from the owners of a mom-and-pop grocery that had been vandalized. In between calls, she tried to work out the knots in the Randi McCafferty case.

It was after eight when she filed her last report and, hiking her jacket around her neck, climbed into her car. The windows fogged with the cold temperature, but the night was clear, stars visible above the lights of the town. She started for her row house, but changed her mind at a red light and turned toward the hospital where Randi McCafferty lay comatose.

There was no longer any evidence of the press as Kelly made her way to the fourth floor to Randi's private room. Seated on a folding chair, flipping through a magazine, the beefy policeman whose job it was to protect John Randall's daughter looked up and recognized Kelly.

"Don't suppose you're my relief," he said with a toothy grin. He checked his watch. "If you are, you're early."

"Not me, Rex, but I'll take over if you want to take a break and refill that." She pointed to an empty paper cup that sat at his feet.

"You don't have to ask twice. You're on." He swiped the empty cup from the floor and swaggered down the hall. As Rex disappeared around the corner, Kelly walked into the private room where the lights were dimmed and Randi McCafferty lay on her back, her breathing regular, her lips slightly parted, her eyes closed.

"Wake up, Randi," Kelly said softly. "You've got some brothers who are worried sick about you and a baby who needs you." She touched the back of one of Randi's hands. Her skin was cool and soft. "You know, I could use some help here, too. I've got questions only you can answer." She bit her lip, wondering about this woman who seemed to be a mystery even to her brothers. No one in Grand Hope knew the ins and outs of Randi's life— who were her friends, what project she was working on, who was her lover? Maybe the answers were in Seattle. Maybe if Kelly was sent there for just a few days she could find answers to the dozens of questions surrounding this case. "Come on, Randi. Wake up, would you?"

"Y'know, she *still* can't hear you. No more than she could the last time you tried to talk to her."

Kelly froze, fought her instinctive reaction to reach for her sidearm and silently cursed her luck as she recognized Matt McCafferty's deep, condemning voice. So he'd caught her again. She dropped Randi's hand and turned to find him framed in the doorway, his shoulders nearly touching each side of the doorjamb, his athletic body silhouetted by the backlight of the hall.

Kelly's stupid heart skipped a beat. Her pulse jumped.

She met cold censure in his chocolate-brown eyes. "Are you the guard?"

"No. His relief for a few seconds."

"You didn't hear me come in. I might have been the killer," he said, his voice tight. "I could've got the jump on you."

"Or my presence could have scared you off," she said. "I'm still in uniform."

His gaze raked down her body. "That you are."

"And I've got a weapon."

He didn't comment.

Rankled, she stepped closer to him and kept her voice low for the patient's sake. "So, are you through dressing me down? Because I'm not in the mood for it."

"What *are* you in the mood for?" he asked, and for the fleetest of seconds she thought he was making a pass at her. But she was probably imagining things.

"I just thought I'd see how your sister was doing and let Rex use the rest room and get a fresh cup of coffee. He's the guard on duty. You have a problem with that?"

Matt seemed to cool off a tad. He glanced quickly around the room, as if seeing for himself that it was secure. "I guess not."

"Good."

He strode to the bedside, bringing the scents of horses, hard work and the cold outdoors with him. "I heard you talking to her."

Now her embarrassment was complete.

"But it doesn't seem to work. We've all tried communicating with her. Over and over again, but she doesn't move. Not so much as a blink." He drew in a whistling breath, then sighed. "Sometimes I don't think she'll ever wake up."

His jaw was tight, his eyes trained on his half sister,

frustration evident in the strain tugging at the corners of his mouth.

"It's just going to take more time."

"So I've heard. About a million times." He rubbed the back of his neck, his fingers delving beneath the collar of his suede jacket. "I'm not sure I believe it." Matt's gaze moved from Randi's bed to Kelly. "And don't give me any lectures about having patience or faith, okay? It's all been stretched thin. Real thin."

"It could be that she can hear all of us," Kelly said. "Maybe she just can't respond."

He lifted a dark eyebrow, then nodded curtly. "I s'pose." He reached for his sister's hand and Randi's palm seemed small and pale in his long, work-roughened fingers. "Come on, Randi gal," he said, seeming awkward in the role of doting brother. "Come on." Kelly's heart ached when she saw the pain etched across Matt's rugged face. He was a complex man, she realized, capable of a hundred emotions, ranging from anger, to guilt and love. Beneath his ranch-tough exterior was a good heart.

If only his sister's eyes would flutter open.

Realizing she was an intruder in a very intimate scene, Kelly started for the door.

"You don't have to go." Again his voice seemed loud and out of place in a hospital where hushed conversation and the faint strains of piped-in music were the backdrop.

"I'll just be outside." Kelly offered him a smile over her shoulder. "I think you need to be alone with her." Then she slipped through the doorway and eyed the nurses' station a few doors down a wide corridor. Two nurses, both women, were on duty, one talking on the telephone while looking at a computer screen, the second writing in a fat binder. An aide pushed a cart stacked with towels and blankets toward the elevator and one older man was strolling down the hallway, his IV stand in tow.

Quiet.

Peaceful.

Nothing strange or sinister.

"Hey, thanks for spelling me," Rex said as he ambled toward his chair. "I brought you a cup of coffee...hope you drink it black."

"Perfect." She accepted the second cup and took a sip of the scalding brew.

"It's supposed to be French roast, whatever the hell that is." Rex touched the lip of his cup to hers. "Here's to police work, which, in this case, includes baby-sitting." He shook his head, a few gray hairs catching the light. "Personally I think this is a big waste of time. I know someone tried to kill her before, but they'd have to be flat-out stupid to try it again. The hospital's beefed up security, and frankly, I haven't seen one suspicious character in this place."

"Let's keep it that way," Matt said as he overheard the last part of the conversation. He was frustrated with the situation, and seeing a big man in uniform sharing a cup of coffee and complaining to Kelly about the guy's duty irritated the hell out of him.

The policeman nodded as his eyes met Matt's. "I intend to," he said. "Rex Stanyon." He shot out a beefy, freckled hand that Matt reluctantly shook.

"Good." Matt squared his hat on his head and tried to ignore the spurt of jealousy that raced through his blood. His reaction to Kelly was all wrong. Way out of line. So she was pretty, so she filled out that drab uniform in all the right places, so what? She was a policewoman, for God's sake.

Ridiculously he felt a tightening in his groin, as he always seemed to whenever she was around. Hell. He clamped down his jaw. She was investigating the attempts on his sister's life; he couldn't think of her as a woman.

"We'll take care of your sister," Rex was saying.

"See that you do." He started for the elevator before he said something to the cop that he might regret.

From the corner of his eye he saw Kelly drain her cup, say something to Rex, then take off to catch up with him as the elevator doors parted and an attendant pushed an empty wheelchair into the hallway.

"That was uncalled for." Kelly strode into the elevator and swatted the button for the ground level.

"What?"

The doors closed and with a groan the elevator car began its descent.

"Rex is a damned good cop."

"If you say so."

"Look, McCafferty," she said, stepping closer to him and jabbing a long finger at his chest. "Everybody's doing the best they can, and believe me, we all want to see the creep who attacked Randi behind bars. But that doesn't mean we don't have the right to grumble a bit."

"I just asked the man to do his job."

"You insinuated that he wasn't." Her lips pursed in fury, her nostrils flared and a soft blush colored her cheeks.

"Cops are supposed to have thick skins."

"So are cowboys!"

Without thinking, he grabbed her. His hands surrounded her upper arms and he dragged her close. "Cowboys are just like cops. Flesh and blood."

"And they have feelings, too. Is that the sorry line you were going to throw at me?"

"No, lady, I wasn't. In fact, I wasn't going to say a

damned thing.'' Without really thinking about it, he yanked her closer still, lowered his head and kissed her. Hard. Full on the mouth while she was gasping and sputtering and probably reaching for her gun. Her lips were firm and warm, the starch in her spine not giving an inch. If he expected her to melt against him, he was disappointed.

She flung herself out of his arms as the elevator landed and her eyes flashed indignant fire. ''Don't you ever—''

The doors parted and Slade McCafferty started to step inside. ''Oh. Matt, I was looking...'' Blue eyes focused full on Kelly and then, as if he read the situation perfectly, Slade had the nerve to grin, one of those crooked, I-know-what-you've-been-up-to smiles that had irritated the hell out of Matt while growing up. ''Well, what's going on here?'' he drawled, and Matt wanted to lunge at him.

''Nothing.'' Kelly found some shred of her pride. ''I was just explaining to your brother that we're doing everything possible to locate the person who attacked your sister.''

Slade's eyes danced and again Matt wanted to knock his block off.

''Well, I was trying to track you down, 'cuz we just got a call from Kurt Striker. He's on his way to the ranch from Seattle. Should be there in an hour.''

''Let's go,'' Matt said.

''I'd like to talk to him,'' Kelly said as they headed along the hallway to the wide front doors of the hospital.

''I don't think—'' Slade started to protest.

''Why not?'' Matt nodded, as if agreeing with himself. ''Maybe you could share some information with him and he could do the same for you.'' Slade was about to argue the point further, but Matt cut him off. ''We just have to catch this bastard. If the police are willing to work with

Striker, all the better." He glanced at Kelly. "You want to ride with me?"

"I've got my car."

He lifted a shoulder and ignored the unspoken accusations in his brother's eyes. "I'll catch up with you at the ranch," Slade said. "I just want to look in on Randi first." Turning on his heel, he started for the elevator.

The electronic doors opened to the cold night. "You were about to tell me where to get off," Matt reminded her as they strode across the parking lot and snow blew across the asphalt.

"Don't ever try to manhandle me, okay?" She zipped her jacket and glanced up at him. "It could be dangerous."

"What? Were you going to handcuff me? Pull out your .38? Use a billy club and knock some sense into me?"

"That's not what I was talking about," she said soberly, then, unexpectedly, chuckled. When she glanced up at him, snowflakes caught on her eyelashes. "But it's not a bad idea. Watch out. I graduated from the police academy with honors in billy-clubbing."

So she did have a sense of humor. Beneath Ms. All-business-I'm-a-member-of-Grand-Hope's-finest-team, the lady appreciated a joke. "I didn't mean to offend."

"Of course you did," she said, reaching her car.

"I just kissed you."

"No way. That wasn't a kiss. That was a slap in the face. You were trying to let me know who was boss. Period. Neanderthal tactics, McCafferty. In case you didn't get the word, they went out with the Stone Age." She yanked a key ring from her pocket and started opening the door.

"No one's ever complained before."

"Have you ever done a poll?"

"Ouch." He winced.

"Just telling it like it is."

The door unlocked, and Matt, his pride stung, wanted to haul her into his arms again but didn't dare. "What is it with you?"

"What do you mean?"

"You're...different."

"From the women in your life? Let's hope." She started to slide into her vehicle when he grabbed the crook of her arm.

"Wait a minute."

She glanced down at his hand and disdainfully peeled his fingers from their grip on her elbow. "I don't go for the macho-man tactics."

"No? Then what?"

She hesitated, bit her lip and studied him through night-darkened eyes. "Since you asked..." Stepping around the door of her four-wheel drive, she held his gaze. "I know I'm going to regret this, but you did bring it up...." She reached upward and placed her chilled hands on either side of his face. Standing on her tiptoes, she pressed her lips to his, softly at first, just brushing her skin over his, and then, as her fingers warmed against his cheeks, she deepened the kiss, ever so slowly slipping her arms around his neck and molding her lips to his. Deep inside, the fire that had been banked for so many years ignited, warm ashes sparking to life. With a groan, he closed his eyes and slid his hands to her waist. Desire licked through his blood and the combination of the frigid night air and the warm woman in his arms was so damnably erotic. He wanted so much from her. Body and soul and—

She pushed him away quickly, and though she tried to cover it up, he saw the quickness in her breath, noticed that her eyes were nearly black, her skin flushed.

"That...that was just a demonstration," she said, her voice husky. She cleared her throat. "So the next time you think about using caveman tactics you might want to think twice."

Chapter Seven

Matt wasn't going to let some woman...some lady cop...best him. Grinning crookedly in the night, he drew her to him again. The ethereal lamplight glistened in the snow covering the parking lot and caught in her eyes. "You're not so tough, are you, Detective?" he asked, knowing he was stepping into dangerous territory. He should just leave well enough alone, but the challenge in her eyes, the defiant lift of her chin, the passionate woman hidden beneath that cop's uniform zeroed in on his male pride. "Don't lecture me about caveman tactics," he warned, "or I might just accuse you of being a tease."

"That wouldn't destroy me."

"No?" His fingers tightened over her arms. "And I'll bet it's not true."

"Wait a minute. I was just—"

"You were just curious and it backfired. You're not as

immune as you thought you were. You're not an ice woman after all.''

''And you're not a gentleman.''

''Never said I was.'' He let her go then, dropped his hands and turned toward his pickup parked two rows over.

Kelly climbed into her rig and bit her lip. He was right, dammit. She had reacted to him. She slammed the door shut and jabbed her key into the ignition with trembling fingers. How long had it been since she'd felt any response to a man? Two years? Three? Five? She couldn't remember, not that there were all that many to consider. She'd only fallen in love twice, and both times when the man started talking marriage, she'd bowed out.

Maybe she hadn't really been in love.

Or maybe love didn't exist.

She kicked herself as she flipped on the wipers. She knew better. Her parents' marriage was proof enough of the commitment and bond that can exist between a man and woman.

Good Lord, what was happening to her? What was she doing thinking about love? Just because Matt McCafferty had kissed her, she shouldn't go off the deep end. Besides, any McCafferty brother, Matt included, was off limits. Definitely off limits. Not only was he the brother of a victim, but he was the son of John Randall McCafferty, the man who had single-handedly ruined her mother's life.

''This is nuts,'' she told herself as she watched him through the windshield. With the athletic prowess that had tamed more than one bucking bronco, Matt climbed into his truck and started the rig. She threw her own car into gear and followed the glow of his taillights as he drove through town toward the main highway leading north to the Flying M. ''Stupid, stupid woman,'' she chastised herself. What had she been thinking? Why had she kissed him? Oh, yeah, feminine and professional pride, that had been her reasoning, she thought as she braked for a red light, then caught up with Matt's truck at the outskirts of town. She didn't like any man coming on to her and McCafferty had been trying to teach her a lesson, so she'd thrown it back at him, only to have it blow up in her face, as he'd so ineloquently pointed out.

Matt drove a good five miles over the speed limit and she wondered if he was taunting her. She thought of pulling him over just to prove that she could, that he couldn't get away with breaking any law, but she tamped down the urge. It wouldn't get her anywhere and she'd already experienced one emotional dressing-down for the night. But…but, if he got reckless or pushed the speed up another five miles an hour, she'd nail him. She'd have to.

Kurt Striker was already at the house, a cup of coffee cradled in his hands as he sat on the edge of a worn-looking chair. Nicole was seated on the piano bench near Thorne, who leaned back in the recliner. The twins and the baby were already in bed, the house quiet aside from the group clustered in the living room around a coffee table, where an enamel coffeepot, several empty cups and a plate of crackers and cheese were situated. A fire crackled and the odors of coffee and smoke wafted in the air. Kelly stood at the fireplace, warming the back of her legs, and accepted a cup from Matt, who handed it to her and stood next to her, his shoulders braced against the mantel.

"Do you think this is a good idea?" Thorne asked, his eyes moving from Kelly to Kurt. Kelly understood what he meant. Kurt was working for the McCaffertys privately; he reported to them rather than the police. Kelly was the law.

"It's fine, as long as the sheriff's department agrees to

share information." Kurt leaned back in his chair and eyed Kelly. He could have been Hollywood's version of a cop. Rugged good looks, straight brown hair, hard-edged features and intense green eyes, he seemed like a man who would bend the law if need be, just to get what he wanted. There was a secretive shadow in his eyes, the kind that Kelly often thought better belonged to criminals. Kurt was lanky and lean, dressed in denim and cowboy boots—as if he were ready for the next take on a weekly detective series.

"We just want to get to the bottom of the attacks on Randi and possibly Thorne as quickly as possible," she said, "and, of course, arrest the assailant and bring him to trial."

"Then we're all on the same page." Thorne flipped the recliner to a more upright position.

"I assume you've already checked my credentials." Kurt was still staring straight at Kelly, and from the corner of her eye, she saw Matt inch a little closer to her.

"Of course we have." Kelly nodded. "We've scrutinized everyone involved."

"Good. Then let's get down to business." He set his cup on the table. "I just flew in from Seattle where Randi worked. I dealt with the Seattle PD while I was there."

He said it, Kelly guessed, to put her at ease, to let her know that he was working on the right side of the law, but his eyes narrowed slightly, as if he was trying to size her up. "Everything I discuss with you here tonight will be squeaky clean. All according to police procedure. You don't have to worry that your professionalism will be compromised."

"Just so we lay out the ground rules." She didn't believe him for a second, but he seemed savvy enough to know where she was coming from. "If you broke any laws, you won't tell me about them and I'm supposed to ignore, not question them, is that it?''

"For the record, I didn't.''

"Duly noted," she replied, though she suspected he was lying. She whipped out a pen and notepad just in case he said anything she might want to check into later. "So what did you find when you were in Seattle?''

He reached into the pocket of his jacket. "To start with, this…" He withdrew a computer disk. "It's a copy. The Seattle PD have the original.''

"That you found where?''

"Surprisingly the door to Randi McCafferty's apartment was unlocked. I knocked, no one answered and I walked inside.''

"And found a computer disk that the police had overlooked?" she asked skeptically. She wanted to accuse him of being a bald-faced liar, tell him she damned well knew that he broke into the apartment, but saw no reason for it. Hadn't she used the same tactics herself? But then she'd bent the law while wearing a badge. This guy was a civilian. She was a cop. Which was worse?

"Not exactly. Let's just say I found a key to a locker.''

"What locker?" Kelly asked.

"One at the train station.''

"And the disk was in the locker?''

"That's right.''

"Did you find anything else?''

"Not so far.''

"What's on it?" Nicole asked, eyeing the computer disk as if it were evil.

"The start of a book. An outline and about three chapters.''

Thorne shoved himself upright. "The book Juanita kept mentioning. I thought it was all just talk.'' He struggled onto his crutches and balanced near the bookcase. "Ever since she was a little kid, Randi had a dream of writing a novel of some kind. When she was in grade school, she kept a diary and was always making up little stories, but I thought she gave all that up when she was in junior high and started showing interest in boys and the rodeo. I figured getting a degree in journalism and writing a column for the newspaper was good enough."

"But she wrote magazine articles as well," Nicole added, pushing up from the piano bench and standing near Thorne. She ran a finger over a dusty volume of an outdated set of encyclopedias. "I'm sure I read one that was so much like her style, written under the name of R. J. McKay."

"I checked it out," Kurt said with a quick nod. "It looks like she did a little moonlighting. Every once in a while she wrote articles under a pseudonym—probably because she didn't want her publisher to find out and give her some grief about it."

"What's the book about?" Kelly asked.

"It's the start of a novel."

"Not a collection of anecdotes and advice from her column with the *Clarion?*" Thorne asked.

"Doesn't seem like it. There's a story, and if I were a gambling man, I'd think it was a blend of fiction and fact."

"Autobiographical?" Matt asked.

"I don't think so. It's certainly not about her life, but it could have been inspired by someone who wrote in and asked advice, or someone she knew personally, or someone she read about. I don't know. At this point everything is conjecture. As I said, the Seattle PD has the original disk and the laptop."

"But you have copies of everything," Kelly guessed. "This isn't the only one."

Kurt's slow grin confirmed her theory. "I said I'd work with you, not give up all my secrets."

Kelly didn't press the issue.

"I'll print it out," Thorne said.

"Already done." Kurt reached into his briefcase and pulled out a sheaf of papers just as Slade burst through the front door. Rubbing his hands together, the youngest McCafferty brother walked into the living room, clapped Kurt on the back and was brought up to date. Within minutes he'd poured himself a cup of coffee and, along with the brothers, Kelly and Nicole, scanned the pages of Randi's book.

"Who's this about?" Slade asked.

"Beats me," Matt muttered under his breath.

Kurt lifted a shoulder. "I'd say the names have been changed to protect the guilty."

Kelly agreed. The first three chapters were rough, and the remainder of the story compressed into a stripped-down idea surrounding a shady rodeo rider who was being blackmailed into throwing competitions. The main character was a poor boy from the wrong side of the tracks, who had all his life scraped to get by. Eventually he'd been forced by circumstances to step outside of the law and was sucked into a world of drugs and crime. The upshot was that no matter how hard he tried to free himself of the vicious cycle of crime and dependence, he failed.

"What an upper," Slade muttered sarcastically as he scanned the last page.

"Overblown melodrama," Matt snorted as he finished reading and tossed his share of the manuscript to Thorne.

Kelly glanced at Matt. "Or a real story that someone doesn't want published."

"Who would know about it?" Kurt asked.

"I suppose her agent. Maybe he's already shopped it around to publishers." Thorne slung his arm around his fiancée's shoulders.

"Maybe," Matt agreed. "Or maybe not. The trouble is, none of us knows what was going on in Randi's life. But these—" he motioned to the pages that were being passed from brother to brother "—are pretty much nothing. So she was writing a book. Big deal. So it might have had some basis in fact?" He lifted his eyebrows. "So what?"

"You didn't find any notes?" Kelly asked Kurt.

"Other than what's on the disk?" He shook his head.

"Or reference books? Research materials?"

"There were books all over her den. Hundreds of 'em. And a stack of magazines in one bookcase. I didn't see anything that I thought significant."

Kelly didn't belabor the point. The Seattle police had already been in the apartment and they'd either missed or dismissed the fact that Randi was writing a book. It was something to check when she got to the city on Puget Sound.

They discussed the case until there was nothing left to say, then Kelly decided to call it a night. "I'll keep you posted if I find anything," she said to the group in general, then, to Kurt, "and I'll expect the same consideration."

"You got it," he assured her, though Kelly wasn't confident she could trust him.

"Good night." She headed for the door, then thought twice about it. Turning to Matt she said, "Could I see her room?"

With a shrug of his shoulder, Matt showed her upstairs

and quietly opened the door to a small room that had been transformed into the nursery. The baby was sleeping soundly, his breathing audible, and Kelly smiled as she looked down at him. Matt glanced at his nephew and the hard lines of his face softened. ''Such a little guy and such a big fuss,'' he whispered, tucking a blanket closer to the baby's chin.

Kelly's heartstrings pulled so tight she suddenly couldn't breathe. Matt's big hands seemed out of place fingering the dainty satin-hemmed blanket. His tanned, work-roughened fingers should have been awkward but weren't, and the tenderness with which he adjusted the bedding was surprising. Someday, whether he knew it or not, Matt McCafferty would make one helluva father.

She darted a look to his face, caught him watching her reaction and, clearing her throat, stepped away from the crib. In the dim glow from the night-light, she searched the walls of the room. A bulletin board that hung near the closet still displayed some of Randi's childhood treasures: a dried, faded corsage, yellowed pictures of friends splashing in a creek and seated around the remains of a campfire, a couple of shots of Randi astride a black quarter horse, tassels from a graduation cap, a lacy garter and several blue-and-red ribbons tacked haphazardly over the corkboard surface.

A desk had been shoved into the corner, and in the bookcase resting above the walnut surface were trophies of various sizes all dedicated to horsemanship.

There was also a dusty cowgirl hat with a rhinestone tiara as the hatband. She fingered the dusty jewels.

''Randi was a rodeo princess in high school,'' Matt explained.

''So your sister had rodeo fever, too.''

''It's in our blood,'' Matt admitted. ''Every one of us

but Thorne. He didn't have much use for anything to do with ranching or horses or that whole part of western culture.'' He slid a glance in her direction. ''He was more interested in making money—in fact, it was his only interest until he met Nicole.''

''She changed his life.''

''In a big way.''

Kelly studied the books on the desk, mostly about horse care and grooming, then with one last sweeping glance, decided she'd learned all she could about Matt's half sister. If only she would wake up—there were so many questions only Randi could answer. ''I guess that's about it,'' Kelly said, with one last smile for the baby as he sighed in his sleep.

''I'll walk you.'' Matt followed her down the stairs and zipped up his jacket as he walked her through the snow to her rig.

''For the most part, you were pretty quiet in there,'' he observed, hitching his chin toward the ranch house, his breath making a fine cloud in the night air.

''I suppose.'' She glanced over her shoulder to the two-storied building where the windows glowed in bright patches against the chill of the winter night. ''I wanted to hear what Striker had to say.''

''So what did you think?''

She met his gaze in the darkness. ''It's all well and good, but I'm going to double-check everything when I get to Seattle.''

''You're leaving?'' He was surprised.

''For a day or two. Compliments of the department.'' At the SUV, she paused, sent him a mischievous glance. ''I know, you're gonna miss me,'' she teased, but she'd struck closer to home than he wanted to admit.

''I'll try to survive.''

"Do that, cowboy."

She smiled and that was all it took. Before he had a chance to think, he grabbed her, hauled her into his arms and slanted his mouth over hers. She gasped and he took advantage of her open mouth, his tongue sliding into her mouth to find hers. There was a second's resistance, her muscles tensing, and then he felt her melt, her body leaning into his for just a second. Matt closed his eyes, drew her closer still, his hands splaying upon her back, his heart pounding, blood thundering through his ears.

Somewhere he heard a door open and voices. Kelly froze in his arms, then pushed away. "I don't think this is a good idea," she said, and glanced to the porch. Slade and Kurt stood under the porch light, Slade lighting a cigarette, Kurt standing with his hands in the front pockets of his jeans. Both men were staring at them.

"Great," Matt said, knowing he was going to catch hell from his younger brother.

"I think we should keep this professional," she said as if reading his thoughts. She opened the door of her SUV and slid inside.

"And I think you're a liar." He leaned closer to her. "Face it, Detective," he said, his voice low. "You want me."

"You're insufferable."

"So I've heard." His grin was cocksure and irreverent.

"Good night, cowboy." She hauled the door shut and gritted her teeth. What was it about that man that got under her skin? Why had she let him kiss her again? He was right.

Jabbing her key into the ignition, she twisted her wrist and the engine sparked on the first try.

Face it, Detective, you want me.

Oh, if he only knew. The taste of him was still on her

lips and her blood was thundering through her veins. Oh, yes, she wanted him, but she couldn't have him. The whole idea was ludicrous and completely out of character for her. She switched on the headlights and wipers, then pushed the heater's control lever to high.

Nimbly, she swung her car into reverse, her headlights slashed across the lot to land on Matt, standing feet spread apart, arms crossed over his wide chest, eyes trained on her vehicle. She threw the car into drive and stepped on the throttle. *Yes, damn it, I want you, but that's as far as it's gonna go. You, Mr. McCafferty, are strictly taboo!*

Matt braced himself as he walked back to the house. He saw the censure in Slade's dark gaze. "What the hell was that all about?" Slade demanded. He flicked his cigarette butt into the air and the red ember arced in the darkness to sizzle in a snowbank.

"What?"

"You and the policewoman, and don't try to deny it. I thought you were keeping your eye on the police department to see that they were doing their job."

"I am."

"By kissing the detective investigating the case?" Slade snorted. "You're trying to get her into bed, for God's sake."

"Back off, Slade. I'm handling things."

"You're stepping over the line. She needs to be thinking about the attacks on Randi and nothing else. And you—" he poked a thick finger at his brother's chest "—keep your head on straight."

"Don't worry about it," Matt said sharply, his back muscles tightening.

"You have a job to do!"

Matt grabbed his younger brother by the shirtfront. "I

said back off and I meant it.'' He pushed his face so close to Slade's that in the porch light he could see the color throb in the scar running along the side of his brother's face.

"Hold on. Both of you.'' Kurt's eyes were narrowed and he was gazing down the lane where the taillights of Kelly's rig had so recently disappeared. "I think this could work out.''

"How?'' Matt demanded, turning his attention onto the detective, though he still wanted to throw a punch.

Kurt's eyes narrowed and he rubbed the stubble of his jaw. "Pillow talk.'' His gaze took in both brothers.

Slade's lips thinned. "I don't like it.''

"Neither do I.'' Matt's fist uncurled and he stepped away from his brother, only to level a killing glare at Striker.

Kurt didn't back down. "Before you do something we'll both regret,'' he said, "hear me out. We all know that sometimes women say things in bed that they wouldn't otherwise. This could definitely work to our advantage, as Detective Dillinger is so involved with the case.''

"That's not the point,'' Matt argued.

"It's precisely the point. We're all working together, right? Toward a common goal. To find out who the hell's trying to kill your sister, and I figure we can do it by any means possible. So you kiss the woman, so you bed her. Big deal. It's not as if you have to fall in love with her. She's here, you live far away, but for the meantime, you could enjoy yourself for a while. At least you'll find out whatever it is the police might be holding back.''

"If she talks,'' Slade interjected.

"She will if given the right motivation. They all do.'' With that Kurt took off and jogged across the snowy park-

ing lot to his four-wheel drive vehicle, leaving Matt with
a bad taste in his mouth.

"I don't like him," he said to Slade.

"You don't have to. Just do what he says." His lips
were compressed, his blue eyes harsh. "You want to bed
Ms. Dillinger, anyway. Now you've got an excuse."

Chapter Eight

Kelly stomped on the accelerator and told herself she'd just won the medal for moron of the century. What had come over her? What was she thinking, flirting so outrageously, *kissing* Matt, for crying out loud? It was just plain nuts! She couldn't, *wouldn't,* let herself fall for Matt McCafferty. To let him kiss her was bad enough, but had she let it go at that? Oh, no, she had to challenge him, and even now, ten minutes later, she felt the heat, tingle and impression of his lips against hers.

"Idiot," she growled, clenching the steering wheel hard. She drove to Grand Hope as if possessed, parked and stormed up the flight of stairs to her living area. This damned case was making her crazy, that was it. She was losing her perspective.

She spent the rest of the night going over the computer printout of Randi's novel, making notes, drumming her fingers, reading passages over and over again, trying to gain some insight into the mind of Matt's half sister. The McCaffertys' housekeeper seemed to think this book was important; Kelly didn't see how. As far as she could tell it was fiction. She found no clues as to the identity of Randi's attacker, nor did she discover a hint about little J.R.'s father.

But the rodeo scenario bothered her. Not only had Randi's father followed the rodeo circuit, but two of her brothers, Matt and Slade, as well. And then there was Randi herself, into barrel racing and crowned a rodeo princess.

Kelly tapped her pencil against her teeth. So Randi found the whole cowboy thing fascinating, to the point that she'd been involved recently, however briefly, with Sam Donahue, a man who had grown up around these parts and joined the rodeo circuit soon after he'd graduated from high school.

So how did it all tie into Randi's book? Or did it? Was it significant? Or another false lead? One of far too many.

"It's a waste of time," she told herself, stretching in her chair at the kitchen table and eyeing the clock. It was well after midnight. She couldn't keep her eyes open and tumbled into bed where she spent a restless night, tossing and turning and dreaming of a rangy cowboy whose kisses stole the breath from her lungs.

By the time she'd walked into the office the next morning and dropped the rough draft of Randi's manuscript on the corner of Espinoza's desk, she'd tried and failed to push Matt McCafferty out of her mind.

"This is about all Striker found," she said as Espinoza picked up the rough draft of the manuscript and riffled through the pages. She placed the disk on top of the printout.

"Does it mean anything?"

"Just that she has a vivid imagination." Kelly leaned against the file cabinet and gave him the blow-by-blow of the night before.

He skimmed the pages and shook his head. "It bothers me that the Seattle police didn't find this."

"Me, too."

"I think you'd better check with them, ask them about Striker when you're there." He reached into the top drawer of his desk and withdrew a thick envelope, then slapped it into Kelly's hand. "Airline tickets," he explained. "You leave tomorrow."

"Son of a bitch!" Matt slammed down the receiver and caught a warning glare from Thorne, who was seated at the kitchen table with Nicole, J.R. and the twins as they all were trying and failing to play Go Fish. Nicole was balancing the baby on her lap while the twins slapped cards willy-nilly. Thorne was attempting to teach the four-year-olds the basics of the game while half-drunk cups of cocoa steamed and the bowl of popcorn had been reduced to a few unpopped kernels sitting in a pool of melted butter.

The scene was way too domestic for Matt. Who would have thought Thorne could become such a family man? But there he was discussing the upcoming wedding with his fiancée, laughing with the twins and taking the time to relax.

"Trouble?" Thorne asked.

"Yeah, there was a major storm in the mountains and it took out a lot of the power and phone lines. I can't get through to Kavanaugh." He glanced out the window to the dark night beyond and silently swore. He'd worked damned hard for that scrap of land near the Idaho border; it had been his pride and joy, his proof that he could make

it on his own, without John Randall's help. Without anyone's. He always figured he'd eventually find a good
woman to settle down there, raise his family and die on
the land he'd claimed as his own. When the time came,
he figured his ashes would be scattered in the wind, near
the pond by the barn.

But lately he'd been thinking of giving it all up, relin-
quishing his dream.

For what?

For Kelly Dillinger.

Hell, what had happened to him in the past couple of
weeks?

"You'll just have to be patient." Thorne picked up a
card from the discard pile and tossed off another. "Mike
will call when he can."

Matt didn't like it. He poured himself a cup of day-old
coffee he didn't want and glared out the window. He
needed to get back to his own place, to check on his stock,
to reconnect with what was his. Day by day he was feeling
less a part of his own spread and more entrenched in life
back here in Grand Hope. His brothers, the kids,
Randi…and, though he hated to admit it, Kelly Dillinger,
all played a big part in his newfound roots at the Flying
M.

"Go fish!" one little voice yelled proudly.

Matt took a swig from his cup, scowled at the bitter
taste, tossed the remainder down the sink and tried to fight
the restlessness that seemed to be his constant companion
these days. "I think I'll go into town," he said, striding
to the back door and grabbing his jacket. "I'll check on
Randi."

"You don't wants to play?" one of the twins—Mindy,
he thought—asked.

"Not right now, darlin'," he said, smiling and tousling

her dark curls. ''I'll take a rain check.'' Her face pulled into a little knot of confusion. ''I mean I'll play with you another time, okay?''

'''Kay,'' she replied, and he felt a tug on his heart. Yep, he was getting way too tied up here. He grabbed his jacket off a hook near the back porch.

A chorus of ''byes'' followed after him until the door slammed shut. On one level he was glad his older brother was getting married. It was about time, and Nicole, even with her ready-made family, was a helluva catch, a beautiful woman who could handle Thorne like none other. That they loved each other was obvious to everyone. They planned to stay here at the house, rent Nicole's cottage in town and, eventually, once Randi woke up, build nearby.

If Randi ever woke up. Matt scowled into the night as his boots crunched through the crusted snow. Clouds covered the moon and stars, but so far the snow had held off. He slid into his truck and tore out of the lot. First he'd drive to the hospital, check on Randi, then he'd cruise by the station and see if Detective Dillinger was working and if not…

What then?

He pulled onto the two-lane highway and headed south toward Grand Hope without coming up with an answer.

''So I was gonna invite you over for a glass of wine, but since you're out, it'll have to wait until I get back from Seattle,'' Kelly said, leaving a message on her sister's answering machine. ''I'll be back the night before Thanksgiving. See ya then.''

Kelly hung up and stretched. She'd poured herself a glass of wine and had hoped that her sister would join her, but since she couldn't reach Karla, she'd have to alter her plans slightly. Instead of girl talk around the fire, or playing a board game with Karla's boys, Kelly decided on a bath and a good book. She hadn't soaked in the tub in ages, rarely had enough time. Instead she showered in the morning and, if she needed it, again at night. Fast, easy, done in five minutes. But tonight, after being chilled to her bones from working all day outside investigating accident scenes and vandalism to property, she decided she deserved the luxury of soft music.

She stripped off her uniform, twisted her hair into a loose knot, lit two white tapers and filled the tub with hot water. She left her glass of wine and book on the rim of the tub, then settled into the warm, scented water.

It felt like heaven.

She sank lower, half closing her eyes as the candles flickered and the heat seeped into her bloodstream, loosening the tension from her muscles. Her mind ran in slower and slower circles, winding down to eventually stop dead center at Matt McCafferty. Despite her warnings to the contrary, she thought about kissing him and her response. Deep. Heartstopping. Breathless. He'd left her with her knees weak and an ache beginning to throb deep inside her.

Oh, she was playing with fire with that man. Kissing him was a luxury she couldn't allow herself again. At least not until the mystery surrounding his half sister was solved, and God knew when that would be. Soon…it had to be soon. She sipped her wine and tried to get into the mystery, but as she read one paragraph over and over again, she thought of Randi McCafferty's unfinished novel and she wondered at its significance. Rodeos. Barrel racing. Bareback broncos. Matt McCafferty. She could nearly picture him, lean body tense and rigid, one hand raised, the other tight around the strap surrounding a muscular, headstrong rodeo horse. With a sigh she gave up on her book and set it on the ledge. "Forget him," she chided. Closing her eyes, she nearly drifted off when she heard the doorbell chime softly over the music playing on the radio.

Her eyes snapped open.

Who in the devil would be dropping by?

Karla.

Her sister had gotten home, heard the phone message and hurried over.

"Coming!" she yelled as she stepped out of the tub, threw on her bathrobe and cinched the belt tightly around her waist. She slipped into scuffs and hurried down the stairs to the door, where she peeked through the peephole. Karla wasn't anywhere around, but Matt McCafferty, larger than life through the fish-eye lens, was staring back at her.

Her silly heart skipped a beat. She threw the bolt and swung open the door before she realized she was wearing nothing—not one solitary stitch—beneath the yellow terry robe.

His eyes widened just a fraction and for a second he actually seemed tongue-tied as he looked down at her. "I didn't realize it was so late," he said, and she swallowed a smile. Obviously he was expecting *Detective* Kelly Dillinger to answer the door, that he would be face-to-face with a no-nonsense officer of the law, dressed in full uniform and probably packing heat.

"Is there something I can do for you?" she asked.

He nodded, his eyebrows knitting into one dark line. "I was in town and I thought I'd…well, I guess I should have called." His lips compressed together and his glance shifted to one side. "I thought maybe you'd like to go out for a drink or a cup of coffee or something."

"Or something?" she prodded, amused and flattered.

"I should have called."

"That's usually the way it's done, yes," she said, not giving him an inch. Her pulse fluttered ridiculously and her heartbeat cranked up a notch as she stood in the doorway.

God, she was gorgeous, Matt thought, wondering what had compelled him to her doorstep. He'd told himself it was because he was keeping an eye on the sheriff department's investigation, that it was all business, but deep inside, he knew there was more to it, more than he cared to admit. He'd argued with himself as he'd driven to her row house, tried to convince himself to turn back to the ranch, but here he was, the victim of his own sexual drive, for that's what it was; he wanted to see her because she was an intriguing, sassy, beautiful woman. He'd expected to find a slim, all-business policewoman dressed in her uniform...but this...this fascinating lady was even more irresistible. Kelly appeared smaller, more vulnerable, incredibly feminine and damned sexy in that thick yellow duster. Her hair was piled onto her head, some strands escaping to curl in damp ringlets around a flushed face with incredible cheekbones, dark-fringed, mocking eyes and a saucy mouth curved into an amused smile.

"I suppose it's too late."

"For a date? Tonight?" she asked, folding her arms under her chest and allowing him just a peek at cleavage where the lapels of her robe overlapped. "I think so."

He felt like a schoolboy as he worked the brim of his hat between his fingers. "Maybe tomorrow."

"I'll be out of town. It's a working vacation. I'll be back in a couple of days...."

"Maybe we can get together then."

"I don't think that would be a good idea."

"No?" He couldn't help himself. Something in the defiant tilt of her chin challenged him.

"Well, you know, it might not be the proper thing to do."

"You're worried about propriety?" He didn't believe it.

"I wouldn't want to do anything where my professionalism or objectivity might be questioned."

Was it his imagination or did her eyes twinkle with a dare? The scent of jasmine reached his nostrils and he couldn't help himself. "The hell with professionalism," he growled. His arms surrounded her.

She gasped. "Now, wait a second."

"And damn objectivity." He slanted his mouth over hers. Her lips were warm and tasted faintly of wine. She moaned quietly and he kissed her harder, rubbing his mouth over hers, wrapping his arms more tightly around her body, feeling her melt against him.

The fire in his blood ignited. His fingers curled in the soft folds of her robe. He felt her quiver and it was his undoing. Deftly, he reached down, picked her off her feet and crossed the threshold.

"Hey," she said breathlessly. "What do you think you're doing?"

With a heel he kicked the door closed. "What I've wanted to do from the first time I saw you," he said, carrying her up the stairs and unerringly to her bedroom. Candles from the adjoining bath gave off a soft, glimmering illumination that reflected in the foggy mirrors and windows as he tumbled with her onto an antique bed covered with a plush comforter.

Kelly knew she should object, that she should resist the temptation of his touch, but his lips were magic, his hands warm and persuasive. He kissed her eyelids, her cheeks and neck as he somehow shrugged out of his jacket and let it drop to the floor. Work-roughened fingers scraped her robe open and he pressed his lips against the curve of her suddenly bare shoulder.

Flames of desire licked through her blood.

He untied the knot of her belt and lowered himself onto the bed. His breath was hot against the cleft between her breasts and she tingled inside, felt the first dark stirrings of want.

Don't do this, Kelly. Don't. This is the biggest mistake of your life! Think, dammit.

But she couldn't. His hands and mouth were seductive, chasing away all doubts, and try as she might, she couldn't find credence in any of the reasons she called up that might put an end to his lovemaking. She knew that her father and mother would disapprove, that her boss would consider this an act of betrayal insofar as she would compromise the investigation and her badge, that her sister would remind her that a McCafferty was the worst possible choice of a lover and yet…and yet…his lips were so warm and seductive, the ache deep within her impossible to deny.

He pulled the pins from her hair with his teeth just as the knot holding her robe together gave way, parting as his hand skimmed her skin beneath the rich cotton. A jolt of desire shot through her bloodstream. Kissing her cheek, he glanced down at her body. "I knew you'd be beautiful, Detective," he said, touching one nipple with the flat of his hand. "I knew it." He squeezed the dark bud gently and her entire breast began to ache. Oh, she wanted this man. She bucked up and he leaned forward, his mouth surrounding her nipple, his teeth lightly scraping her skin, his tongue laving.

Damn, but she was melting inside, feeling warm, moist

heat coiling between her legs. As if he understood, he trailed one hand lower, fingers skimming her abdomen to delve deep into the curls where her legs joined. Lower still he probed, searching her cleft expertly, finding the nub that drove her wild, kissing her breasts as lust stormed through her blood. She moaned deep in her throat and shifted, anxiously wanting more...so much more...everything he could give...everything he would. Her skin was on fire, sweat dampening her forehead.

Her fingers tore at the buttons of his shirt, delving beneath the cotton to touch a hard-muscled chest covered in springy black hair. She touched taut, sinewy muscles, felt him tremble, but it wasn't enough. She needed to feel him, all of him, rubbing against her—skin on skin, heartbeat to heartbeat. And still he touched her deep inside. She gasped. Gripped his shoulders hard.

"Oh...oh..." She swallowed hard and felt as if her entire being was centered in that small spot that he rubbed intently. She writhed, sweated as if in a fever, felt the storm brewing hotter, and wilder.

"That's a girl," he whispered across her breasts, fanning the flames. "Just let go..."

The world seemed to spin. His lips found hers again, his tongue rimmed her mouth, his breath hot and wild against her already flushed skin. "Please," she murmured, her voice so low she didn't recognize it. "Please... Matt...oh, please..."

"Anything for you, darlin'."

She reached for the waistband of his jeans, felt his erection straining against the worn denim. "Then..."

With his free hand he grabbed her wrist. "In time, darlin', in time." His ministrations increased and she lolled back, closed her eyes, writhed and cried out as the first spasm jolted her, sending her skyrocketing through space, her soul streaking through the heavens.

"Oooh," she sighed, gasping, trying to take in any air.

But he wasn't finished. His fingers delved again, deeper, faster, pushing her to the limits again. Her fingers dug into his bare shoulders and she cried out as convulsion after convulsion ripped through her.

"Matt...oh...Matt..." She couldn't breathe, couldn't think, but knew she needed him, all of him, wanted the feel of his hard body joining with her.

She found his belt and her fingers fumbled with the huge rodeo buckle that held the strap together. Before he could protest, she kissed him, touched the tip of her tongue to his, invited him to enter her.

Groaning, sweat sheening his skin, he stretched out beside her, giving her better access, no longer fighting her.

Click.

The buckle was open.

Pop. Pop. Pop.

His fly gave way.

He felt a rush of cool air against his skin and bit his lips as her fingers brushed over his bare shaft.

Ding.

Somewhere a bell began to chime. A doorbell.

"Oh, no." Kelly's hand fell away. She turned a dozen shades of red.

"Expectin' someone?" he asked lazily, amused.

"No."

The bell chimed again. Insistently.

"Someone wants to see you real bad."

"Oh, damn. Karla! I—I left her a message earlier, on her machine...she's probably got her sons with her." She shoved her hair out of her eyes.

"Who's Karla?"

"Oh. My sister. Just…just wait." Kelly hurled herself off the bed, dashed to the closet, grabbed a shirt and a pair of jeans, then darted to the bathroom.

Matt zipped up his pants. Hooked his belt. The damned bell rang again and this time a woman's worried voice followed after it. "Kelly? Are you there? It's me."

"I know. I know," Kelly grumbled as she emerged from the bathroom. Barefoot but dressed, she was snapping her hair into a rubber band. Then, spying Matt still lounging on the bed, she hissed, "You, go sit in the living room for goodness' sake and pour yourself a glass of wine or something. Look like you've been in there all the time. Make it look…like we've been discussing the case, for crying out loud, and then…and then—" she stopped short at the foot of the bed and sighed loudly, then sent him a rueful glance "—and then brace yourself."

She disappeared out the door of the bedroom and he heard her footsteps hurrying down the stairs.

Matt hitched up his jeans, sauntered into the living room and, finding an open bottle of wine, went to a cupboard, plucked a long-stemmed glass from the shelf and heard the door open somewhere downstairs. Female voices reached him.

"Jeez, Kelly, didn't you hear the doorbell ring? I darned well froze my tail off waiting for you!" Footsteps pounded up the stairs. "What took you so long to…" A small woman with short red-blond hair and wide green eyes that landed full force on Matt appeared. "Uh-oh." She stopped dead in her tracks and the playful smile that had been tugging at the corners of her mouth faded. "Kelly…what's going on here?" Her eyes narrowed a fraction and zeroed in on the wineglass in Matt's hand.

"Oh. Well. Matt came over to discuss the case."

"Matt?" the woman repeated.

Kelly entered the room and despite the circumstances seemed cool. "Yes. Matt McCafferty, this is my sister, Karla."

"Pleased to meet ya," Matt drawled as Kelly's sister seemed all the more disconcerted. He had the manners to reach across the counter and clasp Karla's reluctantly offered hand.

"Oh, yeah, me, too," Karla said, rolling her expressive eyes before catching a hard look from her sister. "Wait a minute, is this for real?"

"What do you mean?" Kelly said. "Is what for real? Matt and I were going over—"

"Whoa." Karla held her hands up, the fingers of her right pointing into the palm of her left. "Time out, okay?" She skewered both Kelly and Matt in her hard glare. "Don't give me any garbage about the case. I've got eyes, Kelly." She gave her sister an exaggerated once-over. "I just hope you know what you're doing."

"Of course I do."

"Care for something to drink? A glass of wine?" Matt offered as he grabbed another stemmed glass from the cupboard and began to pour from the bottle of chardonnay.

"I think I need something stronger, but yeah, okay."

"There isn't anything stronger. I already asked."

Karla didn't so much as blink, just took the drink from Matt's hand and, with one last condemning glare at her sister, plopped down in a rattan chair covered with a plump green cushion. "So how is the investigation going?" she asked with more than an edge of sarcasm.

"There are some snags, of course, and we keep coming up against dead ends, but I think we're making progress."

"Ummm." Karla swirled her wine but obviously wasn't buying her sister's story.

Matt emptied the bottle into another glass and gave the drink to Kelly.

"I'm leaving for Seattle tomorrow," she explained, and fielded the questions Karla shot at her. From the gist of the conversation he gathered that Karla, after hearing Kelly's open invitation left on her answering machine, had decided to stop by. The younger Dillinger sibling had pawned her kids off on her folks and driven over, only to find Matt already here. For some reason his presence rankled Karla, and there was more to it than disappointment at having to share her sister for the evening. No, there were undercurrents of resentment running through the conversation and pooling in her eyes.

Rounding the kitchen bar, he joined the women in Kelly's small living room. He'd expected her apartment to be neat and tidy, functional yet spartan, but, as with everything about this woman, he'd been dead wrong. The row house wasn't cluttered but definitely had a lived-in feel. A raised counter separated the living room from the kitchen. Along with the rattan chair, there was an antique rocker, a tan couch with floppy pillows and a beveled-glass coffee table that appeared to match a lawyer's book-case, crammed with all manner of paperbacks and criminology texts. A fussy walnut secretary occupied one corner and a collection of candles and photographs graced the mantel of a small fireplace.

"You said in the phone message that you'd be back in time for Thanksgiving," she said to her sister.

"That's the plan."

"Good." Kelly's sister relaxed a bit, sipping from her wine as Kelly took a seat on the couch and Matt leaned against the counter. "I wouldn't want to explain to Mom and Dad that you weren't going to show up at the house because of work."

"Dad would understand. He was a cop."

"Eons ago."

"So you come from a family tradition of fighting crime," Matt observed.

"Mmm. Dad, his father and, I think, my great-grandfather."

"It beat mining," Karla said. "Until Dad got shot and had to retire early. Disability." She finished her glass of wine with a flourish. "So, how about you?" she asked him, though she expected she knew a lot more about his family than he did about hers. Like it or not, the McCafferty name was nearly legendary around this part of western Montana, and Karla was fishing. The smile on her face was about as warm as the bottom of a Montana well in the middle of winter. "What is it your family does?"

She didn't bother to hide the bite in her words.

"Dad was a rodeo man turned rancher, bought the Flying M over fifty years ago and expanded that to include some other businesses around Grand Hope."

Karla's lips compressed and she cast a hard, darting glance at her sister. "He doesn't remember, does he?"

"Remember what?" Matt demanded.

Little lines of irritation surrounded Karla's lips but it was Kelly who answered. "Mom worked for your dad for a few years."

"Not just a few," Karla said, setting her empty glass onto the table. "She dedicated her life to that man, to her job as his secretary, or personal assistant, yeah, that's what he called her." She snorted. "And what happened when things started to go bad for your father's businesses? Mom was history. Just like that." Karla snapped her fingers for emphasis and her cheeks had turned a bright, hot scarlet. "No job, no retirement fund, no damned golden parachute. Nothing."

"Wait a minute—you said she was his secretary?"

"And more. She was like his right-hand woman, his executive assistant. Surely you remember her. Eva. Eva Dillinger."

"Eva?" The name did have a familiar ring, but Matt had never spoken to the woman. He'd only heard her name a couple of times in passing when John Randall had mentioned her, but Matt hadn't paid much attention. He was too self-involved at the time. "I guess Dad did mention her once in a while."

"Once in a while? I hope to shout he did," Karla said with a shake of her head. She glanced at the open bedroom door where Kelly's yellow robe was sliding off the messed bed. Her lips puckered even more. She seemed about to say something, then thought better of it and stood. "Maybe I'd better leave," she said, and some of her anger dissipated. "I think I interrupted something."

"You stay." Matt glanced at his watch. "It's time I was heading back, anyway." He drained his glass and set it on the edge of the counter. Reaching for his jacket, he said to Kelly, "Just let me know if you learn anything else about what happened to my sister."

"I will." Kelly walked him to the top of the stairs where he paused to zip his jacket.

"I'll talk to you later, oh…" He held up a long finger. "There is one more thing."

"What's that?" she asked, visibly tensing.

"Have a good trip."

"I will."

He turned to Karla. "Nice meetin' ya."

"You, too," she said, though the words seemed to

strangle her. She was watching him as if he were the devil incarnate and Matt couldn't let it go.

With an exaggerated wink toward Karla, he turned on his heel, slipped his arms around Kelly's waist and dragged her close to him. "Thanks for the hospitality, Detective. Now, don't you forget me." He leaned forward and kissed her. Hard. Like he intended to ravish her body and never stop. She stiffened, then slumped slightly. He let her go, she stumbled back a step, then he winked at Karla again and headed down the stairs.

"Oh, my," Karla whispered, her gaze following him as he disappeared. Her eyes rounded and one hand covered her heart. "Oh...my."

Kelly steeled herself for the barrage she was certain was headed her way.

"You're in love with him, aren't you?" Karla accused, but some of the fury had left her voice and it was replaced by an emotion akin to awe.

Downstairs the front door opened, then slammed shut. Matt McCafferty was gone. A few seconds later an engine sparked to life.

"Well...you are, aren't you?" Karla demanded.

"No, of course not," Kelly snapped, stunned as she found her wineglass, polished off the last drops of chardonnay and gathered her wits. In love? With Matt Mc Cafferty? Her heart pounded a million beats a minute at the thought. Oh, God, was she? Could she possibly have fallen for the smart-aleck, rogue of a cowboy? "That's ridiculous."

"I see it in your eyes," Karla countered as she walked to the window and peeked through the blinds to the wintry night outside. "I can't believe it, Kelly. Someone's managed to melt the ice around your heart and he's a damned McCafferty." Folding her arms across her chest, she clucked her tongue, cocked her head and eyed her sister as if she'd never seen Kelly in such a state. "Another time, I'd say we should celebrate, but since the man of your dreams is John Randall's son, I think it would be a better idea if I called a priest and asked for an exorcism."

"Very funny," Kelly grouched.

"It's not, I know, but *really,* are you out of your ever-lovin' mind? Mom and Dad are gonna flip when they find out and your boss will probably fire you. I mean, come *on,* what about the investigation?"

"Mom and Dad don't run my life, my boss can't tell me what to do when I'm not on duty and the investigation is still ongoing. I haven't compromised anything."

"Yet," Karla said, unconvinced. She walked to the bedroom door and looked pointedly inside. "But it wouldn't be long."

"It's none of your business and you're borrowing trouble." Kelly carried the wineglasses to the sink and her sister padded after her.

"I don't think I have to borrow any. You've got enough to last us both for the rest of our lives. Oh, Kelly, don't be dumb, okay?" Karla rapped her fingers around her sister's upper arm. "The McCaffertys are bad news, all of them. You can't trust any one of them as far as you can throw them."

"I've heard this lecture before."

"Excuse me, I thought *you* were the one who gave it. Just listen, for God's sake. Whatever you do, Kelly," Karla advised with all the wisdom of someone who'd made more than her share of mistakes when it came to affairs of the heart, "don't fall in love with Matt Mc-Cafferty."

"I won't."

"It would be a devastating mistake."

"I said, 'I won't.'"

"And I think you're a liar. It's probably already happened." Karla held up her hands as if to ward off any further protests. "But if you are in love with him, you're in trouble. Deep trouble. All you'll get out of it is a broken heart. That, I can guarantee."

Chapter Nine

"Where are you going?" Slade asked as Matt, hiking the strap of his duffel bag over his shoulder, hurried down the stairs. Slade was standing by the fireplace in the living room with a clear view of the foyer and bottom step. Standing in stocking feet, warming the backs of his calves by a slow-burning fire, he cradled a cup of coffee in his hands and had been paying attention to Larry Todd, who, Matt gleaned from the tail end of the conversation, was explaining the need for a new pole barn.

"So it wouldn't cost that much, as it's basically a roof on poles. It would just give the stock some more shelter and make feeding easier."

"I don't see why not," Slade replied, then looked past Larry to the bottom of the stairs.

Matt paused in the archway and explained, "I hope you and Thorne can hold down the fort. I'm gonna be spending a couple of days in Seattle."

"Don't tell me, the lady detective is there." Slade's smile was downright evil, and with the scar running down one side of his face and the antlers mounted over the mantel seeming to be growing out of his head, he looked even more fiendish. "Right? Detective Dillinger is there."

Matt didn't bother to answer. "On my way back, I'll stop by my place, check in with Kavanaugh, and be back by Thanksgiving."

"That's only few days away. And Nicole mentioned something about both of us going into town to make sure our tuxes for the wedding fit."

"Did she?" Matt wasn't deterred.

"She'll be mad as a wet hen if you don't take care of this. The wedding's set to go as soon as Randi wakes up."

"The tux will fit fine, the wedding will go on without a hitch, and they'll get married," Matt bit out, his temper starting to control his tongue. "Tell her not to get her knickers in a knot. Randi is not even conscious yet. As I said, I'll be back in a couple of days." He clomped down the hall toward the kitchen and the seductive scent of coffee. He'd woken up in a bad mood, having slept poorly, his dreams peppered with images of Kelly—sexy, hot images that had forced him to a shower that felt sub-zero this morning.

He passed the den. From the corner of his eye, he saw Thorne, his casted leg propped by a corner of the desk, a phone crammed to one ear, his black eyebrows pulled into a thick line of consternation as he read the monitor of his computer.

"I'm outta here," Matt said, and Thorne, absorbed in his conversation, took a second to glance up. He held one finger aloft, signifying Matt should wait a second. Probably for orders. Matt wasn't in the mood. "Be back in a couple of days."

"Hold on, Eloise, looks like I've got a crisis here," Thorne said into the receiver, then turned all of his attention on his middle brother. "Where the hell are you going?"

Matt repeated himself. "Striker says I should keep an eye on the police, and since the sheriff's department is sending Kelly Dillinger to Seattle, I decided that I should tag along."

"Does she know it?"

"Nope."

"Thanksgiving is in three days."

"I know, I know, and Slade was already on my case about the tux. I'll take care of it when I get back."

"You'd better." Nicole's voice preceded her, and Matt inwardly groaned as he turned to face his soon-to-be sister-in-law. Her hair was pinned back and she was wearing a crisp white blouse, dark slacks and a wide belt. A briefcase swung from her fingers, as she was on her way to the ER at St. James Hospital. She took her place in the doorway next to him. "If you don't," she warned, her lips quirking as she fought a smile, "I'll just have to tar and feather you, *then* skin you alive."

"Thanks, *Doctor*. Anything else?"

"That should do it. For now."

"Are you always this much fun?" Matt grumbled.

"Only when I want something." She smiled sweetly, then rested a shoulder against the door frame and turned her attention to Thorne. "I'll look in on Randi, and Jenny should be here any minute to see to the twins and the baby. Juanita's feeding him right now. I kissed the girls goodbye, but they both fell back to sleep, so they shouldn't give you too much trouble."

"I wouldn't count on it," Thorne grumbled, but his eyes had brightened at the sight of Nicole.

She chuckled, the sound deep and low. "I'll call them later." Sliding a glance at her brother-in-law-to-be, she added, "You might want to say goodbye to your nephew."

"I will."

"Good." She blew a kiss to Thorne, then walked briskly down the hallway toward the kitchen.

Thorne's gaze followed her, his important call temporarily forgotten as he watched the sway of her hips. Boy, did he have it bad. When the lovebug bit Thorne McCafferty, it wasn't just a tiny nip. Thorne had been swallowed whole.

"I'll call," Matt said, and followed his future sister-in-law to the kitchen. As Nicole stated, Juanita was cradling the downy-haired baby in her arms and singing something that sounded like a Spanish lullaby to J.R. The baby blinked his round eyes and stared at the housekeeper-cum-nanny as if he was mesmerized.

Matt poured himself a cup of coffee from the pot simmering on the coffeemaker. Juanita was doing a helluva job with the kid, and Jenny Riley, Nicole's baby-sitter, was a godsend. But, by rights, little J.R. should be with his mother. Right now Randi should be the one singing to him, cuddling him, even nursing him. The muscles in the back of Matt's neck tightened as he thought of the bastard who'd tried to kill his sister. Not once, but twice. Who the hell was he? Could he possibly be J.R.'s missing father? That would be a bitch. The poor kid would be screwed up for life. Matt couldn't imagine saying, *Yeah, J.R., we didn't know who your father was, but it turned that he didn't claim you and tried to kill your mother while she was pregnant with you, and when that didn't work, tried again when she was in a coma in the hospital.*

Still in a black mood, Matt took two long swallows from his cup, then tossed the dregs into the sink.

"You're leaving?" Juanita asked, eyeing his duffel bag.

"*After* he gets fitted for his tux," Nicole said. She was half-serious, half-teasing. She sipped from her coffee cup and rested a hip against the counter.

"I'll take care of it." Tapping J.R.'s button of a nose, Matt said, "Don't give anyone any trouble, okay?" The baby cooed and Matt felt that familiar pull on his heart-strings that had become a part of his life here at the Flying M, new emotions that both J.R. and Kelly evoked in him.

Damn it all, anyway, what was happening to him? Ever since he'd heard the first news of Randi's accident, he'd changed. Angry at himself and the whole damned world, he squared his hat upon his head and ignored Juanita's protests that he needed a real breakfast before he left.

A broken heart indeed, Kelly thought the next day as she slid behind the wheel of her rental car at the Sea-Tac airport. *That would be the day.* But as she drove through the tangle of traffic toward downtown Seattle, flipping on her windshield wipers against the steady rain, she knew there was a smidgen of truth in her sister's concerns. She was falling in love with Matt McCafferty and it was a monumental mistake. Mon-u-men-tal.

But, no matter how she tried to talk herself out of see-ing him again, she knew she wouldn't. It was all part of that moth-and-flame scenario where she was attracted to something that would ultimately burn her. "Fool, fool, fool," she admonished as she switched lanes, brake lights flashed in front of her, and someone honked loudly. She found the address of the Seattle PD, and after scouring the parking lot, squeezed the rental into a tight spot. Dashing through the rain, she headed into the building.

She spent the next five hours at the police station talking with a friendly, heavyset detective who had been handling information on Randi McCafferty. Oscar Trullinger told her that so far no one could see that the book Randi had been writing was connected to the attacks upon her in any way and that they had no new information. Of the men she'd been associated with, none seemed likely to hold a grudge against her. Sam Donahue was currently living in western Washington on a ranch outside of Spokane; Joe Paterno, the photojournalist, was on assignment in Alaska; and Brodie Clanton, whose great-grandfather had founded the *Clarion*, was out of the country, vacationing in a villa in Puerto Vallarta, Mexico.

How convenient that all of the men Randi McCafferty had dated weren't anywhere near Seattle. *Too convenient*, she thought as she drove to the offices of the *Seattle Clarion*. Located on the third floor of a brown brick building near Pioneer Square, the offices of the newspaper weren't much different from what she expected. Inside, the once-open rooms were broken up by modular units of soundproof walls where cluttered desks were occupied by a dozen or so reporters all typing on keyboards of computers, or talking on the phone, or scanning news reports on small television sets. Through the windows, views into other buildings and a few glimpses of the gray sky and green waters of Puget Sound were visible.

"Can I help you?" a sober receptionist with doelike eyes asked.

"I'd like to speak to Bill Withers," Kelly said, and flashed her badge. "Detective Kelly Dillinger. I'm from Grand Hope, Montana. I have some questions about Randi McCafferty."

The receptionist offered what might be considered a smile. "Mr. Withers isn't in right now."

Kelly wasn't surprised. "How about Joe Paterno or Sara Peeples?" she asked, though, again, she anticipated the answer.

"Joe's on assignment, won't be back until tomorrow. But Sara's in. I'll let her know you're here." Without waiting for a reply, she pushed a button and left the appropriate message.

Within two minutes a small woman with a long face, oversize features and tousled blond curls appeared. She wore a short fitted dress, boots, jacket and half a dozen bracelets that jangled as she walked.

"You're Detective Dillinger?" Sara asked. "I'm Sara, and I'm really glad you're here. How's Randi?"

"Holding her own."

"Come on back, my desk is a mess, but we can talk there." She led Kelly through a maze of desks and past a fax machine and copy center to a desk in the corner, near what appeared to be an adjacent office dedicated to photography. "I heard Randi's still in a coma. That someone might have tried to kill her."

"That's what we're looking into," Kelly admitted.

"Wow." Sara's smile twisted at the irony. "You know, the paper reports this kind of thing all the time, but it doesn't really touch you until it's someone you know. Someone who's your friend or relative."

"I know. I was hoping you could tell me a little about Randi. Who she hung out with, who she was dating, who were her friends and enemies."

"And who the father of her baby is," Sara said. "That's the million-dollar question, isn't it? And I don't know." She seemed earnest, her eyebrows knitting, her lips pursing as she thought. "You know, I don't know who would want to hurt Randi and I would hope it wouldn't be the father of her kid, but the world is made up of all kinds...."

For the next two hours Kelly talked to Sara and others in the office and left without much more information than she came in with. No one had any idea who would want to hurt her, who the father of her baby was, who she'd inadvertently ticked off. She had girlfriends from college, one in particular, Sharon Okano, whom she was close to, an aunt and female cousin on her mother's side who weren't related to any of Randi's brothers, and it was generally thought that she was writing a novel, a fictional story against a backdrop of the rodeo circuit. Aside from her regular column, she occasionally wrote a freelance piece.

It was dark by the time Kelly checked into a hotel overlooking Elliott Bay, where she made her way to her room and tossed her purse onto the table.

She stood at the window, stared at the gray water for a few seconds, then placed a call to Randi's friend, Sharon, who, according the recorded message, would call her back "as soon as possible." Kelly left her name and the number of her hotel along with the telephone number of the sheriff's department in Grand Hope, then called the department and left a voice-mail message for Espinoza. Those tasks completed, she decided to explore the city. Windows ablaze, skyscrapers knifed upward from the steep hills, traffic whizzed past, and pedestrians huddled in raincoats and, carrying umbrellas, hurried along the wet pavement.

Kelly made her way to the waterfront, where a stiff breeze blew across the white-capped sound and ferries chugged through the dark water. Though it wasn't quite Thanksgiving, there were already hints of Christmas in the store windows, and there was a buzz in the air, an electricity that seemed to charge the night.

She bought a cup of chowder from a small restaurant located on Pier 56 and hiked back to her hotel, feeling wound tight and wondering what Matt McCafferty was doing. She thought about the fact that she'd nearly made love to him and knew in her heart that given a second chance, she'd do it again. Jamming her fists into her pockets, she considered the consequences of that one fateful act.

What would be the harm?

She was an adult.

He was an adult.

But you're a cop and he's the brother of a victim, perhaps even a suspect. Not that she believed the local gossip. Her hair was wet by the time she reached the hotel, her cheeks chapped and her fingers icy. She walked through the rotating door and started for the elevator when she sensed, rather than saw, someone fall into step with her. A hint of musky after-shave, and just the wisp of the scent of leather and horses. "How did you find me?" she asked, her heart skipping a beat as she caught his reflection in the elevator doors.

"A little detective work."

She nearly laughed. "Oh, yeah, right."

The doors parted and she stepped into the waiting car. Matt was beside her and she looked up into his dark eyes. They sparked with humor and something decidedly more dangerous.

"You think you've got the market cornered on snooping?"

"I don't think of it as snooping."

He pressed a button for the top floor of the hotel and she reached forward to poke a different one, but he grabbed her hand. "I thought you might want to come up to my room for a while. Have a drink."

Her throat tightened. "Did you?" She shook her head. "I know that we got a little carried away the other night, but it's really not a good idea for us to…" She lifted her shoulders and one hand as the elevator rumbled ever upward. "Well, considering the circumstances, it just wouldn't be smart for us to get involved."

"We already are." He was standing next to her, not touching her, just seeming to fill the whole damned car. Kelly felt claustrophobic, as if she couldn't breathe.

"Okay, then, maybe not any *more* involved. Until this case is solved, I don't have any business losing my objectivity."

"Too late." He grabbed her then, and though she knew she should tell him to go jump in the proverbial lake, she didn't. Instead she tilted her chin upward and met his warm mouth with her chilled lips. His arms wrapped around her, and as the elevator car landed on the uppermost floor, he kissed her. Hard. Long. With enough passion to send tingles to the deepest part of her.

The battle was over and she knew it, didn't bother to protest or resist as he lifted her from her feet and, like a groom carrying a bride on his wedding night, carried her over the threshold of the penthouse suite.

She closed her eyes and lost herself in him. They were alone, and what would one little night together harm? Groaning, he worked at the zipper of her jacket, peeling the unwanted garment from her easily as he kissed her. First the jacket, then her sweater, her boots and jeans, all piled onto the plush carpet, and she didn't stop him, just kissed him as fervently as he kissed her.

She was vaguely aware of the dimmed lights, hissing fire and flowers scenting the room as she stripped him of his clothes, but those images were lost in the touch and feel of his work-roughened hands caressing her body, his lips and tongue touching and tasting her, the length of him pressed hard against her. Slowly he pressed her backward onto the satin comforter stretched across a king-size bed.

"How...how did you find me?" she asked again as they tumbled together.

"When I want something, I go after it." He caressed her chin with one long finger. "You told me you were leaving, I decided to follow."

"Seattle's a pretty big city."

His smile was wickedly delicious. "I'm a pretty determined guy."

"With connections."

"Lots of 'em." He kissed her shoulder and she shivered with want.

"And you use them."

"When I have to." He leaned toward her, kissing the top of her breast and lowering her bra strap, exposing more of her. Kelly swallowed hard as his hands sculpted her ribs, sliding behind her back, drawing her closer, and he finally took her nipple into his mouth.

She thought she would die.

He suckled and she arched her back.

"Kelly," he whispered across her abdomen, and lowered himself, brushing his mouth across her skin, touching her, tasting her, teasing her, dragging her panties down her legs and tossing them onto the floor. She writhed at his ministrations and she felt herself melting, wanting, aching for more of him. The corners of the room began to fog and she knew only the sensations he evoked from her.

Sweat dotted her body and her blood pounded through

her veins, pulsing in her eardrums, thundering through her brain. She heard a moan before she recognized her own voice. Heat spread from the back of her neck through her extremities and she moved against him, wanting so much more.

"Matt, please..." she whispered throatily, and he came to her, slid up against her and somehow kicked off his jeans. His lips found hers, muscular arms circled her body as he poised above her for a heart-stopping moment. In one thrust, he entered her and she gasped against his skin. He began to move and she caught his tempo, her blood on fire, her heart thudding. Her fingers scraped his back and he held her tight, breathing in counterpoint to her own ragged gasps, his rhythm increasing, his sinewy body straining with each rapid thrust.

She stared into eyes that looked down at her, deep brown, intense, searching her soul. Deep inside she convulsed, and behind her eyes a thousand colors splintered, a million lights danced, and she was certain the universe collided. He let go and with a roar as untamed as the wild Montana wind, he fell against her, wrapped his arms around her and buried his face in her neck. "Kelly," he whispered. "Oh...Kelly."

They lay spent, entwined until at last their breathing had calmed. She nestled against him, resting her cheek on his bare shoulder as he caressed her face and brushed the hair off her cheek.

A dozen recriminations assailed her, but she ignored them. Instead, she slid him a mischievous glance. "So...tell me, cowboy," she teased. "What do you do for an encore?"

He barked out a laugh. "You want to see?"

"Mmm." She ran fingers through the curling hairs of his chest. "If you've got it in you?"

"You're asking for it, lady."

"Again. I'm asking for it again," she clarified with a giggle.

Quick as a rattler striking, he surrounded her, pressed his mouth against hers, and as she gasped, said, "Then you're gonna get it."

"Wait a second—" But her protest was cut off by his kiss, and within a heartbeat her blood had heated again, her heart was pounding and she lost herself all over again, realizing as she did so that there was no doubt about it, she was hopelessly, helplessly in love with him.

Chapter Ten

"Randi's awake." Slade's voice echoed through the telephone wires and pounded through Matt's brain the next morning. Matt glanced to the side of the mussed bed where Kelly, her red hair splayed around her face, was stretching, yawning, those beautiful brown eyes blinking out of a deep sleep.

"When?"

"Just a little while ago."

"Has she said anything?" he asked, and Kelly was instantly alert, all traces of slumber disappearing. She'd reached over the side of the bed for her clothes.

"Not yet. I'm on my way to the hospital now."

"We'll catch the next flight out."

"We?" Slade repeated, and Matt winced.

His brother chuckled and the sound grated on Matt's nerves. "You can tell me all about it when you get back to Grand Hope, brother." Slade hung up and Matt reached for his clothes.

"Randi?" Kelly asked.

"She's awake."

She was suddenly all business. "What are we waiting for?"

"Maybe you'll tell me what's going on," Randi said as Matt and Kelly walked into her already-crowded hospital room. Slade, Thorne and Nicole surrounded the bed where Randi was ready to spit nails. "I want to see my baby."

Not only awake, Randi was ready to tear into any doctor or brother who made the mistake of keeping her from her child from limb to proverbial limb. In a private room, the top half of her bed elevated, she was glaring at the small gathering of people around her bed, and Matt felt as if a ton of bricks had been lifted from his shoulders.

Randi's brown eyes were clear, her face only slightly swollen, her short mahogany-colored hair sticking up at odd angles. Her jaw, which had previously been wired, was now working with some difficulty as the wires had been removed, and she winced as she lifted her right arm as if her broken ribs still bothered her. However, it was easy to read her expression: she was ticked. Big time.

"Is there any reason she can't see J.R.?" Matt asked, his gaze landing on Nicole.

"We're arranging it."

"Well, arrange it faster," Randi insisted as she read the name tag pinned to her lab coat. "Who are you?"

"Dr. Stevenson," Nicole answered as Randi's eyes narrowed on her.

"I can see that, but I already met two other doctors who claim to be taking care of me." She was speaking with some difficulty, only forcing out the words by sheer will. They sounded a little muffled, but the message was clear: Randi McCafferty was awake, angry and not about to be bullied. Good. That meant she was definitely getting better.

"I was the admitting doctor when you were brought in," Nicole explained, "and you were in pretty bad shape. Aside from being comatose, you had a concussion, punctured lung, broken ribs, a fractured jaw and a nearly shattered femur. Some of your bones have knit, you can talk, but it'll be a while before you can walk, I'm afraid, and then there was the complication that you've just had a C-section. And don't forget to factor in that someone slipped some insulin into your IV and you nearly died, so I think it would be best if you just took your time, listened to the doctors' orders and tried to get well before you start making too many demands."

"So are you the one in charge? My physician of record?"

"You have several. In fact, an entire team. I'm just interested because you were my patient and…and I'm involved with your family."

"Involved?" Randi repeated, her eyes narrowing. "What does that mean—'involved'?"

"Nicole's my fiancée," Thorne explained, stepping closer to the bed rails and linking his fingers through Nicole's. "And believe me, we'll bring the baby in as soon as the pediatrician and your doctors agree."

"Fiancée?" Randi whispered, then winced as if a sudden pain had slammed through her brain. "Wait a minute, Thorne. You? You're going to get *married?*"

"That's right. We've only been waiting for you to recover so that you could attend the wedding."

"Hold on a sec. This is a little too much for me to process. Just how long have I been out of it?"

"Over a month," Slade said.

"Holy Toledo!" She lifted her hand palm outward to stop the flow of conversation. "Now, wait a minute," she said, finally zeroing in on Thorne's cane and cast. "What happened to you?"

"An accident. I was lucky. My plane went down."

"What?"

"And you…" She turned her eyes in Slade's direction. "Were you hurt, too?"

Slade touched the fine line that ran from his eyebrow to chin. "Nope. Skiing accident. Don't you remember?"

She shook her head slowly.

"It happened last winter, not quite a year ago. You saw the scar at Dad's funeral."

Her eyes clouded. "There's a lot I don't remember," she admitted, then turned her attention to Matt. "Is the whole family falling apart? What about you? Seems like everyone named McCafferty is cursed, so what's happened to you?"

"Nothing," he said.

"No near-death experiences, no injuries, no engagement?"

"Not so far," he drawled, and saw Kelly's shoulders stiffen slightly.

"Good. As for you," Randi said to Thorne, "I'll catch up on your love life later. For now, what I want is to see my son, so you can either bring him to visit me, or I'm walking out of here."

"Hang in for a while, okay?" Slade requested, his voice surprisingly tender. "We named him, J.R., like junior or after dad. He's with Juanita at the ranch, and as soon as we can we'll get you two together."

"Just don't waste any time, okay?" Randi was adamant, but obviously starting to tire. "And we'll discuss the name thing. I don't think I want to stick with J.R. I mean, come *on*. After, Dad?" She swept a skeptical gaze over her brothers. "Whose brilliant idea was that?"

"Mine," Thorne said.

"Figures. You always were a Dudley Do Right. Even though you couldn't stand the guy."

Thorne started to argue but held his tongue, and Kelly stepped forward, closer to Randi's bed. "I'm Kelly Dillinger, with the sheriff's department," she said clearly as she offered an encouraging smile. Matt had a quick mental flash of another grin, one much more naughty, that she'd rained on him last night. His thoughts strayed for a second to their passionate night in Seattle, but he forced himself into the here and now. With Randi. "When the doctors agree," Kelly was saying, "I'd like to speak to you about the accident."

Randi's eyes clouded. "The accident…" she said, and shook her head.

"Up near Glacier Park. You were forced off the road, we think," Thorne added.

"You mean you think that someone purposely tried to kill me?"

"It's a possibility," Kelly said. "Or possibly it was a hit-and-run accident and the guilty party took off. But that seems unlikely, since someone walked into your hospital room and injected you with insulin. We're approaching this as an attempted homicide."

Randi's gaze traveled from one somber-faced half brother to the next. "Tell me she's exaggerating."

"'Fraid not," Matt replied, his blood cold at the thought of how close the would-be murderer had come to snuffing out Randi's life.

"Oh, God." The starch seeped from Randi's body and she leaned back on her pillow. "I...I can't remember...." Her eyebrows slammed together in concentration. "In fact...I don't remember much," she admitted. "I mean, I know all of you and realize I'm in a hospital and I know that I'm a writer, that I usually live in Seattle, but...so much else is blurry."

Thorne's shoulders stiffened. "How about the father of your child?" he asked, and the room was instantly so quiet that the noise from the hallway—the rattling gurneys, carts and the hum of conversation—seemed suddenly loud and intrusive. "Who's J.R.'s dad?"

Randi swallowed and turned suddenly pale. She glanced down at her hands, one strapped to an IV, the other bound by plaster and tape, her left hand bare, no wedding band surrounding her third finger. "The baby's father," she whispered, biting her lip. "I...I can't remember...I mean...oh, damn." She blinked rapidly, as if fighting a sudden wash of tears.

"That's enough," Nicole interjected. "She needs to rest."

"No!" Randi was adamant. "Are you a mother?" she asked her soon-to-be sister-in-law.

"Yes. I have twin girls."

"Then you understand. I want to see my baby. And as for you—" she swung her gaze to Kelly "—I'll answer anything I can, but right now I can't remember a thing. Maybe seeing my baby will jog my memory."

Matt knew a con when he saw one, and unless he missed his guess, his half sister was conning all of them, bargaining by trading on their emotions. Randi wanted to be reunited with her child, and she'd pull out all the stops, including lying about what she remembered, to attain her goal. Matt didn't blame her. The best medicine in the world for baby and mother was to get them together. "I'll take care of it," he said.

"Wait a minute." Nicole was suddenly in his face. Nicely, but with emphasis on each syllable, she added firmly, "Of course we'll bring J.R. here as soon as possible."

Matt glanced over Nicole's shoulder to the battered, determined woman lying on the bed. "I'll see to it," he said to Randi, and he meant it. To hell with hospital procedure and damn the police investigation. Right now, all that mattered was to get J.R. into Randi's eager arms.

"So that's about the size of it," Kelly reported to Espinoza later in the day. He, too, had visited St. James, only to be rebuffed by hospital personnel. He hadn't gotten so much as a word with Randi and now sat in his chair, one leg crossed over the other, fingers tented under his chin, as Kelly told him about her dealings with the Seattle PD, the people at the *Clarion* and later, her short conversation with Randi McCafferty.

"You think she's an amnesiac?"

"I don't know." Kelly was seated on the corner of a visitor's chair on the other side of his cluttered desk. She lifted a shoulder. "Randi obviously remembered her brothers, her job, where she worked, but the accident seemed to elude her. Any references to foul play stopped her short, but she was bound and determined to see her child. Until she and J.R. are reunited, I don't think we'll get much out of her, including the name of the baby's father."

"Odd," Espinoza commented, clicking his pen as he concentrated. He was beginning to grow a mustache again, his upper lip darker than it had been a few days earlier.

"Not really. I think the motherhood instinct is the strongest on the planet."

He sent her a look silently begging the question *How would you know?* but had the presence of mind not to ask it. They talked for a while longer and he asked her how she'd gotten the information on Randi, as he'd tried to call her hotel room and no one had answered. Kelly couldn't dodge that one, admitting that she'd heard the information from Matt McCafferty, whom she'd bumped into in Seattle. Espinoza's eyebrows had lifted, inviting further details, but Kelly hadn't offered any. She was still trying to sort out her own emotions on her involvement with Matt. She didn't want or need any fatherly or brotherly advice from anyone. Especially not her boss, who seemed edgy and out of sorts.

"Some people still think one or maybe all of the McCafferty men should be suspects."

"Why?" She couldn't keep the snap from her voice.

"Because the half sister inherited so much, for starters. She was obviously the old man's favorite. If she was out of the way, everything would be left to her child, and since there's no father stepping forward, Randi's brothers would probably be appointed guardians."

"I think I told you before that theory's way off base."

"Just reminding you."

"Fine. I'm reminded," she snapped, then caught the censure in his eyes. He'd been testing her and she'd risen to the bait like a stupid trout to a salmon fly.

Irritated at Espinoza, her job, herself and life in general, she left her boss's office without slamming the door, collected a cup of coffee, received the local gossip and phone messages from Stella, then holed up in her office where she typed reports, returned calls and generally caught up. She worked through lunch, then spent the afternoon following leads in the McCafferty case. Who was trying to kill Randi or terrorize the McCaffertys and why? Something Espinoza had said triggered her to search through her notes. Motive. That's what they needed. Who besides the brothers would benefit by Randi's death? Was there someone angling for her job? A boyfriend who'd been jilted? J.R.'s father, whoever he was? Someone with an old grudge against the family?

Like your own mother?

John Randall had made his share of enemies during his lifetime, but he was dead. Certainly no one would seek revenge against his progeny. But what about Randi? Had she offended someone in her columns, inadvertently triggered a homicidal response in someone who had written to her seeking advice? What about the book? Did someone know that she was writing about graft and corruption, and if so, who?

With more questions than answers, she finally gave up and stretched, her back popping as she shut off her computer and climbed out of her desk chair. The night crew had arrived and she waved to some of the officers she knew, then, zipping up her jacket and yanking on her gloves, made her way to her four-wheel drive.

The temperature was nearly ten degrees below freezing and she didn't want to think what the windchill added. Snow was beginning to fall again, dancing in front of her headlights and sticking to the windshield.

Adjusting the heater, she listened to the local news, only to be reminded by a newscaster that Randi McCafferty, the local woman who'd been in a coma for over a month, had woken up.

It was after seven by the time she reached her house, climbed up the stairs, peeled off her clothes and took a long shower. She'd just opened a can of soup when the phone rang. Her heart skipped a ridiculous beat at the thought that it might be Matt, and when she answered, she was disappointed to hear her sister's voice.

"About time you got home," Karla reprimanded.

Kelly stretched the phone cord so that she could stir her soup as it heated on the stove. "I do work for a living."

"So do I."

"It wasn't a dig."

"I know that," Karla said quickly.

"I'm just in a lousy mood."

"And I thought you'd be euphoric what with Randi McCafferty waking up."

"So you heard."

"Everyone's heard. I wondered what she had to say," Karla said.

"Not much." Kelly turned the burner down. "Come on, Karla, you know I can't discuss a case with you."

"Yeah, but I heard over at the Pub'n'Grub that Randi hasn't told anyone who the father of the baby is."

"You shouldn't listen to gossip."

"Oh, right. I work in a beauty parlor, Kelly."

"Then you should know everything already."

"Very funny. Besides, I heard a report on the television at noon. The anchors were hinting that there would be more information, even an interview with Randi on the evening news."

Kelly leaned a shoulder against the wall of her kitchen and looked out at the snow swirling around her window. "They'll have to break through a barricade of half brothers and hospital security to get to her, and then, believe me, she won't have a lot to say."

"What do you mean? Why not?"

"Look, I've said more than I should already." Then,

hoping to change the subject, Kelly asked, "How're my favorite nephews?"

"In trouble. *Big* trouble," Karla said, as if her boys were hovering nearby and could hear the conversation. "Aaron found some extra tubes of hair dye here at the house and Spencer took it upon himself to give the bunny a new hairdo. He tried to change the color of Honey's fur from tan to red—I think the official name of the color is Heavenly Henna or something like that, but let me tell you, it's more like Hellish Henna. You should see the poor thing—all those red blotches. This year we won't be dyeing Easter eggs, we'll color rabbits for Thanksgiving instead," Karla joked.

"But Honey's okay?"

"Yeah. Just as embarrassed as all get out. I think she might have to go to one of those animal psychiatrists, she's so traumatized. I'm afraid Honey Bunny will be in therapy for years to come." Kelly chuckled and Karla added, "I guess I should count myself lucky the boys didn't decide to give her a perm. Think how that would've turned out." She sighed. "It's really not funny. They could have gotten some of that stuff into her eyes. I took all my supplies down to the shop and I'll have some more closets built—better yet, safes with combination locks, but, enough about all this, tell me about your love life."

"What?" Kelly should have expected the question from her straight-shooting sister, but it still caught her off guard.

"You were in Seattle yesterday, right? And so was Matt McCafferty. I happened to overhear that bit of news at the coffee shop. I figured it wasn't just a coincidence."

"You're fishing again."

"And you're dodging the question."

"Since when is my love life any of your business?"

There was a pause, then all of the humor left Karla's voice as she said, "Since you fell in love with that son of a bitch, Matt McCafferty."

Thanksgiving was a nightmare. Though Kelly enjoyed being with her family, she felt distant, somewhat removed from the festivities. Her mother and father had each other, Karla had the boys, and though Kelly was a part of it, she also felt alone.

Because of Matt.

A part of her wanted to share the holiday with him and his family. She'd ordered an apple pie and pumpkin pie from the local bakery, and had spent the morning helping her mother stuff the turkey and prepare the sweet potatoes, but still there was something missing.

The family had prayed together, and her father had made a big show of carving the bird, but Kelly felt, for the very first time in her life, as if she belonged somewhere else, which was just plain stupid.

"Something's bothering you," her mother said as she loaded the dishwasher. Karla was wiping the table and couldn't help but overhear the conversation as her boys were in the den with their grandfather, making out their Christmas lists. One holiday was about over, so on to the next.

"I'm okay," Kelly argued as she angled a serving dish into the overloaded washer.

"Is it the case?" Eva Dillinger prodded.

Karla snorted. "Not exactly."

"What does that mean?" Her mother's smooth forehead furrowed with concern. "Kelly...?"

"It's nothing, Mom."

Karla snapped her dish towel, then folded it over the handle of the oven door. "Kelly's in love," she said.

"You are?" The worry lines disappeared and Eva Dillinger's mouth curved upward in anticipation. This was news she'd been hoping to hear for years.

Kelly shot her sister a warning look.

"Who's the lucky guy?" Eva persisted.

"Karla shouldn't have said anything. I'm not in love," Kelly lied.

"But you're seeing someone. Who?"

Kelly squared her shoulders. "It's nothing serious, okay, so don't freak out." She wanted to strangle her sister, and if looks could kill, Karla would be six feet under.

"I wouldn't..." But Eva's voice faded with her smile and she glanced to the doorway.

"What?" their father said, rolling into the room. "What are you talking about? Kelly's got a boyfriend?"

Inwardly groaning, Kelly lifted a hand. "Not a boyfriend. Not really. I've just been spending time with Matt McCafferty. Because of the case."

No one said a word. From the den the sound of the television could be heard. Other than that, nothing. Karla had the sense to wince, as if she finally understood the magnitude of her faux pas. "I shouldn't have said anything."

"No. No, it's good you did." Ronald's face had turned scarlet, while his wife had paled to the point that she had to lean a hip against the counter for support. "You know, Kelly girl, your mom and I, we only want the best for you and...and I can't imagine why you would take up with—"

"Hush, Ron. Don't. Kelly's old enough to make her own decisions," her mother reprimanded softly, and her support of her daughter along with the wounded look in her eyes cut Kelly to the bone. She wanted to apologize, and yet she knew she had no reason to offer up any kind of "I'm sorrys." Her father clamped his jaw and wheeled in silent agony back to the den.

"Happy Thanksgiving," Karla muttered under her breath, then added, "I'm sorry. I should have kept my big mouth closed."

Amen. But Kelly didn't say it out loud. Instead she said, "At least it's out in the open."

The rest of the evening was tense, conversation revolving around Aaron and Spencer, and Kelly couldn't wait to escape. She felt claustrophobic and restless and, for the first time in her life, undecided about her future. She'd grown up always knowing she wanted to be a cop, and she'd never let anything deter her. No man had derailed her from her objective. But then she'd never let any man as close as she'd let Matt. She drove home hardly aware of the city lights or the traffic. On autopilot, she pulled onto her street and hit the button of her remote garage door opener.

Somehow, she'd have to figure out what she was going to do with the rest of her life. Worse yet, she thought, as she steered into the garage, she'd have to figure out if Matt McCafferty would be a part of it. But how was that possible? His home, his *love* was his ranch. She couldn't, *wouldn't* ask him to give it up and her life was here. The situation was impossible.

She got out of her car and climbed the stairs to the main floor of her home, tossed her jacket and scarf over the back of her couch and saw the red light blinking on her answering machine. Kicking off her boots, she hit the play button and waited, then heard Matt's voice. Her heart skipped a beat.

"Hi, it's Matt. I thought maybe you'd like to join me and my family for Thanksgiving dinner." Her heart plummeted as she glanced at the clock. After nine. Too late. ''We're celebrating in about three days or so, I'm not quite sure yet, but whenever Randi's released from the hospital. It just didn't make sense to go through all the folderol twice. Anyway, I'll let you know when we pick a day…and…well, I'll be talkin' to ya.'' The machine clicked and automatically rewound.

Kelly played the message again.

So he was inviting her to a family get-together. ''Heavy stuff,'' she muttered under her breath, and caught her reflection in the mirror. She saw the glint of hope in her eyes, the flush on her cheeks that couldn't be entirely attributed to the cold weather she'd just endured.

''Oh, Dillinger,'' she said on a sigh. ''You've got it bad. Real bad.'' She'd have to steel her heart. No matter what happened, Matt would eventually leave. He was tied to his ranch hundreds of miles west of Grand Hope and this was her home. There was no future with him for her. Absolutely none.

Yet, what they'd shared was nice. Intimate. But it meant nothing in terms of commitment. He was a cowboy who lived a nearly solitary life in the wilds of western Montana; she was a cop, a dedicated officer of the law, whose ties were here in Grand Hope. Fleetingly she thought of her mother and father, Karla and the boys. They were her family.

She glanced at her left hand and her ringless third finger. Did she really harbor the ludicrous notion that she would some day marry Matt McCafferty?

Because they slept together?

She knew better.

Squaring her shoulders and tossing her hair off her face, she told herself it didn't matter. For the moment, if not the rest of her life, she'd enjoy the sensation of falling in love.

Even if it was one-sided.

After all, what was the worst that could happen?

Chapter Eleven

Matt forked hay into Diablo Rojo's stall and the two-year-old eyed him warily.

"Still don't trust me, do ya, boy?"

The Appaloosa snorted and pawed the straw.

"Then that makes two of us. I don't trust you as far as I can throw you."

Diablo lifted his head and shook it, jangling his halter and causing a nervous nicker from the bay in the box next door.

"Now look what you've done," Matt grumbled, but Diablo, ever the headstrong colt, didn't appear the least bit sheepish. Not much intimidated, that one. Maybe why Matt felt a connection with the beast.

He finished feeding the stock and walked outside. It was early morning, not yet light, the moon giving off a ghostly light that created shadows on the snow. Matt's breath fogged and his boots crunched as he followed the path he'd broken from the back porch. At the back door, he paused long enough to stomp the snow from his boots and walk inside, where a solitary light over the range was the only illumination. He'd gotten up early after a restless, sleepless night. When he had dozed, he'd dreamed of Kelly, and when he'd been awake, his brain had run in dizzying circles of memories of making love to her over and over again. In his mind's eye he'd seen her flawless white skin, her pink, puckered nipples, the teasing spark in her eyes and the way her red hair had spilled over her shoulders. Only pausing long enough to throw on clothes and plug in the electric coffeemaker, he'd trudged out to the barn and stables, intent on working out Kelly's image.

But it hadn't happened. With every lift of the pitchfork or ration of oats he'd poured into the mangers, he'd thought of her and the fact that he was, whether he would admit it to himself or not, falling in love with her.

He ground his back teeth at the realization and poured himself a cup of coffee from the carafe steaming in the coffeemaker. Kicking out a chair by the window, he drank his coffee and wondered what he'd do about her. He'd always planned to marry. Someday. When the time was right. He figured he'd find a local woman who was pretty, yes, and smart, but certainly not one so headstrong and career-minded. Never a cop. Never.

And not a woman who was tied so closely to Grand Hope. Her entire family lived here. She would never leave her home for a remote outpost in the western hills. And then there was the bad blood between the families.

Too much baggage.

Too much water under the bridge.

Too much…oh, hell.

He just couldn't get any more involved with her than he already was. He didn't want a long-distance love affair, nor, he guessed, did she. She was the wrong woman for him and that was all there was to it.

But even now, as he was trying to talk himself out of falling in love with her, his pulse jumped a notch and his groin tightened. Hell, he was horny as a schoolkid, always fighting his damned arousals. He hadn't felt this way in years. Or maybe ever. Not about one woman.

Nor had he ever in all of his thirty-seven years invited a woman to share the holidays with him. He'd considered it a time or two, but never had extended an invitation, always figuring the woman would see it as a sign of some kind of commitment or intent to commit. He'd also never accepted an invitation to be a part of some woman's family celebrations, either. Yet, even with the trouble between the McCaffertys and Dillingers, he'd be willing to take that step. And he'd make it right with Kelly's family. Somehow. Yep, this time it was different.

He took one final scalding swallow and forced his mind to other issues. Randi was coming home this morning, going to meet her son for the very first time. He'd have to concentrate on that reunion, of getting Randi into the house. Some of the staff at St. James weren't happy that she was being released, but she'd been adamant and chomping at the bit. Since Nicole was living on the ranch, all the release papers were being signed by the appropriate docs. The empty guest room on the main floor was being converted to Randi's bedroom, and a hospital bed was being transferred this morning before the guest of honor arrived.

Hopefully then, she'd be safe and get well. At least being close to the baby should help her peace of mind, maybe even jog her memory…if in fact she was telling the truth about her amnesia. Matt wasn't so sure. Randi had been John Randall's favorite child, the only one conceived with his second wife, Penelope, and the only girl to boot. Though she'd been raised in part as a tomboy, probably more because of the fact that she lived with three older half brothers than anything else, she'd also been pampered, the "princess," as John Randall had often referred to her. She'd grown up believing she could do anything she damned well wanted and that everyone in the world would treat her with the same regard and adoration as her father.

And she'd been proved wrong. Whatever had happened between her and little J.R.'s father couldn't have been good. Not good at all. That was the trouble with relationships—even with the right intentions, they usually went sour. His father had had two marriages and two divorces to prove Matt's point.

Headlights reflected against the side of the barn and shortly thereafter Juanita's station wagon slowed to a stop near the garage. Within minutes she hurried into the house. Blowing on her hands, she shivered, then unwound the scarf covering her head.

"You are up early," she said, and poured a cup of coffee.

"Big day."

Her smile was wide. "Señorita Randi will come home."

"That's the plan." He stretched from his chair. "I guess I'd better start moving some of the furniture out of the guest room to make room for some of the other stuff."

"And then, once she is home, we can have the wedding." Her dark eyes shone at the thought of the first McCafferty nuptials. *"Sí?"*

"Sí." Matt nodded. "You bet."

"And you, perhaps you will be next."

"To what? Get married?" He shook his head quickly,

by habit, as he always did when anyone brought up the subject of him getting married. "I don't think so."

Juanita didn't comment as she hung up her coat, but he didn't miss the smile that played upon her lips and the knowing glimmer in her eyes. In her mind, he was only one step away from the altar. Was it so obvious?

He thought of Kelly. God, he wanted her. Ached for her, but he couldn't imagine that she would ever want to be a rancher's wife, marry and settle down so far away...no, he concluded for the dozenth time, it just wouldn't work.

He heard the sound of a baby crying and made his way to the nursery where J.R. was starting to wind up, his little voice making coughing-hiccuping noises. "Hey, big fella," Matt said, picking up the baby and holding him to his shoulder. "What's wrong, hmm? Hungry, are ya?" While the baby stared up at him, Matt carefully placed him on the changing table and, with more dexterity than he ever thought possible, unsnapped the tiny pajamas, removed the wet diaper, cleaned the baby and fastened a clean diaper in place. J.R. kicked while Matt refastened the pajamas and carried him downstairs where Juanita was heating a bottle. She handed it to Matt and he carried the baby into the living room, plopped down in the old rocker and sat by the banked fire in the old stone grate. J.R., eyes bright, suckled hungrily as Matt stared down at this little wonder. "Mama's coming home today," he whispered, and the baby moved one tiny fist beside the bottle. "And then watch out. She's gonna take one look at you and melt." But that wasn't all, he decided, keeping his thoughts to himself. When Randi returned home, he was certain all hell would break loose. "You and I, we'll have to take care of her, won't we?"

He leaned back in the chair and rocked, wondering if

he'd ever do the same for his own infant. Thinking of Kelly, he imagined a baby—maybe a girl—with bright red hair and wide, curious brown eyes.

Surprisingly the thought wasn't frightening at all. If anything, it was downright seductive.

"Listen, I've told you and Roberto Espinoza everything I remember," Randi McCafferty insisted. Her hospital bed was propped up and she was no longer attached to an IV. Wearing a jogging suit, peach lipstick and a don't-mess-with-me attitude, she skewered Kelly in her stare. "I'm going home and meeting my son for the first time, tomorrow my family's celebrating a belated Thanksgiving, and right now I'd like to forget all this for a little while, okay? I know you're just trying to do your job, but give me a break."

"Detective Espinoza and I are just trying to help," Kelly said, unswayed. "Trying to protect you and your baby."

"I know it. Really. But please, don't give me any lectures about taking care of myself or my baby or my safety, okay? Believe me, I've heard all the reasons I should stay in the hospital, comply with the police and live my life a virtual prisoner until whoever it is that's taking potshots at me is caught, a million times over from my brothers. But that's not going to happen." She stopped suddenly, sighed and jabbed stiff fingers through her short locks. "Look, I don't mean to come off ungrateful, or like some kind of bitch. I do appreciate what you're trying to do." She let her hands drop into her lap. "It's just that I want to see my son. I'm going crazy sitting here. I haven't had the chance to be a mother yet and he's over a month old. I think the most important thing for me to do is bond with my baby." The honesty in her dark eyes got to Kelly.

"Would it be too much of a hassle for you to drop by the ranch in a few hours, after I've settled in and he and I have...well, you know, started to get used to each other?"

Kelly wasn't immune to what Randi was feeling. Espinoza wouldn't like it, but Kelly wasn't feeling particularly interested in keeping on his good side. She was still stung by his insinuations about her love life the other day.

Not a love life, she reminded herself. *Don't kid yourself. You had a good time the other night, but it was sex, nothing more. At least to Matt.*

She'd just finished the thought when he strode through the door, larger than life, bringing with him the scents of leather, musk and memories that she should best forget. His dark eyes found hers, and for a second she felt the same heat, the intensity that she had before. Her stomach tightened and she swept her gaze in Randi's direction again. "I understand. I'll drop by later. After dinner."

"Thanks," Randi said. "I'm sure my brothers will take care of me until then."

"We'll try," Matt drawled, then offered Kelly a smile that silently reminded her of the passion they'd shared. Ridiculously, she felt her cheeks stain. She was a cop, for crying out loud, she couldn't let some macho cowboy make her act like a silly schoolgirl. "How're you doin'?"

"I'm fine. I just want to get the heck out of here...oh, you weren't talking to me," Randi said.

"I was talking to both of you."

"I'm fine," Kelly replied. "I'll be in the hall, and I'll see that she gets to the car without any problems with the press."

"We can handle it. Slade's making sure all the discharge papers are ready and we've parked near a rear entrance."

"All right." She gave Randi a professional smile. "I'll be over about seven tonight, will that be okay?"

"Yes. And thanks."

Kelly walked out of the room stiffly. Why did she feel so awkward around Matt? So she'd spent a night with him. So they'd made love. So what? This was the twenty-first century, for heaven's sake. She was thirty-two years old, had graduated from college years ago and was a detective. She had every right to do whatever she wanted, sexually or otherwise, and yet she'd never been promiscuous, hadn't believed in sex for sex's sake, hadn't let herself have "flings" without any emotional attachment. In fact, other than a boyfriend in high school, another in college and one man since, she'd never been emotionally involved. While her sister had fallen in love a dozen times and been married twice, Kelly had been cautious and had lived her life by using her head instead of listening to her heart.

Until now.

Until Matt, damn him, McCafferty.

He caught up with her before she could leave. "I just wanted to double-check. We're planning a belated Thanksgiving celebration tomorrow and you're invited. Six o'clock."

"I don't get off until five, but, yes, I'd love to come."

"Good. And then…" He shifted his weight from one foot to the other. "Saturday night's the wedding. Thorne and Nicole are going to tie the knot. I thought you might want to be my date."

"You did, did you?" she teased.

"Unless you have other plans."

She laughed. What was it about this man? One minute she was tongue-tied and felt awkward around him, the next she was flirting as she'd never done in her life. "I'll cancel them," she joked, and started to walk off, before he caught her by the arm, spun her around and kissed her until she couldn't breathe.

"Do that," he whispered, and turned on his heel to disappear into Randi's room. Kelly cleared her throat, saw two nurses look quickly away, pretending they hadn't seen the open display, then caught sight of Dr. Nicole Stevenson striding down the hallway.

"Arrogant S.O.B., isn't he?" Nicole said as Kelly tried to regain some of her professional integrity.

"The worst."

"Like his brothers," Nicole said, and then managed a smile. "I know that I've come on a little strong sometimes, especially when it comes to my patients. I hope you understand it's nothing personal."

"I do."

"And I hope you'll come to the wedding. I know it's short notice, but Thorne and I wanted to wait until Randi could attend. It's this Saturday night."

"I'll be there," Kelly promised, and refused to second-guess herself.

She returned to the office and holed up, closing the door and the blinds so that she could plow her way through some paperwork on various cases, but as usual ended up flipping through Randi McCafferty's file. The same old names leaped out at her—friends and family, college roommates, peers and associates, but none leaped off the page as potential enemies. Aside from her half brothers she had an aunt, Bonnie Lancer, on her mother's side, and one cousin, Nora, who was Bonnie's daughter. Her friends were a small group who stayed in touch primarily through e-mail and an occasional phone call. Kelly had talked to everyone who had called or e-mailed Randi in the three months prior to her accident and had come up dry. The maroon Ford product that was thought to have been used to force her car off the road had so far proved to be a bust, and she couldn't figure out how Randi's book could possibly come into play. What had she written that would make someone angry enough to try to kill her.

She was about ready to call it a day when Stella buzzed. "Detective Dillinger...Kelly, there's someone here to...oh, no, don't you do it again—" She had a visitor just as the door to her office burst open and Matt strode in.

"You really have to stop doing this," Kelly admonished, ignoring her elevating pulse as Stella, once again sheepish, filled the doorway and lifted her palms. "It's all right," Kelly said to the receptionist before the poor girl had a chance to apologize, and Stella hurried back to her desk.

"This is the sheriff's department, you can't just keep barging in here," she said, centering her gaze on the cowboy who in his sheepskin jacket, snow-dusted Stetson and faded jeans seemed to fill up the entire office. "I mean, you're giving poor Stella fits."

"We need to talk."

Her throat constricted. "I assume this is business."

His nostrils flared a little. "Partly."

"I'm at work," she reminded him as she leaned back in her chair, and waved him into a seat on the other side of her desk. "It's got to be all business. A hundred percent."

"Does it?" he challenged, and she saw the glint of a dare in his dark eyes. Her heart nearly stopped and she knew in an instant that he was remembering the night they'd been together. Her throat went dry at the memory of his hot skin, fevered touch, deep groans.

"Yes, well, I think that would be best." She cleared

her throat, tossed an errant lock of hair over her shoulder and flipped open Randi's file. "What can I do for you?"

The man had the audacity to smile. Slowly. One side of his mouth lifting into a crooked and decidedly wicked smile. "Now, that's a loaded question."

"I assume you have a reason, and it had better be a good one, for barging in here, bullying Stella and taking up my time," she said.

Leaning against the file cabinet, he said, "I heard you say that you were coming out to the house."

"Later. Around seven."

"How about now?"

"Why?"

"It's Randi. She's not cooperating."

"Meaning?" Kelly prodded.

"She doesn't seem to be taking the attacks on her seriously. She's refused to have a bodyguard and has been snapping everyone's head off. She claims we're all paranoid and that everything's just hunky-dory."

"Even though someone forced her off the road and then slipped insulin into her IV?"

"Yep."

"Why?"

"I don't know, probably just that damned McCafferty stubborn streak, but I thought maybe you could talk some sense into her. She seemed to listen to you at the hospital."

"Not much, she didn't."

"She's always been headstrong, but I thought a woman might be able to get through to her. Nicole's at the hospital, Jenny's watching the twins, but she's too young, really a kid herself, so…how about it?"

"Give me ten minutes. I'll follow you."

"Fine." He started for the door, and not knowing what

got into her, she caught the crook of his elbow, spun him around and, standing on her tiptoes, kissed him hard on the lips. He gasped and she took advantage, slipping her tongue between his teeth for just the briefest of seconds. His arms tightened around her.

"You're asking for trouble," he warned as he kissed her.

She pulled back and skewered him with a vampish look. "And who's gonna give it to me?"

"Just watch."

"Slow down. I was only giving you a little of your own back," she said. To her surprise, he laughed, a deep warm sound that rippled through the offices.

"Don't lose that thought." With a tip of his hat and a low, mocking bow, he exited. "I'll see you at the ranch."

That you will, cowboy, she thought, and reached for the phone and flipped through her notes until she found Kurt Striker's number. She needed to get in touch with the P.I., just in case he'd come across any new information. She dialed his motel, waited and left a message when he didn't answer.

She'd get back to him later, she decided, hanging up and reaching for her jacket and gloves. As she left her office she ran into Roberto Espinoza striding through the front doors of the building. The scent of cigarette smoke clung to him and snow covered the shoulders of his down jacket. "Don't tell me, you're on your way to the Flying M, right?" His lips were compressed, his eyes dark, and his gaze landed like a ton of bricks on Kelly.

"Randi McCafferty was released from the hospital today and now she's not cooperating with her doctors, her brothers or anyone."

"And lover-boy thought you could talk some sense into her, right?"

Kelly bristled. "I need to question her again."

Espinoza looked about to spit nails. His dark eyes flashed and he sighed loudly. "As long as it's business."

"And what if it isn't?" she said. Who the hell did Espinoza think he was? "I am a professional, Bob."

"I know, it's just that…" Whatever it was he was thinking, he let the idea drift away. Frowning, he took off his hat, hung it on an ancient hook and raked stiff fingers through his hair. "It's your funeral, I guess."

"I'll remember that." Fuming, she held on to her temper. Blowing up now would only make things worse. For the moment, she had to maintain her composure, meet with Randi McCafferty and try to figure out how much the woman honestly didn't remember, because Kelly had a gut feeling that Randi knew a lot more than she was saying.

It was Kelly's job to find out just what it was and she was damned well going to do it.

Chapter Twelve

"I told you, I don't remember," Randi insisted, but Kelly wasn't buying it. Propped up in a hospital bed in the guest room of the ranch, her baby cradled in her arms, Randi McCafferty was lying through her teeth. And she wasn't particularly good at it. Then again, Randi wasn't interested in anything but her son. Cradling and cooing to her baby, Randi couldn't have cared less who had tried to kill her. She probably wouldn't have paid any attention if the world stopped spinning.

As Kelly stood near the bed, Matt filled the doorway, leaning a broad shoulder against the frame. He sent Kelly an I-told-you-so look as Harold sauntered in and circled a few times before lying on the rug at the foot of the bed.

"You asked me to stop by and promised you'd answer some questions," Kelly reminded Randi.

"I will, when J.R., and that's *not* his name, goes to bed. And don't look at me like I'm insane, okay? Lots of people go home without naming their babies first.'' At her brother's skeptic lift of an eyebrow, she amended, ''Well, okay, not *lots,* but some. And I want the right name for my son. So don't give me any grief. Go ahead and call him J.R. if you want, but as soon as I come up with the perfect name, we're changing it.''

''It might be too late,'' Matt drawled.

''Never. I've dealt with this in some of my columns,'' she said, then added, ''the value of a name and all that.''

''Didn't you have one picked out?''

''Yeah. Sarah. Somehow it doesn't seem to fit. Oh.'' Randi grinned as Juanita brushed past Matt and hurried through the door carrying a warmed bottle of formula. ''*Gracias,* Juanita. You're a doll.''

The housekeeper flushed as Randi accepted the bottle, adjusted the baby in her arms and offered him something to eat. With wide eyes, little J.R., or whatever she was going to name him, stared up at her. He suckled hungrily, but stopped every so often to observe the woman beaming down at him.

''Isn't he beautiful?'' Randi whispered, awestruck at her infant, and Kelly, feeling just the trace of envy, silently agreed.

One side of Matt's mouth lifted. ''And smart as the devil and no doubt athletic as all get out. I figure Harvard will be cablin' any day now.''

Randi giggled. ''I wouldn't be surprised. How about you, pumpkin?'' she asked her baby as Juanita, too, smiled down at mother and child.

''Oh, no, you can't call him that. 'Sport' or 'big fella' or something else, they're okay, but not 'pumpkin' or 'precious' or any of those cutesy-sissy names, okay?'' Matt insisted.

"You hush," Juanita snorted. "He is an angel. *Perfection.*"

"And the least you two will give him is a big head," Matt grumbled. "Look what happened to Slade."

"I heard that," the youngest McCafferty brother grumbled as he paused at the door by his brother.

Kelly realized she wouldn't get any more information until she was with Randi alone. "I'll talk to you later, once he's—" she hitched her chin in the baby's direction "—asleep."

"Thanks." Randi was more than appreciative.

"And I...I had better look in on the pies for tomorrow," Juanita said, bustling off toward the kitchen.

Kelly stepped out of the room.

"See what I mean? She's not taking anything seriously," Matt growled, walking into the foyer with her.

"She just wants to take care of her child."

"And bury her head in the sand. If we don't find out who tried to kill her and he strikes again, she won't be worrying about anything, baby or no." He rubbed the back of his neck in agitation.

"You don't feel she's safe here?"

"No, actually, it's better than the hospital. Not so many people coming and going. No strangers. No reporters."

"So far," Kelly said, "but that might not last."

"Damn. The problem is that Randi doesn't realize that the most important thing right now...the *only* thing, is finding out who's got it in for her. *Nothing* else can be a priority."

"Not even a baby?"

Matt's jaw turned to granite. His lips thinned. "This is all about the baby and keeping him safe. What do you think would happen if Randi lost him?"

"Let's not even consider that," Kelly said, her heart stopping at the thought.

"No matter what it takes, we have to find whoever's behind this." Frantic footsteps pounded overhead and echoed on the stairs. Over the thunder, the phone jangled somewhere in another room as the twins appeared.

Nicole, carrying two small pairs of jeans, was trying to shepherd her two rambunctious daughters, who, once they reached the bottom step, flew by in a blur of dark curls, rosy cheeks and mischief sparkling in two sets of bright eyes. Neither was wearing anything but a sweatshirt and panties.

"Never a dull minute around here," Nicole said, shoving her hair from her eyes as her daughters tore down the hall. "All I want them to do is try on their dresses for the wedding and you'd have thought I'd asked to handcuff and shackle them."

Matt's grin spread wide. "Maybe you should let their stepfather handle that."

"Now, that's a great idea!" Nicole said as Thorne, appearing in the hallway from the doorway to the den, called, "It's Kavanaugh on the phone for you, Matt."

"Excuse me," Matt said, and hurried off toward the den.

"I'll be right back, after I corral the girls." Nicole added, "Why don't you meet me in the kitchen and we can get to know each other?"

"In a minute," Kelly promised, thinking she might try to speak with Randi one more time. Matt was right. Finding out who was trying to kill his half sister was her top priority. It was also her job, something she was losing sight of a bit. Because of her feelings for Matt.

All her life she'd wanted to follow her father's footsteps

and become a cop. She'd been focused. Determined. Hadn't even let any relationships deter her. Until now.

God, she was hopeless.

Loving Matthew McCafferty had changed everything.

She lingered at the doorway, hoping Slade would say his goodbyes and exit. From the kitchen she heard the twins talking and giggling as the scents of cinnamon and nutmeg mingled with the fragrances of baked apples and pumpkin. She couldn't hear what Matt was saying, but every once in a while heard the low rumble of his voice. It had been so easy, *too* easy to fall in love with him.

She stared at the pictures mounted on the wall—the McCafferty photo gallery—and stopped at the one of Matt astride the bucking bronco. He was much younger then, of course, a wild cowboy, as untamed as the animal he was astride. A hell-raiser. And a heartbreaker. Anita Espinoza was just one of many women who'd hoped they'd be the one to capture his wayward heart.

Just like you.

As the noise from the kitchen muted, Kelly couldn't help but overhear the conversation between Randi and Slade through the open doorway of her bedroom.

"I mean, what's going on?" Randi was asking. "I was out of it for little more than a month and I wake up not only with this precious little guy, but to find out that Thorne, *Thorne of all people,* is head over heels in love and planning to get married! Who would have thought? He was as confirmed a bachelor as anyone I've ever seen. And then there's Matt—what in the world's going on with him? I was under the distinct impression that the ranch he fought so hard to buy was the most important thing in his world, that nothing and no one could hold a candle to it, at least not in his estimation. He practically sold his soul to Satan to buy the damned thing. Now all that's changed.''

"He's just worried about you," Slade said, and Randi laughed.

"My eye! I see the way he is around that detective—the one who was in here earlier.''

"Kelly," Slade supplied, and Kelly stiffened.

"Yes, Kelly. Matt's a different man around her. In fact, you'd think she was the only woman on the planet from the way he looks at her.''

Kelly smiled and silently reprimanded herself for eavesdropping. Yet, she couldn't help herself.

"It might not be as serious as you think.''

"What, because of that woman…Nell, in the town where he lives?''

"That's been over for months.''

Kelly froze. Matt had never mentioned another woman. No one had. *But you knew he'd had lots of affairs, didn't you? He's a virile man. Why wouldn't there be a woman back home? Damn it, why wouldn't there be half a dozen, considering that you're thinking about Matt McCafferty?*

"I have eyes, Slade. The guy's in love, whether he knows it or not.''

"Or it's an act. You know how he is with women. One comes along and he's in love, head over heels for a few weeks until…until…''

There was a long pause. Kelly felt her chest constrict.

"Until she becomes just another notch in his belt.''

"I wasn't going to say it that way.''

Kelly's heart plummeted.

"Okay, so let's say a scratch on the bedpost, a conquest, a quick roll in the hay, any way you say it, it comes out the same, doesn't it? All part of the old, sick double standard.'' Randi's voice inched up an octave and fairly shook with outrage at her brother's actions. Meanwhile, Kelly wanted to die.

"Hey, wait a minute, what's got you so riled?" Slade demanded.

"I just don't like the whole idea."

Amen, Kelly thought.

"It's degrading. Demeaning to women. In my job I see it every day. Women write me in reams about men who use them, pretend to be interested, make the woman think he's falling in love, then up and turn tail and run the other direction the minute she starts to get serious. It's age-old, Slade, and it's common."

"I'm just filling you in, but I thought you didn't remember much about your job. About your life. You know, I'm starting to think that's a crock, little sis. Don't tell me, let me guess, someone did a number on you. Right? Like maybe the baby's father?"

There was a tense, thick moment and Kelly wished she could witness Randi's expression. Despite her own embarrassment, Kelly still needed to know about the father of Randi's child. "We were talking about Matt and his women...I was hoping he was over all that love-'em-and-leave-'em adolescent garbage."

"It was Striker's idea," Slade explained. "He thought one of us should stay in tight with the police, keep an eye on the investigation."

"Why? Because you don't trust the police?" she asked, just as the baby started to cry.

"We just want to know what's going on. Sometimes the cops can be pretty closemouthed."

"So Striker *suggested* that Matt fall in love with...no, wait a minute, that Matt get the policewoman into bed... Oh, God, Slade, tell me that's not what it was all about. Tell me that Matt isn't using that detective, because she's pretty damned clever and she won't fall for any of that, besides which, it's just…just disgusting.''

Kelly wanted to drop through the smooth patina of the old plank floorboards.

''He was hoping there might be a little pillow talk,'' Slade said over the baby's wail.

Sick inside, Kelly felt her knees start to go weak. *Don't do this, Dillinger. Chin up. Spine stiff. Shoulders square. You're a professional. A detective.*

''Then he's an idiot, because that woman impresses me as way too sharp to fall for that. In fact, she's probably too good for him!'' Randi added, obviously furious. ''And whether he knows it or not, he's falling in love. I'd like to throttle him and you and Striker and whoever else is involved.''

You and me both. Heat flooded up Kelly's cheeks and she was mortified. What a fool she'd been.

The baby was still crying, and Randi must've turned her attention to her child, because she said, ''Now, now…shh.'' Kelly had heard more than enough. On silent footsteps she moved into the living room and pretended interest in some farming magazine as Slade strode out of the bedroom. From the corner of her eye she caught him send her a dark glance, then take off toward the kitchen just as Matt emerged from the den into the hallway.

Her heart wrenched and she silently called herself the worst kind of fool imaginable.

''Sorry about that,'' he said, and there wasn't a glimmer of a smile in his voice. ''The guy who's supposed to be taking care of my spread called from his place. He slipped, fell and broke his leg, so it looks like I'm going to be taking the next plane home.''

She forced a smile she didn't feel. ''I understand.'' *More than you know, McCafferty. A helluva lot more.*

"I won't be around here tomorrow for the belated Thanksgiving festivities."

And your invitation is withdrawn. He didn't say it, but it was there hanging in the air between them.

She grabbed her jacket from the hooks near the door. Shoved her arms through the sleeves. Reached into a pocket for her gloves. "Don't worry about it. I already celebrated," she said, inwardly cringing when she heard the drip of ice in her voice. *Get over it, Dillinger. It wasn't that big of a deal.* She pulled on her gloves. "I'd better shove off. Randi's not interested in talking to anyone in the sheriff's department right now. I'll be back."

She started for the door, and when he tried to reach for her elbow, she yanked her arm away from his outstretched fingers; she'd fallen for that trick one too many times as it was. Then she remembered how she'd turned the tables on him, spun him around by his arm just a few hours earlier and kissed him hard. Oh, what an idiot she'd been.

"Kelly?"

"I'm wise to you, McCafferty." She reached for the door, not bothering to explain. Let him think that she was talking about his little trick of whirling her into his arms. It didn't matter that she meant something much more serious.

With a hard yank she opened the door and walked into a biting wind that snatched the breath from her lungs and rattled the panes of the windows. But she didn't care. The sting of the icy blast felt good against her hot cheeks, shook her out of her dark reverie, reminded her that she wasn't dead, though she was beginning to feel hollow inside.

"I'll walk you." He was beside her, not bothering with his jacket and matching her short, furious strides with his longer ones.

"Don't bother."

"It's no bother."

"I'm a cop, McCafferty. I can make it to my rig alone."

"Wait a minute."

She didn't; she just kept walking, plowing through the crunchy blanket of white, barely noticed that small, icy crystals were falling from the dark sky again.

"Kelly, what the hell happened?" he demanded when she threw open the door of her SUV.

"I woke up," she said as she climbed behind the steering wheel. "Look, Matt, I've got to go. I'll be back to talk to Randi and I'll keep you posted on everything that's happening with the investigation, but I've done some thinking and I really don't think it's a good idea for either of us to become too involved right now."

"Wait a damned minute—"

"Look, Seattle was nice, but I think I'd better keep my perspective." *And my distance.* She ignored the questions in his dark eyes, the play of night shadows across his strong features, the pain ripping through her heart. "I'd hate to do anything to compromise my professionalism."

"I thought we'd talked this through already."

"And I rethought it. The thing is that you and I have different interests. We're at different places in our lives."

"This sounds like a canned speech."

"It's not. I've got my job. You've got your ranch."

"So?"

"That's all there is to say. I'm going to wrap up this investigation or die trying, and you're going back to the Idaho border." She twisted the keys in the ignition. "Goodbye, Matt." Her heart wrenched at the words and she saw the mixed emotions crossing his features. Disbelief, distrust and a seething anger evident in the throb of a vein at his temple.

Tough.

He'd get over it, she decided as she jammed the SUV into gear and cranked on the steering wheel.

He always did.

What in the hell just happened? Matt threw a couple of pair of jeans, two shirts and his shaving gear into his duffel bag and couldn't make heads nor tails of Kelly's change in attitude. One minute she'd been flirting with him and he'd been coming close to being envious of Thorne and Nicole, because they, not he and Kelly, were getting hitched; the next minute, after he'd taken the call from Kavanaugh, she'd been as cool as the proverbial cucumber, telling him in so many words that their love affair—so hot and torrid only days before—was over.

He wasn't buying it.

No woman would respond the way she did, then turn away. Not without a reason, and a damned good one.

He yanked the zipper closed and slung the strap of his bag over his shoulder. With one last glance around the room he'd reclaimed, he ignored the feeling that he was leaving more than a scarred old double bed and a collection of ancient, dusty rodeo trophies.

Nope, there was more here. Not only his brothers and half sister, but the twins, the baby and Kelly. God, why did it hurt to think that he wouldn't see her for a few days, and worse yet he might never get to kiss her again, touch her, make love to her?

Get over it, she's just a woman, he tried to tell himself, but the pep talk didn't work. Because that was the crux of the problem. She wasn't just a woman.

Hell.

He didn't have time to second-guess himself. He had to go back to his spread tonight. He'd put it off too long already, and Striker was camping out here at the ranch. Along with Thorne, Slade and their father's arsenal supplied by Remington and Winchester, Randi and the baby should be safe.

And Matt was coming back. Soon. Because of his family. Because of the unanswered questions surrounding the attempts on Randi's life, but most important, because of Kelly.

"What do you mean you're not going to the wedding?" Karla asked, checking her watch and shoving the remainder of the pizza she and Kelly shared across the table toward her sister. They were seated in Montana Joe's, not far from the glassy-eyed bison head, while the noon lunch crowd swarmed the counter, stomping snow from their boots and unwrapping their scarves to expose red noses as they tugged off gloves and ordered from plastic-covered menus. An old Madonna song played over the buzz of conversation and the shout from a loudspeaker for an order to go.

"I thought you were all hot to trot to do anything you could with the McCafferty clan."

"You make it sound like I'm a traitor."

"Are you?" Karla lifted an eyebrow, then reached across the table and pulled a piece of ham off the leftover pizza.

"I don't think so. But I did think that mixing business and pleasure wasn't such a hot idea."

Sighing, Karla plopped back on the cushions of the booth. "That's depressing!" She tossed her napkin on the remaining slices of the Hawaiian Paradise they couldn't quite finish.

"I didn't think you approved."

"I didn't. Don't. But…oh, damn, I was beginning to believe that there was such a thing as true love again, you know? I mean…it was kind of like one of those star-crossed-lovers things with the feuding families. Kind of a Romeo and Juliet scenario."

"In your rose-colored dreams."

"I thought maybe I'd just been unlucky and that there was still a chance. You know, that if you found love, maybe I would, too, and that the third time would be the charm."

"Sorry to dash your hopes," Kelly said, then sighed as she checked her watch. "You know, Karla, you're a hopeless romantic."

"I know it's my one serious character flaw."

"You've only got one."

"Absolutely."

"More bad news. It's ten till one."

"Oh, damn. I gotta run. I've got a wash and set for one of my regulars." Karla scrambled out of her side of the booth and threw on a wool poncho and floppy-brimmed suede hat.

"You look like a bad guy out of one of those old, old Clint Eastwood movies."

"Make my day."

"Older," Kelly said, "one of those spaghetti westerns."

"Guess I missed it on the late-late show," Karla said as she adjusted the string. "But seriously, Kelly, you might want to rethink this Matt McCafferty thing. Mom and Dad will get used to the idea. No one's had a heart attack or a stroke over it. Well, not yet, anyway."

"What's with the turnaround?" Kelly asked, standing

and reaching for the jacket she'd slung over the back of the booth.

"It's simple. I just want you to be happy, and these past few weeks you've been a whole lot more light-hearted. It's nice to see you smile."

"I do."

"Not all the time. The job gets to you whether you want to admit it or not. And you're alone. That's not good. Your work is your life, I know. You practically work twenty-four-seven and that's also not good. It's bringing you down, Kell. You look half dead as it is."

"Thanks a lot."

"I'm not kidding. You can't be a policewoman day in and day out."

Kelly wanted to protest but didn't. For once, Karla was making a lot of sense. And she had been working long hours. Ever since leaving Matt at the Flying M the other night, she'd thrown herself body and soul into the case, digging up information on friends and family of the McCaffertys', searching out anything she could about Randi's job and her work acquaintances. Someone wanted her dead. Kelly was determined to find out who it was. And soon. She'd had less than five hours' sleep in two nights, but she was getting closer to the truth, she could feel it.

"It's a hard job and you're good at it, but it's bleeding you dry," Karla was saying. "I've seen it. You need some fun in your life. We all do. I don't think it's a coincidence that you lightened up about the same time that Matt McCafferty rode bareback into your life!"

"So now you know what's best for me."

"I always have." Karla flashed her a smile as they walked through the heavy doors to the outside. "I just wish I could figure out what's best for *me*."

With a wave, she jaywalked back to her shop and Kelly, surprised at her sister's turnaround, unlocked her four-wheel drive and drove out of town. She had avoided the Flying M on the day the McCaffertys had designated for Thanksgiving, but she wasn't giving up on talking to Randi. She still had a job to do, and it would be considerably less difficult with Matt out of the picture. If she was lucky, she could avoid him all together.

At that thought her throat tightened and the heaviness in her heart, the ache she'd tried to ignore, throbbed painfully. "You'll get over it," she told herself as she took a corner a little too fast and felt her rig shimmy before the tires took hold. "You've got no choice."

With her own words ringing in her ears, she drove to the Flying M and made her way into the now-familiar ranch house. Jenny Riley, a slim girl with a nose ring and tie-dyed tunic over a long skirt, let her inside. "Randi's in the living room, and Kurt Striker is talking with Thorne in the den," she explained when Kelly stated her business.

Great. The P.I. who didn't trust the police and who had egged Matt on to get some "pillow talk." Kelly would like nothing better than to strangle that lowlife. He might be a hell of an investigator, but he was the one who'd suggested Matt get close to her to glean information about his sister's case.

"Do you want me to tell them you're here?"

"No. I'd rather speak to Randi alone."

"Then could I get you something? Coffee, tea or cocoa? I'm on my way to take the girls to their ballet lesson, but I have time to bring you a cup, and Juanita will skin me alive if I don't offer you something."

"I'm fine. Really. Just ate," Kelly said, and as a shriek from one of the twins soared to the rafters of the kitchen,

Jenny took off down the hall while Kelly, hauling her briefcase with her, walked into the living room.

Randi was half lying on the couch, a small cradle near her side where the baby was sleeping quietly. Kelly couldn't help but smile at the crown of reddish hair peeking from beneath an embroidered quilt. "He's adorable," she said, wishing she had a child of her own.

"Isn't he?" Randi waved Kelly into a chair near her, one that faced the fireplace where embers glowed red and flames crackled and hissed. "Sit," she ordered and, as Kelly dropped into the chair with its back to the foyer, asked, "Would you like something?"

"Just answers, Randi." Kelly sat on the edge of one of the rockers and leaned forward, her gaze locking with the new mother's. "I know you want to keep the baby safe, and I think you know more than you're saying. Either you're covering up or afraid to say the truth, or don't realize how much danger you and your boy are in, but I've got to tell you that without your help the investigation is stymied." Randi glanced away, her gaze traveling from Kelly to the window and beyond, where snow was drifting against the fence and barn.

She hesitated. Tapped her fingers on the edge of the couch.

"Do you know anyone who would want to kill you?"

"You mean other than my brothers?" Randi joked.

"I'm being serious."

"I know." Her smile disappeared. "I probably have some enemies, but I don't remember them."

"Do you remember the man who fathered your child?"

Randi stiffened, picked at a scratch in the arm of the leather couch. "I'm…I'm still working on that."

"It won't help to lie."

"I said I'm working on it." Randi's index finger stopped working on the scratch.

"Okay, so what about the book you were writing?"

Was it Kelly's imagination or did Randi pale a bit?

"It's fiction."

"About corruption in the rodeo circuit."

"That's the backdrop, yes."

"Does it have anything to do with your father or your brothers?"

"No. Other than I got the idea for it from Dad, I think— Look, this is all kind of fuzzy."

"How about Sam Donahue? He's a cowboy and was involved in rodeo work. He still supplies stock to the national competitions, doesn't he?"

"I said it was fuzzy."

"You and he dated."

"I...I think that's true. I remember Sam."

"Could he be the father of your child?"

Randi didn't answer, and in true McCafferty fashion, her jaw slid forward in stubborn defiance.

"Okay, so what about your job? Do you remember anything about it? Anything that you might have been working on that would have caused someone to want to kill you?"

"I wrote advice columns. I suppose someone could have taken offense, but I don't remember them."

"What about Joe Paterno? The photojournalist you worked with? Do you remember him?"

Randi swallowed hard.

"You dated him."

"Did I?"

"When he was in town. He's gone on assignment a lot. Rents a studio over a garage in one of those old homes in the Queen Anne's district of Seattle when he's in the Northwest.''

''As I said, I really don't remember. Not details. Names are familiar, but…'' Kelly was ready. She snapped open her briefcase and slid three pictures across the coffee table. One was of Joe Paterno, his camera poised as he was about to snap a shot, while someone took a picture of him. The second was a color copy of a photo from a newspaper in Calgary. The grainy shot was of Sam Donahue, a rangy blond with a cowboy hat tilted back on his head and his eyes squinted against a harsh, intense sun. In the background penned horses and cattle were visible. The third photo was a glossy eight-by-ten of Brodie Clanton. Wearing a suit, tie and the thousand-watt grin of a lawyer with political ambitions, he stared into the camera as if it were his lover.

''Well,'' Randi said, leaning forward and separating the photos and eyeing each one. ''You've certainly been busy.''

Chapter Thirteen

"I want to find the bastard who tried to kill you, Randi, but I can't do it without your help," Kelly said. "So tell me, who do you think it is?"

Randi eyed the pictures on the table. She chewed her lower lip as Kelly felt eyes on her back. At that moment, Randi turned her attention to the archway that separated the foyer from the living room. She froze.

"Who are you?"

Kelly glanced over her shoulder and found the private investigator standing at the foot of the stairs. "Kurt Striker."

"The private detective," Randi said, her eyes snapping and her chin inching higher. "My brothers hired you to try and figure out who's trying to kill me."

"That's right." Kurt sauntered into the room and extended his hand. Kelly gritted her teeth to hold her tongue.

Randi didn't bother shaking his hand. Her lips flattened

over her teeth and she said, "I don't know what my brothers were thinking, but we don't need anyone investigating the accident."

"It wasn't an accident," Kurt asserted.

Randi's gaze zipped back to Kelly. She asked, "You're certain?"

"Fairly." Kelly nodded.

Randi shot a look at the private detective. "I think the police can handle it."

Kurt smiled crookedly and had the audacity to sit on a corner of the coffee table, placing his tough-as-leather body directly in front of Randi. "You got a problem with me, lady?"

"Probably." She reached over and adjusted the edge of the blanket near her baby's chin. "I just want things to be calm. Peaceful. For me and him. And for the record, don't call me 'lady' again. I consider it demeaning."

"I meant it as a compliment."

"I have a name."

He ignored the jab. "Okay, you want things to be back to normal, then let's wrap this up. The detective was asking a good question when I walked in. Who do you think tried to kill you?"

"I...I honestly don't know," Randi admitted.

"But you should remember the father of your child."

"I should."

Kelly smiled inwardly. Randi wasn't giving an inch for Striker. She leaned closer to the youngest McCafferty heir. "This is important. We think the vehicle that ran you off the road was a maroon Ford product. Maybe a van or SUV. Do you remember anything about the day of the accident?"

"Just that I was in a hurry. I had this feeling of urgency," Randi said, leaning back on the couch and looking at the fire. But Kelly suspected she wasn't seeing the hungry flames licking at the mossy chunks of oak, or the charred bricks in the grate. Her eyes were turned inward.

"I remember I was in a hurry. I was just a few weeks before term and I had a lot to do." Her brow furrowed and her eyes squinted as she thought. "I wanted to get to Grand Hope without going into labor."

"But your ob-gyn is in Seattle."

"I know. That was a problem. I mean, I think it concerned me, but I thought if I could...could spend some time here and finish the synopsis, you know, an outline, kind of, for my book, then once the baby was here, while I was on maternity leave, I thought I could polish the first few chapters and send them to my agent. He thought he might be able to find a publisher who would be interested...but that's about all I remember."

"No car or truck following you or pushing you onto the shoulder?"

She shook her head slowly. "No."

"You don't know anyone who had a maroon car?"

"Not that I can remember." She glanced at the three pictures still spread upon the table. "Do you know something else? Do any of these men... No, surely not someone I dated...but...do any of them own the car that pushed me off the road?" she asked, her color draining as she considered the possibility.

"None of these men has ever owned title to anything resembling what we're looking for," Kelly admitted, "but that doesn't mean the culprit couldn't have borrowed a friend's car or stolen one. The department has done a pretty thorough search of all the local body shops, in a wide arc around Glacier Park, Grand Hope and Seattle. Sure, there are some vehicles that needed repair that *could* have been the car or truck involved, but so far, we haven't been able to make a connection.'' She reached into her briefcase again and handed Randi a list of names. ''Do you know any of these people? Do any of the names jog any kind of memory?''

Randi looked over the computer printout. ''I don't think so,'' she said. ''I mean, I don't remember any of them.''

Kurt reached for the printout. ''Mind if I have a look?''

Kelly wanted to tell him to go jump off the highest bridge, but didn't. There was a chance he could help. ''See for yourself.''

He eyed the report and Kelly envisioned the gears turning in his mind as he scanned the documents. When he finished he looked over the sheets at Kelly. ''Good work.''

''Thanks,'' she said, nearly choking on the word. She didn't trust this guy a bit. He had no scruples as far as Kelly could tell.

''I'm looking for a partner.''

In your dreams. ''I've got a job.''

''I could probably make it worth your while.''

''Not interested.''

''A lifer, eh?''

She didn't respond, just said to Randi, ''Let me know if you remember anything else. And you can keep those —'' she motioned to the pictures and printouts ''—I've got copies.''

''Thanks. I'll let you know.''

''I'll walk you out,'' the detective offered.

''It's not necessary.''

But he was with her stride for stride, and as the front door shut behind them, he said, ''I don't know why you've got a burr under your saddle when it comes to me, but it's not helping anything. We can work together or separately, but it might be easier, faster and damned more efficient if we pooled our resources.''

"You mean I should give you all the information I have, all the access the sheriff's department has, and make your job a whole lot easier, so you can 'solve,' and I use the term loosely, the case, take the credit and the money for it, without putting in the hours and the effort.''

"I just want to get to the bottom of it," he said, and his expression was as dark as the night.

"Right," she muttered under her breath. "I'll keep it in mind.''

She was down two steps when his voice caught up with her. "You know, Detective, unless I miss my guess, you're ticked off and it doesn't have so much to do with me as it does with Matt McCafferty.''

She bit back a hot retort and just kept walking. There was just no reason under heaven to rise to the bait. Because, damn him, he was right.

"I'll give you top dollar, McCafferty. I already had the place appraised by two local real estate firms, but if you don't like what they've come up with, you can have someone else do it.''

Mike was seated in his old pickup, the engine idling, with his crutches and old hunting dog, Arrow, on the front seat beside him. Matt stood in the snow-crusted lane of his house talking through the open window, his breath fogging in the clear air. Kavanaugh reached into a side pocket of the truck and withdrew a manila packet.

"What makes you want this place so badly?''

Kavanaugh grinned as he handed the thick envelope to Matt. "Carolyn's expecting and we're outgrowing my place. I figure we can live there while I remodel the farmhouse.'' He nodded toward the rustic house Matt called home. "It'll take some doin', but I'll finish off the top story, add a bath and let Carolyn decide what she wants to do downstairs. By the summer after next, about the time the baby will be on his feet, we'll be ready to move and I'll rent out my place to my foreman."

"You've got one?"

The grin in Kavanaugh's freckled face widened a bit. "I will have by then. If things go right. You know, I would have bought this the last time it came up for sale, but you beat me to it. Now I've come into a little money, you're never here, anyway, and I figure it's the right time." He stared through rimless glasses and the open window. "You're not telling me I'm wrong, are ya?"

Matt frowned and glanced around the hilly acres he'd ranched for the past few years. The house was big enough, two stories, but the upstairs had never been finished; it was three rooms separated by a framework of two-by-fours. Downstairs the kitchen needed to be gutted. Ditto for the bathroom, which was little more than a closet by today's standards. And the whole place needed new wiring, plumbing and a helluva lot of insulation.

It had been fine for him. He liked roughing it. But it probably wouldn't do for a wife and kids. Along with two barns, one a hundred years old, the other five years old, there were rolling acres backdropped by dark forests. The creek that ran through the property eventually meandered over to Kavanaugh's place.

He opened the envelope and saw Mike and Carolyn Kavanaugh's offer. It was fair. He knew what his place was worth, at least in terms of dollars and cents. And emotionally, he was ready to move on. He owned the spread outright.

"Now, I'd need a contract. It's all outlined in the offer," Kavanaugh said, "but I'd make a balloon payment in five years, either pay you off out of my pocket or get a real mortgage.''

Matt's jaw slid to one side and he eyed his place one last time. ''All right, Mike. You've got it.'' He stuck his hand through the open window and Kavanaugh's fingers clasped his.

''Just like that?''

''Just like that. I'll call the attorneys who drew up the papers when I bought this place, a firm named Jansen, Monteith and Stone in Missoula. Thorne worked there when he first got out of high school and they handled all my dad's legal work.''

Kavanaugh gave a curt nod. ''I've heard of 'em. See what you can work out.''

They talked for a few minutes, then Kavanaugh took off. Matt wandered up the short walk and the three steps to the front porch. Inside he listened as the old furnace growled and the windows rattled with each gust of wind. His furniture was used, most of it had come with the place, and there just wasn't much to tie him here any longer. He didn't waste any time, but dialed the number of the law firm. After going through two receptionists, he was connected with Bill Jansen, the man who had handled splitting up the Flying M in accordance with John Randall's wishes.

''So what is it I can do for you?'' Bill asked after a few polite preliminaries about health, the weather and the NFL.

Matt outlined his request. What he wanted, he explained, was to take the money he made on this property and offer to buy out his brothers for their share of the Flying M, and he wanted to set up some kind of trust for Eva Dillinger, in accordance with whatever agreement his father had made when the woman worked for him.

"That might be tougher than you know," Bill admitted. "I understand John Randall and Eva had spoken about some kind of retirement, but it was never drawn up legally."

"But you heard about it, right?"

"He'd mentioned it."

"Then let's figure out how to make it right. I'm not trying to set Eva up for life, just give her what's due. I'll talk to my brothers. And this has got to be anonymous. Completely."

"I don't think that's possible."

"Anything's possible."

"Not really. Not only will the recipients want answers but the government, as well."

"Can't you dummy up some blind corporation?" Matt said, then laughed as he heard himself, talking like some big corporate hot shot. "Never mind. I just didn't want to deal with it now," he admitted. It was the truth; he had too much to think about, didn't want to stir up that particular hornet's nest. But he had to. If he was going to right his father's wrong. "Don't worry about it. I'll explain."

"Then it's not anonymous."

"Right. I'll handle it," Matt said. "Is it possible to get the paperwork to me in the next few days? Fax it to the ranch and I'll see that my brothers sign it. Can you work that fast?"

"Unless we encounter unforeseen problems."

"You shouldn't."

"One of the junior partners is going to be in Grand Hope in a couple of days. I'll tell her what's going on, and if there's any problem, you can meet with her while she's in town. Her name is Jamie Parsons and she spent her senior year of high school there. Maybe you know her.''

The name was slightly familiar, but Matt couldn't recall why. ''I don't think so.''

''I'll have her give you a call when she gets into town. She'll be staying there for a few weeks, as she's going to be selling her grandmother's place.''

''Parsons,'' Matt repeated.

''Her grandmother was Nita Parsons.''

''As I said, the name's vaguely familiar.''

''Nita passed away a couple of months ago. Your father might have known her.''

''Possibly.''

''Anyway, I'll get on the sale and transfer of property right away. All I'll need is your brothers' signatures.''

''You'll have them,'' Matt said, though he hadn't mentioned his plan to either Thorne or Slade. He was certain it wouldn't be a problem. Thorne had already mentioned moving to a spread close by and Slade wasn't one to put down roots. Matt was the rancher of the lot. He'd buy out his brothers and own half of the Flying M.

Matt hung up and his gaze swept the interior of the old house. He'd spent a lot of years here. Alone. And it had been fine. But he wanted something more from life right now, and that something was a red-haired lady cop.

There wasn't any reason not to start the ball rolling. Quickly he dialed the number of the Flying M, connected with Thorne and stated his business. ''Get Slade on the extension. I've done a lot of thinking while I've been gone. Kavanaugh's buying my place, so I want to transfer my operations to Grand Hope. Come up with a fair price. I'll buy the two of you out.''

''Just like that?''

''If you'll sell,'' Matt said.

Thorne hesitated, then said, "I don't see any problem. Let me get Slade on the phone and we'll work something out."

"Just like that?" Matt threw back at him.

"Yep. It's the way I do business."

Kelly was burned. Big time. The last place she wanted to be was at Thorne McCafferty's wedding, but she didn't have much of a choice. Espinoza had insisted.

"Look, the investigation is still wide open," he'd told her while smoking a cigarette in his office. "The potential killer could be there. This is a chance for you to meet those people closest to the family."

"At a wedding?" she'd protested.

"At a wedding, dressed as a guest, mingling at the reception, keeping your ears and eyes open." He'd drawn hard on his smoke, exhaled and looked up at her through the cloud. "Do you have a problem with that, Detective?"

"No problem at all," she said aloud to her reflection, repeating the exact phrase she'd spoken to Espinoza less than three hours earlier. So here she was wearing a midnight-blue silk dress, braiding her hair and wrapping it into a thick chignon at the base of her neck and dreading the thought of seeing Matt again.

You'll get through it; it's just business. But as she dusted her nose, applied brown mascara and touched up her peach lipstick, she felt like a fraud. Her stomach was tense, her skin felt flushed. She—a girl who had taken on men twice her size while training for her job, a female officer who had been known to take a bead on a suspect and demand "Drop it" when she'd been threatened with a weapon, an officer who wasn't afraid to drive more than a hundred miles an hour if a high-speed chase was necessary—was intimidated by a simple wedding and reception.

It was only one night. Somehow she'd get through it. As she reached for her coat and checked to see that she had her car keys, the phone rang. She nearly ignored it, then picked up on the third ring.

"Kelly?" her sister said breathlessly, as if she'd been running.

"This is my house. You called. Right?"

"What do you know about some trust being set up for Mom?" Karla asked, undeterred.

"A trust?"

"That's right. She got a letter from an attorney in Missoula, Jamie Parsons, that says she's the recipient of some trust fund."

"Why?"

"That's what I'm asking you."

"Didn't they say?"

"No, and when Mom called the law firm and talked to the lawyer, he was evasive, wouldn't give her any information. Said it would be coming in a few weeks. Isn't that strange?"

"Very."

"I told Mom and Dad not to look a gift horse in the mouth, but you know how they are. They're certain there's been some mistake. What do you think?"

"What's the name of the law firm?"

"Jansen, Monteith and Stone." Karla hesitated just a second, then added, "Mom said that when she worked for John Randall McCafferty, that was the firm he used. You think it's a coincidence?"

"I'm a cop, Karla. I don't believe in coincidence."

"I'm a beautician, Kelly. I believe in past lives, reincarnation, split personalities, winning the lottery and, in case I forgot, coincidence.''

''I'll check it out for the folks.''

''Figured you would. Now, have fun at the wedding.''

''It's *not* going to be fun.''

''You're right. If that's the attitude you're wearing. Come on, Kell, lighten up. It wouldn't kill ya.''

Kelly wasn't so sure.

Matt hooked two fingers under the collar of his tuxedo shirt and twisted his neck to give him some breathing room. Small places made him claustrophobic, and this anteroom off the chapel where Thorne was about to be married was barely big enough for the minister and the three McCafferty brothers. Maybe it was because Matt didn't have such a great relationship with God, maybe it was because the thermostat in the room must've been broken and the heater was pumping out air that felt at least a hundred degrees, or maybe it was because he was faced with the fact that he'd be seeing Kelly again.

Kelly. Detective Kelly Ann Dillinger.

The woman who hadn't returned his calls.

He'd been back in Grand Hope all of twelve hours, and in that time he'd left three messages for her. He'd gotten no response, but Nicole was certain Kelly would show up.

Good.

Because he wanted answers.

''So we'll sign the papers next week,'' Slade said as he glanced in a small mirror, frowned and brushed a wayward lock of black hair off his forehead.

''As soon as the lawyer contacts us.''

''Bill Jansen?'' Thorne said, though it was obvious his thoughts were elsewhere.

''No, his associate. A woman. Jamie Parsons.''

Slade froze. "Who?"

"Jamie Parsons. She's here on business as she's going to sell her grandmother's house." He caught a shadow chase across Slade's blue eyes. "Do you know her? She lived here her senior year of high school. Her grandmother was named Anita."

"Nita."

"Yeah, that was it. So you've heard of her."

"It was a long time ago," Slade admitted, his lips thinning as the sound of organ music filtered through the walls. "This is it," Slade said to Thorne, as if eager to change the subject. "Your last few seconds as a single man."

Thorne's grin was as wide as the whole of Montana.

"You can still take off," Slade offered.

"I don't think so." Thorne laughed and Matt wondered if he'd ever seen his brother so happy. Joy came with difficulty to Thorne; it wasn't an emotion Matt would have attributed to his eldest brother. Until Nicole. He'd changed since meeting his fiancée. And the change was definitely for the better.

The door to the chapel creaked open and the minister, a tall scarecrow of a man with wild gray hair, rosy cheeks and thick glasses, walked into the anteroom. "Are we ready?"

Thorne nodded. "You bet."

"Then let's go."

Thorne only hesitated long enough to predict, "It'll happen to you two, too. Your days as bachelors are numbered."

Slade snorted.

Matt didn't comment.

"Not for me," Slade argued.

"The bigger they are, the harder they fall."

"Well, maybe for Matt, he's already half-hitched as it is."

For once, Matt didn't argue. Yes, he was ready, but the woman he wanted for his wife seemed to be avoiding him.

"Don't they say something like pride goes before a fall?" Thorne said, adjusting his tie. "You might remember that, Slade." Squaring his shoulders, he led his brothers through the arched doorway and stepped into the candlelit chapel. It was small, more than a hundred years old, and the stiff-backed, dark wood pews were packed with family and friends.

Matt zeroed in on Kelly and his heart skipped a beat at the sight of her. The rest of the crowd seemed to disappear. Even when Matt's attention should have been drawn to the two bridesmaids, Randi and a woman doctor, Maureen Oliverio, Matt could hardly drag his gaze away from Kelly. God, she was beautiful. He forced his eyes to the back of the church as Nicole, dressed in a long cream-colored gown that shimmered in the candlelight, walked slowly to the front of the church to take Thorne's hand. Yet, from the corner of his eye, he noticed Kelly.

This should be me, he thought ridiculously. *Kelly and I should be up here exchanging vows.* He remembered the day his father had studied him trying to break Diablo Rojo and how the old man had advised him to settle down, to start a family, to ensure that the McCafferty name would go on.

Matt swallowed an unfamiliar lump in his throat.

The old man had been right.

He'd found the woman he wanted to live with; he just had to find a way to make her his wife.

Somehow he got through the ceremony. He watched tears spring to Nicole's eyes as Thorne slipped a wide gold band over her finger and felt a deep jab of envy as

Thorne kissed his bride in front of all their guests. The ceremony completed, Matt followed the bride and groom outside and into the cold winter air.

He fell silent as Slade drove him to the Badger Creek Hotel where the reception was to take place. Built on the banks of the stream for which it was named more than a century earlier, the hotel had once been a stop on the stagecoach line and had enjoyed a colorful past. In its hundred-and-twenty-year history, the hotel had been renovated and updated every other decade and now had been restored to its original nineteenth-century grandeur.

Slade stopped for a smoke in the parking lot, but Matt hurried up the stairs to the ballroom, hoping to catch up to Kelly. He was surprised to see her at the wedding and hoped that she would come to the reception.

A crowd had already gathered in the cavernous room with its coved ceiling nearly thirty feet high. Tall windows ran the length of the room and thousands of tiny lights glittered from three immense chandeliers that sparkled with cut glass and dripped crystal. A small combo played music from an alcove in one corner while a fountain of champagne bubbled near an ice sculpture of a running horse.

He saw her the minute she entered. Without her coat, in a long shimmery gown of dark blue, she was exquisite. A silver necklace adorned her long neck and her hair was pulled away from her face, not severely, but with an element of sophistication that got to him.

Snagging two long-stemmed glasses from a linen-draped table, he walked up to her. "Well, Detective," he drawled, "you look…fantastic."

She cocked a reddish brow. "Oh, come on, McCafferty, you miss the uniform. Admit it."

So she still had a sense of humor. "I miss you."

"I don't understand."

"Liar." He handed her a glass and she started to take a sip.

"Wait. I think a toast is in order."

"To the bride and groom?"

"That'll come later." He didn't explain, just took hold of her hand and drew her through a draped French door and onto a snow-covered veranda.

"Wait a minute."

"Nope. I've waited too long." Balancing his glass in one hand, he wrapped his other arm around her and drew her close. Before she could protest, he kissed her, waiting until he felt her loosen, her bones melt against him. Only then did he lift his head. "Isn't that better?"

"No, I mean…look, Matt, I've been trying to tell you that it's over. You can drop the charade."

"Charade?" he asked, and felt the first drip of premonition in his blood.

"I know that you courted me just to get close to the investigation."

"No, I—"

"Don't deny it. I overheard a conversation between Randi and Slade." Anger surged through his veins. "I know that this flirtation or whatever you want to call it was because Kurt Striker told you to play up to me. To get me into bed."

"You believe that."

"Yes."

Anger roared through his blood. He opened his mouth just as she looked up at him with sad eyes. "Don't play me for a fool, okay? It's just not necessary."

"I wouldn't."

"Good. Then we can go on and forget what happened between us."

"Nope."

"Matt, really." She turned toward the door, and he didn't bother reaching for her.

"I'll never forget it, Kelly. Never." She'd reached the door but turned to face him. Tears glistened in her eyes.

"Don't do this," she whispered.

"I love you."

She closed her eyes. A tear, caught in the moon glow, wove a silent course over the slope of her cheek.

"You don't have to—"

"I love you, dammit."

She leaned against the door. "I don't want to do this, Matt. I only came tonight because my boss asked me to. Because of the investigation."

"Have you seen any suspicious characters?"

"Just the groom and his brothers," she said, but the joke fell flat. "Look, I know that you set up some kind of trust fund for my mother, probably because of a guilty conscience over what your dad did to her, and…and that's all well and good, really, but you shouldn't have. It was your father's problem, not yours."

"You're mine."

"A problem…I imagine I am."

"That's not what I meant!"

"The past is over and done. My family is fine…we can take care of ourselves. We don't need any kind of Johnny-come-lately charity."

"That's not what it is."

"It doesn't matter."

"Like hell!" He dropped his champagne glass and his shoes crunched through the snow as he walked to her. "You came here to see me. I did what I did for your mother to right a wrong, my brothers agreed to it, and as for leaving well enough alone, I can't. Not until you tell me that you'll be my wife."

"What? Oh, God, your ego just won't quit."

"I love you," he said again, and Kelly felt her heart rip into a thousand pieces. If only she could believe him, trust him, but she knew better. She opened her mouth to protest again but he snatched the glass of champagne from her fingers, flung it over the rail toward the creek, and pulled her into the circle of his arms. "What will it take to convince you?"

"You can't."

"Sure I can. We'll elope tonight."

"You're crazy."

"I'm serious."

Her throat felt as if it were the size of an apple. Could she dare believe him? Trust him?

"I—I don't believe that's possible," she whispered.

"Anything is." He stared at her long and hard. "I sold my ranch. I'm moving back to Grand Hope. For good. And I want you to be my wife and the mother of my children. You do love me?"

"Yes."

"Then we'll get married."

"I—I'd like that."

"Then that's settled." He smiled down at her with his crooked, damnably sexy thousand-watt grin.

"I...I don't...I don't know what to say," she whispered, stunned at the turn of events.

"Then don't say anything, just kiss me."

She nearly laughed through her tears, but tilted back her head and felt his mouth cover hers. Music filtered through the open door and he started moving, dancing with her, alone on the snow-blanketed veranda with the cold winter air swirling around them, and high overhead the stars twinkled in the night-darkened Montana sky.

Kelly leaned against him. She thought of the investigation, of the danger still surrounding the McCafferty brothers and of Randi and little J.R. Now, knowing she would soon marry Matt, she was more determined than ever to find the culprit who was terrorizing his family...her family.

But...for tonight, she'd dance with Matt, laugh with him and know that whatever fate had in store for them, they would face it together.

"Should we make the announcement?" he asked.

"Tonight?"

"Why wait?"

Why indeed?

"Let's wait until tomorrow. Tonight belongs to Thorne and Nicole," Kelly said as she glanced through the windows and saw the bride and groom gliding around the dance floor. Nicole's eyes were bright, her cheeks flushed, and as the song ended Thorne swept her into a backbreaking dip. The crowd clapped.

"Then tomorrow," Matt agreed.

"Yes, tomorrow."

He kissed her then and she wound her arms around his neck. "All right, Detective. Let's join the party. It looks like you lost your champagne. Besides, aren't you supposed to be looking for the bad guys tonight? Wasn't that your assignment?"

"Right you are, cowboy."

"I don't supposed you've seen any suspicious characters."

"Only the McCafferty brothers," she teased, linking her arm through his as they walked into the ballroom.

"And you'll never meet a sexier, more disreputable bunch of *hombres* in your life!"

"I suppose you're right." Matt laughed, then gave her a conspiratorial wink. "Welcome to the gang."

"My pleasure," she assured him as he wrapped his arms around her and they joined the other guests, who were dancing under the dimmed lights of the chandeliers. Her heart pounded, her head spun and she fought to keep tears of happiness from sliding down her cheeks. As he guided her easily across the floor, she smiled up at the man she loved, the man she'd been waiting for all her life, the man who would soon be her husband, a cowboy after her own heart.

Mrs. Matt McCafferty.

Detective Kelly McCafferty.

Either way, the name sounded right.

Epilogue

A horse nickered softly as Matt entered the darkened stables. He flipped on the first switch, allowing only half the bulbs to illuminate the musty interior. Mares and colts rustled in their stalls and the wind whistled outside. Diablo Rojo stuck his head over the stall door and snorted.

"Yeah, yeah, and I'm glad to see you, too." Matt reached into his pocket for a bit of apple he'd pilfered from the kitchen as he walked to the Appaloosa's box. He tipped his hat back a bit to look the feisty colt square in the eye. "Juanita's making a pie, but I figured she didn't need this." Opening the flat of his hand, he added, "However, she might just disagree, and if she did, we both know she'd skin me alive." Soft lips swept the morsel from his palm. "So we're friends, are we, Devil?"

The horse tossed his head. His dark eyes were still bright with a fire no man would ever tame. Not even a McCafferty.

"That's what I thought."

He rubbed the colt's wide forehead and surveyed the stock. A few of the broodmares were penned within, their swollen bellies indicating that they'd soon deliver the next generation of McCafferty foals.

Matt smiled as his boots rang on the concrete aisle between the stalls. God, he loved these animals. In the spring he'd transfer his own herd here. By that time he'd be married, maybe have a child of his own on the way.

The door creaked open and Kelly slid inside, bringing in a rush of bitter cold air. Snowflakes collected on the shoulders of her jacket and melted in her red hair. Matt's heart pumped at the sight of her, just as it did every time since the first time he'd laid eyes on her.

"I figured I might find you here," she said as she made her way between the boxes, her fingers trailing along the top rails. When she reached him she stood on her tiptoes and planted a kiss on his cheek.

Not good enough. Before she could pull away, he wrapped his arms around her and dragged her tight against him, his lips finding hers instinctively. Her perfume invaded his nostrils and her warm body caused his to respond with a dire need to have all of her. Every day. For the rest of his life. "You came in here so we could have some privacy," he charged when he finally lifted his head and noted the flush on her cheeks.

Her laughter rang to the dusty cross beams high overhead. "Well...that, too, I suppose, but I just wanted to check on you, see how you're doing."

"Fine. Why wouldn't I be?"

She lifted a shoulder. Wrinkled that damnably cute nose of hers. "I want to make sure that selling your place is something you want to do." She was suddenly serious.

"I mean, I could move if you wanted to keep your ranch and—"

"No way. This is home." Still holding her, he glanced around the boxes filled with horses and, high above, to the hay mow. "I did what I had to. Proved my point that I could make it on my own. Now I want to be here." He stared deep into her eyes. "With the woman I love."

"Who's that?" she teased, one side of her mouth lifting.

He barked out a laugh and squeezed her. "Besides, I'm not the only one making sacrifices." He was talking about her decision to quit the police force and take a position as junior partner with Kurt Striker. They'd aired their differences and Kelly was convinced this was the right move. She needed more free time, a more flexible schedule, and less stress on the job as she became Mrs. Matt McCafferty. "How did Detective Espinoza take the news?"

"Not well," she admitted.

"Tried to talk you out of it?"

"Mmm. Offered me a promotion."

"And you turned him down?"

"In a heartbeat. Roberto knew it wasn't going to happen, anyway. My mind was made up. I think he realized he couldn't change it."

"But he gave it a try."

She grinned.

"How about your folks?"

"They're another story." She giggled, snuggled closer to him. "They're adjusting. And even though they're grateful for the trust fund, they're not sure they can trust anyone named McCafferty."

"Even their daughter?"

"We'll see. It'll take some time."

He pressed a kiss to her forehead and she sighed. "Will they come to the wedding?" he asked.

"With some arm twisting."

"Really?"

"No...I'm kidding." Her breath was warm against his chest. "Neither one of my parents would miss my wedding for the world and Karla's excited about being my maid of honor, though she did have a few choice words about marriage and broken dreams."

"Funny, my family's all for it," he said as Diablo stretched his neck, stuck his head over the stall door and, with nostrils flared, searched Matt for another piece of apple.

"Your family is just grateful to marry you off."

"Very funny."

"They thought you were hopeless."

"They were probably right, but it could be something else, you know. It could be that you captivated my brothers and sister."

"Oh, right," she countered, but seemed to glow under the compliment. She checked her watch and sighed. "Got to run."

"You just got here."

"I promised Randi I'd baby-sit. Does he have a name yet?"

"She's, and I quote, 'working on it.' Until she does, we're all still calling him J.R. She doesn't like it too much, but she's going along with it. Doesn't have much choice."

"I haven't given up on finding who's been threatening her," Kelly said, her eyes darkening thoughtfully as she twisted a button on his jacket. "I'll just be working with Kurt instead of the sheriff's department."

"We'll get him," Matt said, and meant it. "Together." He pushed a lock of hair from her face. "Just like we'll do everything."

"Everything?" she teased, her brown eyes sparkling in

that mischievous way he found so intoxicating. One arched brow lifted in naughty anticipation.

"Everything." He meant it. To prove his point, he pressed her against the wall, let her feel the want in him.

"Oh...oh..." He kissed her and she melted, sagged against the old siding.

"Wh—what about when we have children, and the baby needs to be fed or diapered and it's one in the morning?" she asked breathlessly as he lifted his head.

"No problem."

"Spoken like a true man. What about running them all over the map when they've got piano and soccer practice and you're dealing with a sick horse or cattle that have escaped through a hole in the fence?"

"Bring it on," he said.

"What about—"

"What about this?" he said, wrapping his arms around her more tightly. "You and I, we should quit worrying about what will happen when we have the kids and start concentrating on making a baby."

"Now?" she asked as he kissed the side of her face.

"Now."

"Here?"

"Anywhere." His lips brushed over hers, and as he bent down to lift her off her feet, he felt his father's rodeo belt buckle press into the muscles of his abdomen. "Anywhere. Anytime. Anyhow. Just as long as it's you and me."

"You got it, cowboy," she whispered into his open mouth, and removed his hat, before dropping it onto her own head and kissing him as if she'd never stop.

* * * * *

Don't miss

THE McCAFFERTYS: SLADE

by Lisa Jackson,
available from Silhouette Special Edition
in December 2001

Turn the page for
an exciting sneak preview...

Chapter One

*T*he McCaffertys! Why in the world did her meeting have to be with the damned McCafferty brothers?

Jamie Parsons braked hard at her grandmother's small farm and swung her wheezing compact into the drive. Tires spun in the snow that covered the two ruts where dry weeds had the audacity to poke through the blanket of white. The cottage, in need of repairs and paint, seemed quaint now, like some fairy-tale version of Grandma's house.

It had been, she thought as she grabbed her briefcase and overnight bag, then plowed through three inches of white powder to the back door, where she found the extra key over the window ledge where her grandmother, Nita, had always kept it. "Just in case…" she'd always said in her raspy old-lady voice. "We don't want to be locked out, now, do we?"

No, Nana, we sure don't. Jamie's throat constricted

when she thought of the woman who had taken in a wild, rebellious teenager, opened her house and her heart to a girl whose parents had given up on her. Nana hadn't batted an eye, just told her that from the time she stepped over the front threshold with her two suitcases, one-eyed teddy and an attitude that wouldn't quit, things were going to change. From that moment forward Jamie was to abide by her rules and that was that.

Not that they'd always gotten along.

Not that Jamie hadn't done everything imaginable behind the woman's broad back.

Not that Jamie hadn't tried every trick in the book to get herself thrown out of the only home she'd ever known.

Nana, a God-fearing woman who could cut her only granddaughter to the quick with just one glance, had never given up. Unlike everyone else in Jamie's life.

Now the key turned easily and Jamie walked into the kitchen. It smelled musty, the black-and-white tiles covered in dust, the old Formica table with chrome legs still pushed against the far wall that sloped sharply, due to the stairs running up the other side of the house from the foyer. But the salt and pepper shakers, in the shape of kittens, had disappeared from the table, as had all other signs of life. A dried cactus in a plastic pot had been forgotten and pushed into a corner of the counter where once there had been a toaster. The gingham curtains were now home to spiders whose webs gathered more dust.

If Nana had been alive, she would have had a fit. This kitchen had always gleamed. "Cleanliness is next to godliness," she'd always preached while pushing a broom, or polishing a lamp, or scrubbing a sink.

God, Jamie missed her.

The bulk of Nana's estate, which consisted of this old house, the twenty acres surrounding it, and a 1940 Chevrolet parked in the old garage, had been left to Jamie. It was Nana's dream that Jamie settle down here in Grand Hope, live in the little cottage, get married and have half a dozen great-grandchildren for her to spoil. "Sorry," Jamie said aloud as she dropped her bags on the table and ran a finger through the fine layer of dust that had collected on the chipped Formica top. "I just never got around to it."

"Oh, Nana," Jamie whispered, glancing out the window to the snow-crusted yard. Thorny, leafless brambles scaled the wire fence surrounding the garden plot and the henhouse had nearly collapsed. The small barn was still standing, though the roof sagged, and the remaining weed-strewn pasture was thankfully hidden beneath the blanket of white.

Nana had loved it here, and Jamie intended to clean it up and list it with a local real estate company.

She checked her watch. She had less than an hour before she was to sit down with Thorne, Matt and Slade McCafferty, and the Flying M Ranch was nearly twenty miles away.

"Better get a move on, Parsons," she told herself, though her stomach was already in tight little knots at the thought of coming face-to-face with Slade again. It was ridiculous, really. How could something that happened so long ago still bother her?

She'd been over Slade McCafferty for years. *Years.*

Seeing him again would be no problem at all, just another day in a lawyer's life, the proverbial walk in the park. Right? So why, then, the tightness in her chest, the acceleration of her heartbeat? For crying out loud, she was acting like an adolescent and that just wouldn't do.

She changed from jeans and her favorite old sweater to a black suit with a silver silk blouse and knee-high boots, then wound her hair into a knot on her head and gazed at her reflection in the mirror over the antique dresser. It had been nearly fifteen years since she'd seen Slade McCafferty, and in those years she'd blossomed from a fresh-faced, angry eighteen-year-old with something to prove, to a full-grown adult who'd worked two jobs to get through college and eventually earned a law degree.

The woman in the reflection was confident, steady and determined, but beneath the image, Jamie saw herself as she had been, heavier, angrier, the new girl in town with a bad attitude and even worse reputation.

A nest of butterflies erupted in her stomach at the thought of facing Slade again, but she told herself she was being silly, reliving her adolescence. Which was just plain nuts! Angry with herself, she pulled on black gloves and a matching wool coat, grabbed her briefcase and purse, and was down the stairs and out Nana's back door in nothing flat. She trudged through the snow to her compact, carrying her briefcase as if it was some kind of shield. Lord, she was a basket case. So she had to face Slade McCafferty again?

So what?

*   *   *   *   *

Feel like a star with Silhouette.

We will fly you and a guest to New York City for an exciting weekend stay at a glamorous 5-star hotel. Experience a refreshing day at one of New York's trendiest spas and have your photo taken by a professional. Plus, receive $1,000 U.S. spending money!

Flowers...long walks...dinner for two... how does Silhouette Books make romance come alive for you?

Send us a script, with 500 words or less, along with visuals (only drawings, magazine cutouts or photographs or combination thereof). Show us how Silhouette Makes Your Love Come Alive. Be creative and have fun. No purchase necessary. All entries must be clearly marked with your name, address and telephone number. All entries will become property of Silhouette and are not returnable. **Contest closes September 28, 2001.**

Please send your entry to: **Silhouette Makes You a Star!**

In U.S.A.
P.O. Box 9069
Buffalo, NY, 14269-9069

In Canada
P.O. Box 637
Fort Erie, ON, L2A 5X3

Look for contest details on the next page, by visiting www.eHarlequin.com or request a copy by sending a self-addressed envelope to the applicable address above. Contest open to Canadian and U.S. residents who are 18 or over. Void where prohibited.

Silhouette®
Where love comes alive™

Our lucky winner's photo will appear in a Silhouette ad. Join the fun!

HARLEQUIN "SILHOUETTE MAKES YOU A STAR!" CONTEST 1308
OFFICIAL RULES
NO PURCHASE NECESSARY TO ENTER

1. To enter, follow directions published in the offer to which you are responding. Contest begins June 1, 2001, and ends on September 28, 2001. Entries must be postmarked by September 28, 2001, and received by October 5, 2001. Enter by hand-printing (or typing) on an 8 ½" x 11" piece of paper your name, address (including zip code), contest number/name and attaching a script containing <u>500 words or less, along with drawings, photographs or magazine cutouts, or combinations thereof</u> (i.e., collage) on no larger than 9" x 12" piece of paper, describing how the <u>Silhouette books make romance come alive for you.</u> Mail via first-class mail to: Harlequin "Silhouette Makes You a Star!" Contest 1308, (in the U.S.) P.O. Box 9069, Buffalo, NY 14269-9069, (in Canada) P.O. Box 637, Fort Erie, Ontario, Canada L2A 5X3. Limit one entry per person, household or organization.

2. Contests will be judged by a panel of members of the Harlequin editorial, marketing and public relations staff. Fifty percent of criteria will be judged against script and fifty percent will be judged against drawing, photographs and/or magazine cutouts. Judging criteria will be based on the following:

   - Sincerity—25%
   - Originality and Creativity—50%
   - Emotionally Compelling—25%

   In the event of a tie, duplicate prizes will be awarded. Decisions of the judges are final.

3. All entries become the property of Torstar Corp. and may be used for future promotional purposes. Entries will not be returned. No responsibility is assumed for lost, late, illegible, incomplete, inaccurate, nondelivered or misdirected mail.

4. Contest open only to residents of the U.S. <u>(except Puerto Rico)</u> and Canada who are 18 years of age or older, and is void wherever prohibited by law; all applicable laws and regulations apply. Any litigation within the Province of Quebec respecting the conduct or organization of a publicity contest may be submitted to the Régie des alcools, des courses et des jeux for a ruling. Any litigation respecting the awarding of a prize may be submitted to the Régie des alcools, des courses et des jeux only for the purpose of helping the parties reach a settlement. Employees and immediate family members of Torstar Corp. and D. L. Blair, Inc., their affiliates, subsidiaries and all other agencies, entities and persons connected with the use, marketing or conduct of this contest are not eligible to enter. Taxes on prizes are the sole responsibility of the winner. Acceptance of any prize offered constitutes permission to use winner's name, photograph or other likeness for the purposes of advertising, trade and promotion on behalf of Torstar Corp., its affiliates and subsidiaries without further compensation to the winner, unless prohibited by law.

5. Winner will be determined no later than November 30, 2001, and will be notified by mail. Winner will be required to sign and return an Affidavit of Eligibility/Release of Liability/Publicity Release form within 15 days after winner notification. Noncompliance within that time period may result in disqualification and an alternative winner may be selected. All travelers must execute a Release of Liability prior to ticketing and must possess required travel documents (e.g., passport, photo ID) where applicable. Trip must be booked by December 31, 2001, and completed within one year of notification. No substitution of prize permitted by winner. Torstar Corp. and D. L. Blair, Inc., their parents, affiliates and subsidiaries are not responsible for errors in printing of contest, entries and/or game pieces. In the event of printing or other errors that may result in unintended prize values or duplication of prizes, all affected game pieces or entries shall be null and void. **Purchase or acceptance of a product offer does not improve your chances of winning.**

6. Prizes: (1) Grand Prize—A 2-night/3-day trip for two (2) to New York City, including round-trip coach air transportation nearest winner's home and hotel accommodations (double occupancy) at The Plaza Hotel, a glamorous afternoon makeover at <u>a trendy New York spa</u>, $1,000 in U.S. spending money and an opportunity to <u>have a professional photo taken and appear in a Silhouette advertisement</u> (approximate retail value: $7,000). (10) Ten Runner-Up Prizes of gift packages (retail value $50 ea.). Prizes consist of only those items listed as part of the prize. Limit one prize per person. Prize is valued in U.S. currency.

7. For the name of the winner (available after December 31, 2001) send a self-addressed, stamped envelope to: Harlequin "Silhouette Makes You a Star!" Contest 1197 Winners, P.O. Box 4200 Blair, NE 68009-4200 or you may access the www.eHarlequin.com Web site through February 28, 2002.

Contest sponsored by Torstar Corp., P.O Box 9042, Buffalo, NY 14269-9042.

#1 *New York Times* Bestselling Author

NORA ROBERTS

brings you two tantalizing tales of
remarkable women who live…and love…
on their own terms, featuring characters from

CONSIDERING KATE,

part of her heartwarming Stanislaski saga!

Coming in July 2001

Reflections and Dreams

Some women dream their lives away, but
Lindsay Dunne and Ruth Bannion have *lived*
their dreams. Now they're about to discover passion
and romance beyond even their wildest dreams.

Available at your favorite retail outlet.

Silhouette®
Where love comes alive™

where love comes alive—online...

eHARLEQUIN.com

shop eHarlequin

- ♥ Find all the new Silhouette releases at everyday great discounts.
- ♥ Try before you buy! Read an excerpt from the latest Silhouette novels.
- ♥ Write an online review and share your thoughts with others.

reading room

- ♥ Read our Internet exclusive daily and weekly online serials, or vote in our interactive novel.
- ♥ Talk to other readers about your favorite novels in our Reading Groups.
- ♥ Take our Choose-a-Book quiz to find the series that matches you!

authors' alcove

- ♥ Find out interesting tidbits and details about your favorite authors' lives, interests and writing habits.
- ♥ Ever dreamed of being an author? Enter our Writing Round Robin. The Winning Chapter will be published online! Or review our writing guidelines for submitting your novel.

All this and more available at
www.eHarlequin.com
on Women.com Networks

SECRETS

A kidnapped baby
A hidden identity
A man with a past

Christine Rimmer's popular *Conveniently Yours* miniseries returns with three brand-new books, revolving around the Marsh baby kidnapped over thirty years ago. Beginning late summer, from Silhouette Books…

THE MARRIAGE AGREEMENT
(August 2001; Silhouette Special Edition #1412)
The halfbrother's story

THE BRAVO BILLIONAIRE
(September 2001; Silhouette Single Title)
The brother's story

THE MARRIAGE CONSPIRACY
(October 2001; Silhouette Special Edition #1423)
**The missing baby's story—
all grown up and quite a man!**

You won't want to miss a single one….
Available wherever Silhouette books are sold.

Where love comes alive™